INTO THE FLAMES

FIREHOUSE FOURTEEN
BOOK 4

LISA B. KAMPS

Lisa B. Kamps

INTO THE FLAMES
Firehouse Fourteen Book 4

Lisa B. Kamps

INTO THE FLAMES

INTO THE FLAMES
Copyright © 2016 by Elizabeth Belbot Kamps

All rights reserved. Except for use in any review, the reproduction or utilization of this work in whole or in part in any form by any electronic, mechanical or other means, now known or hereafter invented, including xerography, photocopying and recording, or in any information storage or retrieval system, is forbidden without the express written permission of the author.

All characters in this book have no existence outside the imagination of the author and have no relation to anyone bearing the same name or names, living or dead. This book is a work of fiction and any resemblance to any individual, place, business, or event is purely coincidental.

Cover and logo design by Jay Aheer of Simply Defined Art
http://www.jayscoversbydesign.com/

Lisa B. Kamps

All rights reserved.
ISBN: 1537237330
ISBN-13: 978-1537237336

INTO THE FLAMES

Lisa B. Kamps

DEDICATION

For my cousin, Vicki Hansel Bachmeier.
I am in awe of your courage, strength and tenacity in the face of the adversity.
Stay strong and never, ever underestimate yourself.
And always remember: what they say about karma is true!

INTO THE FLAMES

Contents

Title Page iii
Copyright v
Dedication... ix
Other titles by this author xv

Chapter One... 17
Chapter Two... 25
Chapter Three 32
Chapter Four 41
Chapter Five 56
Chapter Six 68
Chapter Seven 86
Chapter Eight.. 101
Chapter Nine... 109
Chapter Ten.. 123
Chapter Eleven 132
Chapter Twelve.. 150
Chapter Thirteen... 167
Chapter Fourteen.. 176
Chapter Fifteen 186
Chapter Sixteen 195
Chapter Seventeen.. 203
Chapter Eighteen.. 212
Chapter Nineteen.. 225
Chapter Twenty 234
Chapter Twenty-One 242

Chapter Twenty-Two 255
Chapter Twenty-Three 268
Chapter Twenty-Four..282
Chapter Twenty-Five...287
Chapter Twenty-Six...295
Epilogue 303

ABOUT THE AUTHOR 309
DANGEROUS PASSION preview 311

INTO THE FLAMES

Lisa B. Kamps

Other titles by this author

THE BALTIMORE BANNERS

Crossing The Line, Book 1
Game Over, Book 2
Blue Ribbon Summer, Book 3
Body Check, Book 4
Break Away, Book 5
Playmaker (A Baltimore Banners Intermission novella)
Delay of Game, Book 6
Shoot Out, Book 7
The Baltimore Banners 1st Period Trilogy (Books 1-3)
On Thin Ice, Book 8
One-Timer, Book 9

FIREHOUSE FOURTEEN

Once Burned, Book 1
Playing With Fire, Book 2
Breaking Protocol, Book 3
Into The Flames, Book 4
Second Alarm, Book 5

STAND-ALONE TITLES

Emeralds and Gold: A Treasury of Irish Short Stories *(anthology)*
Finding Dr. Right, Silhouette Special Edition
Time To Heal
Dangerous Passion

Lisa B. Kamps

Chapter One

Music blared next to his head, the underlying bass rhythm shaking the drywall, reverberating through the headboard and mattress then scraping along his spine and finally exploding throughout his body.

Dale Gannon rolled to his side and threw the covers off with an angry, impatient jerk. He ran a hand over his face, the short stubble on his jaw scratching his palm, and stared at the bright red numbers glowing on the alarm clock.

8:47

He'd managed to get in forty minutes of sleep before the blaring music jolted him awake. It hadn't even been a restful sleep and he felt worse now than he had when he got home. Tired, groggy, his head filled with hazy cobwebs that dulled his thinking and his reaction time. They'd been up all night, running one call after another after another. Shit calls: fire alarms, medic assists, wires down. One auto fire that broke the monotony of the other crap they kept getting hit with.

All he wanted to do was sleep. To get in a few

hours of shut-eye before he went back in this afternoon for more of the same. That shouldn't have been a problem. Up until three months ago, it *wouldn't* have been a problem.

Until the neighbor from hell had moved in.

Dale had yet to meet the guy, whoever he was. All he knew was that the jerk must not have a job, because he was home at all hours of the day and night.

And he had awful taste in music.

Dale rose from the bed, swearing under his breath as he reached for a pair of sweatpants and jerked them on. He curled his hand into a fist and pounded on the wall, hard. Three times. A short pause. Three more.

He held his breath, waiting to see if that would do the trick. A minute went by before the music, whatever the hell it was, finally stopped.

"Thank God." Dale stumbled out of the bedroom and made his way down the short hall to the kitchen. He needed coffee, lots of it. He'd settle for one cup then go back to his room to collapse and try to get back to sleep. Just a few hours, that was all he needed.

He'd taken two long swallows of the strong black brew before the music blared to life again. His back teeth throbbed in time to the bass line. The music built to a loud crescendo that seemed to end in an abrupt scream that caused him to jump. His hand jerked, sloshing coffee over the edge of the mug and onto the floor.

"You have got to be shitting me." Dale clenched his teeth and slammed the mug onto the counter. He once more curled his hand into a fist and banged it against the kitchen wall, hard enough that the pepper shaker fell off the back ledge of the stove. Hard enough that pain shot along the outside of his curled hand.

Dale winced then brought his hand to his mouth, sucking on the knuckle of his small finger with a grunt.

The music stopped mid-squeal, like someone had hit a button and killed all the power. He grunted again then tore off a few paper towels to wipe up the spilled coffee. A little soreness in his hand was a small price to pay for peace and quiet. Finally. Now he could finish the coffee and drag his sorry ass back to bed for a few hours of much-needed sleep.

Sleep. Work. Back home to sleep some more. Yeah, what an exciting way to start his four days off, especially since those four days would probably be spent doing nothing. Unless he called his friend Rick Foster to see if he needed any help on any of his home improvement jobs. Maybe something that involved demolition. Tearing down a wall would certainly help get some of his aggressions out, especially since he wasn't doing much of anything like that at work, not in his position as an engine driver.

He reached for the coffee, not sure if he wanted to finish it or toss it down the drain, when someone started knocking on his door. Only knocking was too subtle a description. It was like someone was pounding at it, or maybe even kicking it, hard enough that Dale was only slightly surprised it didn't fall off its hinges.

A small grin lifted the corners of his mouth, a grin that probably looked as cold and flat as it felt. There was no doubt in his mind who was trying to beat his door down, not so soon after he banged on the wall.

The mystery neighbor from hell. It had to be.

Adrenaline surged through him, better than any jolt of caffeine. This was exactly what he needed to get his mind off things, to knock out the worry and guilt that had been eating at him for the last few months—

ever since his youngest sister Lindsay had pulled that careless stunt and damn near killed his other sister, Lauren.

Dale sat the mug on the counter and did a quick neck roll, preparing for the confrontation he was certain was going to happen as soon as he opened the door. Good. Let it. He couldn't wait to finally meet the neighbor from hell and give him a piece of his mind. To tell him exactly what he could do with the loud obnoxious music that shook the walls at odd hours of the day and night. And if the guy was burly or belligerent—or both—then that was even better.

He stormed over to the door, his steps heavy on the hardwood flooring. He didn't pause, didn't stop to take a deep breath, did none of those things. Why should he, when he was more than ready for this confrontation? He yanked open the door, his mouth already moving before he completely opened it.

"Who the hell do you think—" The words died on his lips as the breath left him in a rush, his stomach clenching as if someone had just punched him. And he had been punched, no doubt about it. Except it wasn't a physical blow—it was complete and utter shock.

Dale blinked, thinking he must be seeing things. This couldn't be the neighbor from the hell. No way in hell. He'd been expecting a burly, belligerent, unkempt man. Someone he would have no problem confronting.

But instead of the man he'd been expecting, Dale found himself staring into the wide ocean blue eyes of an elf.

He blinked again, expecting the image to morph or fade. He was tired, his mind must be playing tricks on him. That had to be it.

The woman in front of him was wiry and petite. Fiery red hair flowed around her face in a halo of loose curls that tumbled around her shoulders and down her back. Her mouth, full and as deep as ripened strawberries, pursed in irritation. A flush spread across her high cheekbones, the color a dark pink against her pale creamy skin. Another splash of color, an electric blue that shone in the light from the hall, was smeared across her chin and jaw and cheek.

Not an elf. A Smurf.

The neighbor from hell was a fucking Smurf.

Or maybe a pixie. Or a siren. Or one of those other ridiculous mythical creatures he could never remember from his days in high school.

And definitely not a burly, belligerent man.

Her eyes narrowed, her feathery brows pulling together in a sharp frown. She leaned forward and waved something at him and for a split-second he actually thought it was some kind of wand. Dale stepped back, his eyes following the movement of her hand. Not a wand. A paintbrush, covered in that same electric blue that was smeared across her face. Her hand kept moving and the brush hit against the door, a line of blue suddenly appearing where it touched. A slash, almost like she was hexing him.

Dale leaned forward and grabbed the brush from her hand. "Watch it!"

Her eyes widened for a brief second then narrowed again. She didn't hesitate at all, even though she was smaller, shorter, more fragile. She jumped just a little and quickly retrieved her brush, then immediately started pointing it at him again, shaking it enough that drops of blue splattered across his bare chest.

"You are the rudest, most infuriating, most annoying person I have ever met!"

"Me? Lady, I'm not the one splattering paint everywhere. And I'm not the one blaring music at all hours of the day. And night."

"Well I'm sorry if the music was too loud. All you had to do was come over and ask—politely—and I would have turned it down. But no, you have to act like a Neanderthal and bang on the walls like a hairy gorilla with no manners!" She waved the paintbrush again, splattering even more paint over the door—and across his bare chest. His bare, hairless chest.

Dale stepped back, frowning, knowing he probably resembled the Neanderthal she was accusing him of being and not caring. Any sane person would be running the other way at the look on his face. Hadn't Lauren told him often enough that his scowl could send children screaming in fright? But the woman in front of him didn't even seem to notice. In fact, she actually stepped closer, still waving that stupid brush at him.

Not only was the neighbor from hell a Smurf, she was freaking insane, too. She had to be. Why else would she still be standing there waving that stupid paintbrush and getting all huffy?

Dale thought about just slamming the door in her face. Yeah, that would teach her. Or at least shut her up. His hand closed around the edge of the door, ready to do just that, but then he looked down and noticed that her feet were right on the threshold of his apartment.

Her bare feet, which peeked out from the hem of the long gauzy skirt she wore. He blinked and looked again, noticing that every single one of her toenails was painted a different color. Ten slender toes, ten outlandish colors.

Dale deepened his scowl and looked back up. "I am not a hairy gorilla."

Smurfette's mouth snapped closed with a soft click, effectively stopping whatever she had been yammering about. Her eyes narrowed for a brief second before she lowered her gaze from his face to his bare chest. Not like she could miss it, since she was less than a foot away and pretty much eye level with it.

The range of expressions playing across her face almost made him laugh. First there was shock, like she just now realized he was standing there in a pair of low-hanging sweatpants and nothing else. Then there was a small flare of feminine appreciation before embarrassment stained her cheeks a bright red, the color oddly matching the flaming glow of her thick hair. Her lips parted and she blinked, her gaze meeting his for a split second. Dale raised his brows in silent question, thought about actually asking her if she liked what she saw. Then her eyes narrowed and her lips pursed and he wondered if maybe he had imagined that look of appreciation.

"You are still a Neanderthal. A mannerless Neanderthal who doesn't even have the decency to get dressed before answering his door. What kind of—"

"Listen, Smurfette. I've been up all night and all I want to do is sleep. The last thing I need is to be listening to that awful screeching you call music—"

"It's opera—"

"And then stand here while you ogle me!"

"Ogle? Ogle!" Smurfette's face scrunched up in an expression of distaste that would have been funny if it hadn't been so insulting. A blush tinted her cheeks once more and she took a step back, opening her mouth to say something else. Dale shut the door with a bang, cutting her off before she could start. He heard her mutter something from the other side of the door, the words too muffled to understand. Thirty seconds later, he heard the sound of her own door slamming shut.

He chuckled then made his way back to the kitchen, feeling oddly energized and more alive than he had for the last three months. For a few minutes he'd been able to forget the drama and guilt and worry that had been plaguing him, the sense that he'd somehow failed. Maybe having Smurfette for a neighbor would actually be good for him.

And then the music started again, loud and obnoxious. He fisted his hand and was ready to bang against the wall when another noise stopped him. Was that really—? Dale leaned closer to the wall, listening.

Yeah, it was. Holy shit, Smurfette was singing, her voice pitched too high and completely off-key. He ground his teeth together and hit the wall, over and over. Only this time, the volume grew louder, overlaid by that awful off-key singing.

Fuck. It was going to be a long day.

Chapter Two

A blast of wind cut around the side of the engine and cut into Dale's bare neck, slicing into his skin. He hunched his shoulders then reached for the collar of his jacket, turning it up one-handed as he adjusted the pressure of the hose lines. Lights pierced the night around him, slicing through the darkness with a coldness of their own. The noise surrounding him was a crescendo of chaos: the loud rumble of engines, the shouts of the crews yelling back and forth, the squawk of radios filled with static and talk. Over it all was the deep roar of a dying fire, being held at bay and pushed back by the crews working to contain it.

Dale pressed the heel of one hand against his eye as he tried unsuccessfully to swallow a yawn. His jaw cracked, nothing more than a small pop that he felt rather than heard. An image of a warm bed in a dark room came to mind, more fantasy than anything else because the chances of them making it back to the station in time to get any sleep before their shift ended in a few hours was practically nonexistent.

Just another day at work.

At least this was better than a bullshit call, giving him something to do, something he could actually focus on. And it would be so much better if sleep wasn't dragging at him, clawing at him in silent demand. Just a few more hours and he could go home and crash in his own bed, undisturbed.

Yeah, probably not. Not with Smurfette blaring her music next door.

Maybe he could go to Lauren's. She'd be working, and her boyfriend, Kenny, was currently on the road. He was a defenseman with the Baltimore Banners, the city's professional ice hockey team. Lauren's place would be blissfully empty, blissfully silent. And he knew she wouldn't have a problem letting him crash for a few hours.

Except she'd probably want to know why and he didn't feel like explaining about Smurfette. Knowing Lauren, she'd make more out of it than it was.

"Here, you look like you could use this."

Dale turned away from the instrument panel and saw Dave Warren and Jimmy Hughes—the paramedics from his shift—standing behind him. Dave held out a Styrofoam cup and Dale took it, holding it to his mouth and taking a long swallow. Hi-test sludge, thick and strong and barely lukewarm. Exactly what he needed. He took another long swallow, frowning at Jimmy over the rim of the cup. The younger man was bundled up, with a wool hat pulled low over his eyes and a thick scarf wrapped around his neck under the bright turnout coat. Dale would have been embarrassed to wear anything that looked so shiny and new but what the hell. Jimmy was a paramedic, not a firefighter, so at least he had an excuse for being clean.

"Really Jimmy? It's not that cold."

"Speak for yourself. I just got back from Key West, I'm not used to this weather. Besides, I thought we were done with winter."

"Don't be such a girl. It's not even April yet, we could still get snow." Dave leaned against the side of the engine and took a sip of his own sludge, his dark eyes bright with amusement at Jimmy's groan.

Dale was inclined to agree with Jimmy's sentiment but he wouldn't admit it, not out loud, at least. Yes, it was late March. Yes, the weather could be fickle and they could still get snow. Just look at tonight, with the below-freezing temps and biting wind. That didn't mean Dale wanted the winter weather. He was as over it as everyone else, especially with everything that happened this winter.

Yeah, he definitely needed Spring. Warm weather, new beginnings. All that other sappy shit that came with it.

No. What he really needed was sleep. Uninterrupted sleep in silence. Maybe then he'd stop having thoughts of sappy shit.

"You look like hell. Everything okay?" Dave's voice was pitched low, loud enough to carry over the whine of the pump but not so loud that Jimmy could hear him. Dale glanced over at him and nodded.

"Yeah, just tired. I didn't get any sleep today. Yesterday. Whatever."

"You sure that's it?" Dave's dark eyes studied him, seeing too much. Of course he would. He had been there the day Lauren had been poisoned, had calmed both him and Kenny down while taking care of his sister, going with her to the hospital. He knew first-hand what had happened, had seen the drama unfold right before his eyes.

Had seen Dale break down and pretty much lose it in the ER once the reality of what his youngest had tried to do sunk in. He didn't need Dave digging deeper, asking too many questions, so he drained the cup and crushed it in his hand, not quite meeting the other man's gaze. "Yeah, that's it."

"Your neighbor from hell still giving you grief?" Jimmy slid a little closer, raising his voice to be heard. Dale gave a short laugh.

"You could say that."

"I don't understand why you don't just say something to the guy. He's obviously an ass. Once he—"

"*She.*" Dale pushed the word through his clenched jaw. "The neighbor from hell is a *she*. I finally met her yesterday morning."

He was pretty sure Dave chuckled, the sound masked by a quick cough when Dale shot him a dirty look. Jimmy nudged closer, a stupid grin on his face.

"Well? Is she hot? Is that why you didn't get any sleep?"

"She's a Smurf."

"Uh…she's a what?"

"A Smurf. You know, those little blue things that live in the woods?"

"A Smurf?" Jimmy repeated the question, his face twisted in confusion. Dave leaned closer, the smile on his face growing.

"Yeah. A cartoon character. A movie featuring them came out a while back, I can't remember how long ago." Dave turned back to Dale, his dark brows raised in question. Or maybe amusement. "So your neighbor from hell is a short chubby blue cartoon character?"

Dale scowled then turned away, refusing to answer. How in the hell had this conversation started? He should have never even said anything to start with, he should have known better, especially with Jimmy.

"So why a Smurf?"

The question came from Dave, which surprised him. Usually it was Jimmy who kept harping on a subject, especially if it had anything to do with a member of the female population. Dave was the more serious one, dark and brooding. At least, he had been until about seven months ago, when he fell in love.

God save him from love-sick men. Dale hoped he never fell into that trap.

Dave nudged him from behind, letting him know he was waiting for an answer. Dale checked the gauges on the instrument panel then released a heavy sigh, his breath a frosty cloud wavering in front of him. "She was covered in blue paint, waving a stupid paintbrush in front of me while she yelled at me."

"She yelled at you?"

"Yeah. Called me a Neanderthal and a hairy gorilla with no manners." The corners of his mouth twitched at the memory, almost forming a smile. He quickly flattened his lips into a straight line.

"Why was she covered in paint?"

"Christ Jimmy, I don't know. I guess she was painting or something. I didn't ask."

"So that's why your neck is splattered in blue. I was wondering about that."

Dale looked over at Jimmy, frowning as his hand automatically went to his neck. All he felt was the rough collar of his turnout coat and under that, the softer material of the hood—which he was using to keep his neck warm instead of his head safe from fire.

Was he still splattered in paint? Probably. He tried to get most of it off when he showered before heading into work, only to realize it was oil-based and not latex. Scrubbing had worked—if that was what you wanted to call scrubbing off the top two layers of his skin.

"So is she hot?"

Dale turned back to Jimmy, scowling as a few choice words hovered on the edges of his mouth. He didn't get a chance to say anything because Dave pulled his partner away, telling him to leave it alone. That didn't stop Dave from tossing a knowing look at Dale, one he chose to ignore.

He spent the next hour by himself, surrounded by nothing more than the steady whine of the pumps and the clouds of his own frozen breath. His crew—Mikey, Jay, Adam—returned to the engine for a quick break, to swap out bottles and pull tools for salvage and overhaul. Their faces were smudged with soot, the odor of smoke clinging to them as they laughed and joked or tossed insults at one another.

And at him.

But they must have sensed his need to be alone, because except for the occasional insult, they let him be. And hell, did everyone know—or suspect—what was going on? Did they know he had too much on his mind, that he couldn't stop thinking about everything that had happened the last few months?

Yeah, obviously they did. Several of them had been there at the charity hockey game. Even if they weren't there, they knew what had happened. They were family, together for long hours, long days and nights. They knew each other, the good and the bad and even the ugly. Of course they knew.

But nobody bothered him, didn't force him to answer questions he didn't want to answer. Which suited him just fine, especially tonight.

Although he had been tempted when Mikey came up and offered him her axe, telling him they could switch positions and she'd look after the engine if he wanted to tear the shit out of something. How had she phrased it? Therapy. Yeah, it had been tempting. But not tonight. Tonight, he just wanted to stay by the engine, doing his job solo.

The solitude suited him fine, except for the direction his thoughts kept taking.

Lauren, so still and pale in a hospital bed, poisoned by their own younger sister.

Lindsay, spoiled and entitled even as she sat in jail, awaiting trial.

And a pair of ocean blue eyes, wide and deep enough to fall into.

Dale shook his head, dislodging the unwelcome image. Where in the hell had that even come from? From being tired, that had to be the only explanation. He couldn't imagine why else he'd be thinking about Smurfette's eyes.

Maybe he should find Mikey and take her up on her offer. Maybe a little physical exertion would do him good, wear him out to the point where he'd stop thinking, at least for a little while. Exhaustion did funny things to the mind. Why else would he be thinking about his neighbor from hell in ways he shouldn't be thinking about her?

No, it was definitely exhaustion. It had to be. And he latched onto that excuse, holding it tight, forcing himself to believe it.

Chapter Three

Anticipation shimmered in the warm air of the upstairs office. The only sound was the rumble of the furnace, a muffled moan that came from somewhere below them in the ancient building. Maybe ancient was the wrong word. The building was just over a hundred years old, worn brick and plaster and rough beams giving it a charm that fairly screamed with atmosphere. It was a perfect building in a perfect location to house a trendy gallery that catered to the perfect people in the surrounding neighborhoods.

Melanie Reeves just wished it wasn't quite so warm.

She pushed the hair from her face and brought her thumb to her mouth, absently chewing on the ragged, stained cuticle. She realized what she was doing and pulled her hand away, curling it into a tight fist and letting it drop to her lap.

Maybe it wasn't the heat coming from the old furnace that caused a fine sheen of sweat to break out along her hairline and the back of her neck. Maybe it was nerves.

Melanie was always nervous when she brought her pieces in, waiting in silence, barely daring to breathe while Anna studied them with her discerning eye.

The silence stretched around them, stretching Melanie's nerves, stretching her patience. Anna James, the gallery owner, moved from one piece to another to another, the high heels of her designer shoes clicking against the polished planks of the wood floor. She paused at the center painting, her head tilted to the side as she studied it. She looked over at Melanie, her hazel eyes curious, then turned back to the painting. Long minutes went by before she moved to the third one, studied it for a few seconds, then went back to the middle one.

She hated it. Melanie could tell. And oh sweets, why had she brought that one with her? She should have left it at home. Should have just scrapped it and started over, pretended she had never painted it.

The colors were all wrong. Dark and light, negative energy fighting with positive in a battle of bold strokes and weak lines. And why, oh why, had she brought it with her?

She'd finished the painting in a day, a frenzy of action and anxiety and anger, aggression on canvas that was so unlike her. And it was all *his* fault. The Neanderthal from next door. She had been so upset, so…so…confused. No, that wasn't the right word. Dismayed? No, that wasn't the right word, either.

She hadn't been herself after their encounter. She'd been angry and upset and off-balance and intrigued and then even angrier because she'd been intrigued and then she had to stop what she was doing and take it out on her canvas and then…then…

Melanie took a deep breath and studied Anna as she studied the middle painting. The one *he* had made her paint. And why, oh why, had she brought it?

"I love this one." Anna stepped back and folded her arms across her thin narrow chest. The dark hair of her neatly trimmed bob swayed just the smallest bit as she nodded, agreeing with her decree. Melanie sat up a little straighter and tried not to frown.

"You do?"

"Absolutely, dear. It's dramatic. Vivacious. Very high energy."

"It is?"

"Absolutely." Anna finally turned toward her, those hazel eyes shining with shrewdness behind the narrow black-rimmed glasses. Melanie blinked and almost asked her if she was overdue for her optometrist appointment.

Anna was the best. Discerning, shrewd, well-connected—and always bringing in top dollar for her artists' work. At least, she used to be. Melanie suddenly worried that maybe she was losing her touch, especially if she liked that…that *thing*.

"It is?"

"You're repeating yourself, dear." Anna removed the glasses and closed the distance between them, lowering herself to the overstuffed chair next to Melanie. She reached out and took one of Melanie's hands in her own, her long narrow fingers cool and confident. "Stop doubting yourself. It's beautiful. It speaks to me like none of your other work has done."

Melanie slumped in the chair, the words deflating her with their implication. She was a fraud, she must be if—"

"Stop." Anna squeezed her hand, almost too hard.

"They are all fantastic, as usual. All your work speaks to me, speaks to those who buy them. But this one—there is something very primitive, very earthy about this one. Very elemental."

"Elemental?"

"Yes, certainly. Do you have a name for it?"

Melanie opened her mouth, almost said she wanted to call it *Neanderthal Unearthed*, then quickly snapped her mouth closed. She shook her head. "No, I don't."

"Then we shall call it *Elemental* and I will charge an obscene amount for it. Or perhaps I will put it on auction."

"Auction? Really?" Melanie's hand automatically squeezed Anna's, an involuntary reaction. The gallery's auctions featured the best of the best, drawing in huge amounts for the featured artists. Melanie's work had never been in one of the auctions before. Not that she still didn't make a decent living but—an auction? Really?

She looked over at the painting, tilting her head to the side and trying to study it from a different perspective. Trying to see whatever it was Anna had seen. Bold strokes of vibrant reds and oranges filled the canvas, broken by slashes of sulfur yellow and smoky black, each color fighting for dominance. The painting was so different from her other works, which usually featured softer colors, softer lines. Pleasing and peaceful. This one was angry, confused.

It was how she had seen her neighbor. Angry, confused. Harsh and strong but hiding something, too. And she hadn't stopped to think, just stormed back to her apartment, set up a blank canvas, and practically threw the colors on it. Instinct and emotion, raw and blinding, had guided her hand.

Melanie tilted her head to the other side, still hoping to catch a glimpse of whatever it was Anna saw. No matter how hard she looked, even if she squinted her eyes and scrunched her face, she couldn't see it. So what did that mean? If Melanie thought this particular work was awful but Anna loved it, what did that say about the works that Melanie loved but Anna only liked?

The breath hitched in her chest, cold and painful. Oh sweets, no. She was a fraud. That had to be it. If she didn't even like what Anna loved, that must mean she was a fraud. A fake. A failure.

"You must stop at once," Anna demanded, her voice cool and direct. She squeezed Melanie's hand then stood, her posture erect and regal as she stared down at Melanie. A determined expression ruled her smooth thin face, demanding that she obey immediately.

Melanie blinked, not even trying to hide her confusion. "Stop what?"

"Questioning yourself. Doubting yourself. Don't lie and tell me you're not, I can see it in those eyes of yours." She leaned down and grabbed Melanie's hand, urging her to her feet. "Now come. We'll drink some champagne and toast your latest works, and the money they will bring in. *All* of them."

Melanie didn't have any choice but to follow so she did, casting one last glance over her shoulder at the paintings leaning against the exposed brick wall. Anna tugged her hand once more, leading her into the back lounge area. She motioned to the sofa then moved to the glass-fronted refrigerator and pulled out one of the many bottles of champagne she kept there. Minutes later, Melanie was sitting next to Anna, toasting her new paintings and sipping champagne. She knew this was part of Anna's routine, a treasured repeating of actions and celebration. One Melanie had learned to dread, because this was usually when Anna asked about her inspiration for each painting.

And usually Melanie struggled with each answer. How could she answer, when she didn't know? The ideas just came to her, ethereal explosions of color in her mind that didn't completely take shape until she placed the brush to the canvas. They weren't conscious creations or ideas. They just *were*.

Her parents, each artists in their own right, completely understood. One or two of her friends mostly understood. Everyone else? No, not really. That included Anna. And how could Melanie explain something she didn't understand? Something she had merely accepted, like she accepted knowing how to breathe without thinking?

Except for this latest piece. *Neanderthal Unearthed*. No, that wasn't right. What had Anna called it?

Elemental.

Melanie wasn't sure she agreed with the name, but she knew exactly what had inspired her to paint it. No, not what. *Who*.

Him. Anger. Frustration. Irritation. He may have inspired it, but the emotions involved were all hers—including those unwelcome sparks of excitement and attraction and curiosity. It didn't make sense. None of it made sense.

Melanie pushed the thoughts away and took a sip of the champagne, the bubbly liquid cold and sweet against her tongue. She looked over at Anna, studying her, wishing she could be more like her.

Anna wasn't ruled by her emotions. Anna didn't shy away from challenges. She was determined and sophisticated and savvy. Independent and controlled. She even looked the part, dressed in a chic feminine business suit that flattered her long legs and lean build. Melanie couldn't even guess how much the designer suit cost. Probably more than she could afford to spend—more than what she would even think about spending. Not that she really thought much about her wardrobe anyway.

Maybe she should reconsider. Anna always looked so put-together, so stylish and young even though she was in her late forties, at least twenty years older than Melanie's own twenty-six. But next to Anna, Melanie looked…frumpy. Scatterbrained. Frazzled.

And oh, for sweet's sake, why was she suddenly so worried about how she looked? She dressed for comfort in flowing skirts and loose tops when she was out, or in stained shirts and flowing skirts when she was home. Her only accessories were the crystal pendant hanging from the leather thong around her neck and the ever-present smears of paint. Always smears of paint, because she never quite remembered to clean all of it off and it never really mattered before.

Why did it matter now?

Her fingers tightened on the fragile stem of the glass and she took a deep breath, relaxing her grip, trying to relax herself. She knew why, and it was silly. So silly.

Because of *him*.

She wished she had never met him. Never gone next door, never saw him standing there in those loose pants and bare chest with his smooth glowing skin and rugged muscles and that ridiculous tattoo across his chest. Latin, of all things. He probably didn't even know what it meant.

Vini. Vidi. Vici.

A little thrill went through her as she wondered what, exactly, he had conquered. She shivered and quickly took another sip of champagne, hoping Anna hadn't noticed. The other woman was watching her, a patient expression on her smooth face, her head tilted slightly to the side. Waiting. Waiting for what, though?

Anna must have asked her a question, a question Melanie didn't hear because her thoughts had been scattered elsewhere. She cleared her throat and smiled at the older woman, hoping she would repeat the question without being asked.

Anna laughed, the sound low and smoky, then moved to sit behind her desk. "You must tell me, dear. What possessed you to paint something so different?"

Possessed. Melanie wasn't sure what to make of that word, worried that it fit too well. "I just, um…my neighbor…I may have been a little angry when I painted it."

Anna laughed again then raised her glass in a small salute. "To your neighbor, then." She finished the champagne then placed the glass near the edge of her desk before pulling her planner close. Her long fingers flipped through the pages, lines creasing her otherwise smooth face. She stopped at one page, a thoughtful expression on her face, then shook her head and turned a few more of the colorful sheets. Her face cleared and she looked up with a satisfied smile.

"Six weeks!"

Melanie stared at her, not understanding. "For what?"

"I will schedule a special auction just for your

works in six weeks. The middle of May. The anticipation will be fabulous. And that will give you time to paint at least one more. Two would be better, but yes, at least one more."

"One more what?"

"Of your fiery creations, dear. Yes, this will be perfect. I can see it now. The auction will be black-tie, of course. Surrounded in mystery. I'll have Carla begin the advertising and PR for it this week."

"But—"

"No buts." Anna stood and made her way over to Melanie, a bright smile on her face as she reached for her hands and pulled her to her feet. "I know you. Stop doubting yourself. Don't be afraid to let your inner turmoil show."

Inner turmoil? Good grief, is that what Anna saw in the painting? How could she see something so far from the truth, something that wasn't there? Melanie had to stop her, had to tell her she was wrong.

She didn't get the chance because Anna kept talking the entire time she led Melanie downstairs and over to the door, shooing her out with a quick kiss and instructions to go home and paint.

To tap her inner turmoil and set it free.

"But I don't have any inner turmoil." A chilly breeze caught the words and carried them away. It didn't matter, because there was nobody there to hear them. Melanie stood outside, barely feeling the chilled air as she stared at the closed door and wondered what she was supposed to do now.

She needed to call her mother. Mom and Dad would know what to do.

She hoped.

Chapter Four

How could she have lost her keys? She couldn't have, they should be right there with her car keys. Right on the same ring. They couldn't be lost.

But they were.

Melanie flipped through the key ring, frowning as she counted each key. Two keys to her car, a key to the small storage space she rented, a key to her parents' house. That was it, just four of them.

Where were the keys to her apartment? Two were missing: one for the main entrance door, and one to the actual apartment door. She kept them on their own tiny ring, which attached to the main ring. They should be there. Think. She needed to think.

She just had them yesterday, when she took them to have copies made so she could give a spare set to her mom to replace the ones she lost. She'd come home from the mega hardware store, used them to unlock both doors and placed them—

Oh sweets.

Melanie's shoulders slumped in defeat. How could

she have been so forgetful? So spacey? She knew exactly where they were: on the small table right by her front door, probably on top of the tiny envelope holding the spare keys she just had made.

How could she not have put them back on her keyring? Yes, she had been distracted. She was always distracted right before she took her work to Anna's. But so distracted she actually forgot her keys?

This was *his* fault. It had to be. She wasn't sure why, only knew she had been completely out of sorts ever since she met her neighbor. So of course it was his fault. She was never out of sorts. Never. At least, not like this, not like she had been.

First that odd, tortured painting that Anna absolutely loved, and now this.

Melanie wished she had never lost her temper and gone next door that day last week. If she had just ignored him, just ignored the barbaric pounding on her walls like she had for the last three months, none of this would be happening.

She wished she had never met him!

The breeze kicked up with a small gust of chilled air, causing her to shiver. She hadn't bothered with a coat this morning, thinking the bulky sweater she had on would be warm enough. It wasn't as cold as it had been last week, the weather finally easing toward Spring. Maybe. Not that it had mattered this morning, because she knew she wasn't going to be outside at all.

Except now she was, and a chill went through her in spite of the sweater. She was stuck. She couldn't even call her mom to bring the spare keys because her mom's spare keys were sitting on that same little table with her own. Melanie could probably hit the buzzer for sweet Mrs. Lillian's apartment. Mrs. Lillian would let her in, and that would at least get her inside.

But she'd still be stuck, with no way to get into her apartment. She'd have to call maintenance and there was no telling how long that would take. And Melanie didn't really feel like sitting on the chilly concrete steps, waiting. Of course, if Mrs. Lillian let her in, she'd probably insist on Melanie coming in for a visit. She'd ply her with weak tea and show her the newest pictures of her grandkids while relating their latest escapades. Melanie would listen and smile and comment, all while she fended off the unwelcome attention of Little Bits, Mrs. Lillian's ankle-biting Chihuahua.

The complex was supposed to be animal-free, but nobody complained about Little Bits. He was such a tiny thing, there really wasn't anything to complain about. And normally Melanie enjoyed spending time with Mrs. Lillian. She was so sweet and friendly. But she talked. A lot. Non-stop. And Melanie just wasn't in the mood, not today.

All she wanted was to curl up on her small loveseat and listen to the strains of La Bohème while she sipped a nice glass of Merlot. And pouted and pondered and brooded.

But first she had to get inside, and she didn't know how she was going to do that without her keys.

She stepped off the small front porch and looked up at her balcony. She only lived on the second floor, and the balcony actually had two doors leading into her apartment: the glass sliders, and the door leading from the kitchen. That was one of the reasons she chose this apartment in Cockeysville. Not that she really had the chance to use either door—or the balcony—that much since moving in, but the idea of having two doors had seemed quaint and appealing.

Another bonus was the fact that the complex wasn't surrounded by a bunch of buildings or businesses, not like the last apartment she had in the city. It was quiet, their building the last one at the edge of the complex, butting up to woods that eventually led to the water shed. Well, to the property surrounding the water shed. The reservoir was further away. But it was still quiet and peaceful, and the apartment was light and open and spacious, with plenty of room for her work.

If only she could get inside it.

Melanie frowned, still studying the balcony. The glass slider was locked, but the door to the kitchen wasn't. Maybe that wasn't very safe, but she didn't live in an area where that was an issue. No, her only issue was her neighbor, the Neanderthal. The very unhairy gorilla with no manners.

And holy sweets, she needed to stop thinking about him and figure out a way to get inside. It shouldn't be that hard. If she could somehow use the railing surrounding the porch to climb up, she could maybe probably reach the railing of her balcony. And if she did that, it should maybe probably be easy enough to just climb over and then she could get inside.

She pictured what she had to do in her mind. Step up on the railing while holding on to the brick wall for support. Lean forward and grab the railing around her balcony. A little stretch, a little hop, then pull herself over.

No problem. She could do this. Absolutely she could.

Maybe.

But not in the flats she was wearing. They had a

hard sole, too slick for what she was going to do. She kicked them off, her toes curling against the cold concrete of the porch. She hadn't expected it to be quite that cold. It didn't matter, she wouldn't be standing here much longer.

She tugged the strap of her small bag and moved it over her head, so it was more like a cross-body bag than a purse. There. Now she was ready. She took a deep breath, telling herself again that she could do this, and stretched her leg up, trying to stand on the first railing.

She ended up straddling it instead, the long skirt twisted high around her legs.

Well. That didn't work.

Melanie looked down, frowning, trying to figure out what to do next. Maybe if she pulled her legs up like she was sitting cross-legged, she could move to her feet and then stand.

Okay, that was a little better. The railing was hard and cold under her bottom, and suddenly seemed thinned than she first thought. That shouldn't matter, though. All she had to do was push herself up and stand. She could do that.

And she did. Except she was facing the wrong way, away from her balcony. And eeks, why did the ground look so far away? It wasn't. It couldn't be, it was just her imagination.

Exactly. Just her imagination.

She took a deep breath and carefully turned around, her hands grabbing onto the brick wall for balance. There, now she was facing the right way. Except her balcony railing was a little higher than she thought, and not quite as close. She should still be able to reach it, though. All she had to do was lean forward and stretch a little, then hop off the railing while she pulled herself up. Gymnasts did things like this all the time. How hard could it be?

Melanie took a deep breath for courage, closed her eyes, and leaned forward, stretching. She probably shouldn't have closed her eyes, because the world suddenly swam in darkness and she felt herself falling. She sucked her breath in as panic swamped her. Her arms flailed and she was certain she was going to fall, waited for the impact of her body slamming against the cold hard ground, waited for the pain to explode through her crumpled corpse.

Did corpses feel pain?

And then her hands closed around something hard and cold. Flaky metal, rough against her palms. Melanie stopped breathing, the heavy pounding of her heart the only sound she could hear.

Because her heart was in her throat, and not in her chest where it should be.

An hour went by, or maybe just a few seconds, before she could finally open her eyes. This wasn't good. This wasn't good at all.

Her body was stretched across a wide expanse of nothing, her hands tightly wrapped around the thin metal spindles of her balcony railing. Her feet were braced against the porch railing but barely, held in place only by the curled toes of her bare feet. Somehow one foot had become caught in the hem of her skirt and she had the brief and silly thought that at least those toes would be warm when she died.

She was stuck. Truly and completely stuck. She couldn't push herself back because she was stretched too far forward. And she couldn't bounce or jump from the other railing because she didn't have any leverage. That, and she didn't think her feet would listen to her. Or that her arms would be able to support her.

Another cold breeze gusted around her, blowing thick strands of hair into her face. Melanie closed her eyes, too afraid to look down. The ground was too far away, too hard and unforgiving. She was stuck here. It was the middle of the week, in the middle of the day. There was nobody around to help her.

She should have just buzzed sweet Mrs. Lillian and called for maintenance. Or a locksmith. She should have played with Little Bits and smiled at his ankle-biting antics.

But she hadn't, and now she'd never see the silly dog again. Or sweet Mrs. Lillian. She was stuck here and she was going to die. Either from exposure from the cold weather, or from her body being battered and crumpled when she plunged to her death. Her parents would be so upset. Would there be a huge crowd at her funeral? Would there be tears and laments? Who would eulogize her? Anna would certainly say a few things. Nothing too sad, she hoped. Something light, uplifting. Maybe a little humorous...except Melanie wasn't the humorous type. She should have learned how to be funny and witty, only now it was too late.

Just one more regret she'd have to bear before plunging to her death. She should stop thinking, in case more regrets came to mind. She didn't want to die with a load of regrets. Maybe the end would come quickly. And be painless. Melanie couldn't bear to think of herself crumpled in a boneless heap on the cold unforgiving ground, suffering as the life slowly seeped away—

"What are you doing?"

The voice came from her left, deep and slightly amused. Was it the Angel of Death? Melanie didn't think so, not unless he sounded exactly like her Neanderthal neighbor. And how odd was it that she knew his voice? She shouldn't. And she shouldn't insult the Angel of Death by comparing his voice to the Neanderthal's. That probably wasn't the best way to make a good first impression.

"I'm sorry." Melanie whispered the apology, hoping the Angel of Death would understand. She didn't expect to hear a deep chuckle in response. Part of her wanted to open her eyes and turn her head to the side, to gaze upon the angelic face before death came to her. That might be pushing her luck, though, so she kept her eyes firmly closed.

"Sorry? Yeah, I'm not even going to ask." The voice came closer, still laced with that humor. Melanie didn't think that was very welcoming of him. "So what, exactly, are you doing?"

"I'm preparing to die. Please don't let it hurt too much."

Silence. She couldn't even hear the sound of the chilly breeze sweeping around her. Was she dead already? Had it happened that quickly? Melanie took a deep breath and eased her eyes open, just a tiny bit. Oh sweets, she was still hanging there, stuck between the railing and her balcony, the ground still too far away. Her cold hands tightened around the spindles of the balcony, her fingers cramping as flakes of paint dug into her skin. She took another deep breath, preparing herself for whatever fate was waiting for her, then looked down again.

Straight into a pair of deep brown eyes that twinkled with amusement. A noise that sounded too much like a squeal escaped her parted lips. The high-pitched shriek embarrassed her and she wanted to close her eyes, to turn her face away. She couldn't.

"Okay Smurfette. Want to tell me what it is you're trying to do?"

It was definitely her neighbor. She was sure there was irony in there somewhere but she was afraid to look too closely and figure out where. Maybe later. If she survived. But for now she just pursed her lips together and shook her head, the movement small and precise.

More laughter, warm and deep. Strong hands closed around her waist and she squealed again, her hands tightening even more against the balcony. Her feet slipped from the railing and she kicked her legs through the air, shrieking in fear. The hands on her waist slipped and she fell, her stomach connecting with something hard. There was a muffled grunt then arms, strong and hard and entirely too dangerous, closed around her, holding her in place.

"Smurfette, let go of the railing."

"No. I don't want to die."

A muttered curse, followed by a deep breath. "You're not going to die. Now let go."

"I'm going to fall."

"No, you're not."

"You're going to drop me."

"As tempting as that might be, I'm not going to drop you. Now let go."

If she wasn't so frightened, she would have kicked him for that comment. She shook her head instead and tightened her hands even more. "No."

"Dammit, Smurfette, let go of the damn railing. Now." She didn't have time to tell him no, didn't have time to argue. He pulled, hard, breaking her death grip. She squealed again, her arms pin wheeling as she searched for something, anything, to hold on to. Something to break her certain fall to death. Her hands fisted into the material of his shirt, gripping the fabric and twisting it. She was hanging upside down, braced over his shoulder, her hair completely covering her face and obscuring her view. She dug her hands deeper into the shirt, feeling rock hard flesh underneath.

"Holy shit. Get your claws out of me!"

"I'm going to fall!"

"You are not going to fall. And stop wiggling before I smack that round ass of yours."

"What?" Indignation flooded her as blood rushed to her face. From his threat, or from being upside down? It didn't matter. Melanie screeched, tried to right herself so she wasn't hanging upside down. His arms tightened around her, his hand dangerously close to her bottom. "I'm going to vomit! Put me down!"

"Smurfette, I swear, if you toss your cookies all over me—" His words ended in a small grunt and she felt herself falling, tumbling. Except she wasn't because he was only trying to set her on her feet. She watched, her eyes drinking in the expanse of hard bare flesh that grew with each inch he lowered her—because her hands were still fisted in his shirt and it was pulling up as he lowered her. She gasped, mortified, and quickly let go. It didn't help, not when her body was sliding down his, not when she could feel every inch of hard muscle beneath the layers of clothes between them.

Muscle wasn't the only thing that was hard between them.

Melanie's bare feet touched the ground, the dirt and grass hard and cold against her skin. She gasped again and stepped back, her heel catching in the hem of her skirt and causing her to stumble. He grabbed her arms, holding her steady.

Holding her entirely too close.

She shook his hands free and pushed at him. "Let go of me!"

"Whatever you say, Smurfette." He stepped back, smiling at her with a crooked grin and twinkling eyes. He reached behind him and tugged at the hem of his shirt, pulling it back into place. Melanie swallowed a moan of disappointment when the shirt fell around him, covering the sliver of sculpted abdomen that she had been staring at.

Ridiculous. She was being ridiculous. Her neighbor was a Neanderthal, she didn't need to be staring at his stomach, no matter how hard and delectable it might be.

She brushed the tangle of hair from her face and gathered it behind her with one hand, then searched for her shoes. There they were, on the concrete porch of their building, right where she left them. She hiked her skirt up with her free hand and made her way over to them, trying not to stub her toe on the steps.

"So what exactly were you trying to do, anyway?"

She glanced over her shoulder as she stepped into the flats, her lips pursed in annoyance. Should she tell him? Not like it would make any difference, not when he was standing there, his hands resting on his lean lips, smiling.

Probably laughing at her.

She raised her chin and folded her arms across her chest. "I was trying to get up to the balcony because I left my keys inside."

"Locked yourself out, huh?"

"I left my keys inside." Which was the same thing, except it sounded better the way she said it. Or maybe not, since he chuckled again, the sound soft and warm.

"And what were you going to do if you made it up there? Play Juliet?"

"Hmph. No, I was going to open the door and get them."

"You left your balcony door unlocked?"

"Of course. Why not?"

"Because it's not safe, that's why not. Anyone could break in."

"Not hardly. It's too high. Only a superhero could make it up there."

He stood there watching her, his eyes too warm, with that annoying twinkle in their depths that let her know he was quietly laughing at her. Let him laugh all he wanted. It certainly wouldn't be the first time she had been laughed at. And it *was* too high. Hadn't he seen how close she had been to certain death?

He turned away from her and Melanie almost called after him, ready to swallow her pride and ask if he could at least let her inside. But he didn't leave. He stepped closer to her balcony then jumped, his hands closing over the spindles. He kicked out with his legs then swung himself up and over, landing on both feet with barely any noise. Her mouth dropped open in shock as he looked over his shoulder with a grin, then moved toward the sliding glass doors. She didn't even have time to tell him they were locked before he moved to the kitchen door and disappeared inside.

How had he done that? Each move had been smooth and graceful and powerful, like he didn't even have to try. Which was wrong. Just wrong. It wasn't fair, not at all.

But wasn't that what gorillas did? Climb things with no effort at all? That was what she had called him, and now she knew why. He really was a gorilla.

Except she had never seen a hairless gorilla with warm laughing eyes and a hard delicious body and a deep chuckle that made her bones turn to jelly and—

"You coming in, Smurfette?"

Melanie jumped then turned, surprised to see him standing at the entrance to their building, holding the door open for her. She shouldn't be surprised, though. After all, he had just jumped onto her balcony and gone inside her apartment. Why wouldn't he be standing there, holding the door open for her?

Probably because she had expected him to just go into his own apartment and forget about her. Isn't that what Neanderthals did?

He certainly wasn't a gorilla. So maybe he wasn't really a Neanderthal, either. Maybe—

No, she couldn't think like that. She wouldn't allow it.

Melanie raised her chin and stepped inside, brushing against him as she headed for the stairs. He chuckled again, the sound doing something much worse than annoying her. She tried to ignore it, to ignore the tingle of warmth that shot through her and swirled through her limbs before settling low in her belly. It would be so much easier to do if he wasn't right behind her, following her too closely.

Sweets, why was she suddenly so aware of him? Melanie shook her head. Her exclamation didn't fit. *Sweets* was too soft, too weak, to describe her frustration. Now, on top of everything else, the man had just ruined her favorite exclamation. How could life be so unfair?

She reached her door then turned around, giving him her best scowl. He paused, his brows raised in silent question, that silly crooked grin still on his face.

"You...you...oh! I don't like you!"

"Well, that's certainly a different way of saying thanks, considering I saved you."

"Saved me? Saved me? You most certainly did not!" Melanie didn't even flinch when the lie fell from her lips. That more than anything told her how much trouble she was in.

"Yeah, you keep telling yourself that, Smurfette."

"Why do you keep calling me that?"

"Because you remind me of Smurfette."

"What?"

"Not what. *Who.* Smurfette. You know. Because you were painted blue when we met."

"Well stop calling me that! My name is Melanie." She had no idea why she told him that. She didn't want him to know her name. She didn't want him to know anything about her at all. But now that she had, she waited for him to tell her his name. That's what good manners called for.

She waited some more but he still didn't say anything. He just stood there, his thumbs hooked into the pockets of his faded jeans, that grin on his face. He was too close, close enough she could feel the heat coming from his body, close enough she could see the subtle shadow of stubble that colored the smooth skin of his jaw.

She opened the door to her apartment and stepped inside, still facing him. "You are such a...a—"

"Neanderthal?" He offered the word nonchalantly, his grin growing to a wide smile that made her stomach tilt and whirl. She scowled at him, opening her mouth to say something, anything. He stepped back, still smiling, and winked at her.

"See you around, Smurfette."

Melanie slammed the door on him, not surprised to hear his laughter coming from the other side.

Chapter Five

Dale leaned back in the chair and raised his feet, crossing them at the ankles and letting them rest on the table. Mikey walked by and swatted his feet, knocking them back off.

"Do you mind? We have to eat there."

"I was going to wipe it down."

"Yeah, sure you were."

"What? I was." Dale dropped his feet to the floor and shifted in the chair. Jay took the seat next to him, sliding Dale's coffee out of the way to make room for his own.

"Don't argue with her. You know you're just going to lose."

"Exactly." Mikey took the chair on his other side, sliding to the edge so she was sprawled on it instead of really sitting. She pushed her hair out of her face, gathering it behind her and twisting it into a ponytail.

They were early for their shift, as they usually were. But there was nothing to do at the moment, since the day crew was out on a run and would be out for at least another half-hour. Technically the shifts ran from six at night until eight in the morning, then eight in the morning until six at night. But pretty much everyone in the field, at each station, relieved at seven and a little before five. He knew a few stations relieved even earlier for the night shift, which generally worked out well.

Unless you got hit with a late call.

Dale glanced at the clock on the wall above the television. Not quite four-thirty yet, so they had some time. Their Lieutenant, Pete Miller, was back in the office catching up on paperwork. Adam Price, the third firefighter on their shift, would probably be here in a few minutes—unless he got hit with a late detail and ended up having to go somewhere else, which was always a possibility.

If the engine was going to be out much longer than thirty minutes, they'd go relieve them on the scene. If not, they'd just wait until they got back. There wasn't much more to do the rest of the night, except for handling any calls that came in. Housework was done during the day, inspections and fire prevention details were done during the day. They didn't have any training scheduled. A light night so far, except for figuring out what they were doing for dinner.

Jay's train of thought must have been travelling in the same direction as Dale's because he leaned forward, his light gray eyes piercing Mikey. "What are we doing for dinner?"

"Why are you asking me?"

"Because you're sitting there."

"So is Dale. You didn't ask him."

Jay rolled his eyes and sat back, not bothering to respond. Dale bit the inside of his cheek to keep from laughing at their antics. The two had known each other for years—too many years. When Dale first transferred here, he had originally thought that maybe the two had something going on. That they were a couple, dating each other outside the station. Jay and Mikey could bicker like an old married couple one minute, then carry on like the best of friends the next while they finished each other's sentences. Which is exactly what they were: best friends. They were each in committed relationships: Mikey with her long-lost love, Nick Lansing; and Jay with Angie Warren—who just happened to be the sister of their paramedic, Dave. It was just a question of which one would be getting married first. Unless they had a double wedding, which wouldn't surprise Dale at all.

"So seriously, what are we doing for dinner? I'm getting hungry."

Mikey rolled her eyes again. "I don't know, you'll have to ask Pete. And how can you be hungry? It's not even five o'clock yet."

"I didn't each lunch."

"That's your own fault."

A wide smile spread across Jay's face. "No, it's Angie's fault."

"Oh God. Knock it off. Please. And you better not let Dave hear you talk that way. He'll kick your ass."

"No he won't. He's cool with it now." Dale noticed that the color drained from Jay's face despite the brave words. He laughed and kicked Jay's foot under the table.

"That doesn't mean he wants to hear the intimate details. No brother wants to hear anyone talking about his sister that way. I thought you would have figured that out by now." And he should have, considering how tense life had been around the station when Dave first learned Jay was seeing his sister. Not just tense, but downright confrontational, considering Dave and Jay had nearly come to blows one day.

Jay opened his mouth, no doubt put his foot in it, but Mikey talked right over him.

"Speaking of sisters, how is she doing?"

And fuck, Dale should have kept his own mouth closed. He should have known that any mention of sister—his or otherwise—would have led to questions. He shifted in the hard seat and reached for his coffee.

"Lauren's fine. Completely recovered, but you already knew that."

"I didn't mean Lauren. I meant Lindsay. How's she doing?"

Dale stiffened, his gaze sliding to Mikey's with a cool glare that should have let her know he wasn't discussing it. She didn't even flinch, just fixed him with a steady gaze of her own, her mossy green eyes boring into him.

He looked away, focused on bringing the chipped mug to his mouth so he could take a sip. Somehow he didn't think Mikey got the message. No, she got the message alright. She just wasn't listening.

"Well?"

"Well what?"

"How is she doing?"

"I have no idea."

Mikey leaned forward, her brows lowering over her eyes. "You mean to tell me you haven't even talked to her? At all?"

"No, I haven't. And I don't intend to." And that was the truth. The last time he had talked to Lindsay was that day at the rink almost five months ago, the day she had poisoned Lauren. He'd seen her since then, two days later at her bail hearing, but only because Lauren had insisted he go because she wasn't capable of going herself. But he hadn't talked to her, had barely even looked at her.

He knew Lauren had gone to visit her at the detention center, at least once, which he still wasn't happy about. For all he knew, she had visited Lindsay again and just hadn't bothered telling him. It was certainly possible, since Lauren knew exactly how he felt.

And he didn't understand it, didn't understand how Lauren could just go see her and act like nothing had happened. Lindsay had poisoned her! Maybe it wasn't deliberate, maybe she hadn't really known exactly what would happen when she emptied an entire bottle of eye drops into Lauren's drink. Maybe. Lindsay claimed she thought it would just give Lauren diarrhea, that was all. Dale didn't know if he believed her not. And when it came right down to it, it didn't matter.

Lindsay had tried to hurt Lauren. Deliberately. That was what mattered. And that was the one thing he still couldn't understand.

Or forgive.

And he couldn't help but wonder if maybe he could have done something to prevent it. If he could have done something to stop Lindsay from tumbling head-first down the path she had taken. He was the big brother, he should have seen it coming, should have done something to stop it.

Guilt gripped him, squeezing the breath from his lungs. He clenched his jaw and forced it away. Guilt did nothing, changed nothing. He told himself again that he wasn't responsible for Lindsay's actions, that she was a grown woman and needed to be held responsible for the choices she had made.

That didn't ease the doubt that clung to him, always there no matter how much he tried to brush it off.

He took a deep breath then looked back at Mikey, noticed she was still watching him, her face carefully blank, her eyes seeing too much. He frowned and stared back, two strong personalities fighting a sudden battle of wills.

Something sharp hit his foot, causing him to jump. Mikey jumped at the same time. They both looked at Jay, who snorted and rolled his eyes.

"You two look like wild animals, staring each other down. Knock it off so we can figure out what we're doing for dinner."

The kitchen door swung open and Pete walked in, his focus on the stack of papers in his hands. He paused, frowning, muttered something under his breath, then shook his head and turned to look at them. They looked back in silence, just watching him. Dale knew that he wasn't the only one counting under his breath, wondering how long it would take for Pete to come back to earth and ask them—

"What are you guys staring at?" They erupted in laughter, which only made Pete frown more. He looked over his shoulder then back at them. "What?"

"Nothing Pete. Nothing at all." Mikey pushed back from the table and moved to refill her coffee cup. Pete slid into the chair she had just left and tossed the papers down.

"So. They're talking about putting a second engine here."

Dale snorted. "Yeah, sure. They've been talking

about that for two years."

"And it looks like they're finally getting serious about it. See?" He pushed the top report toward Dale. He glanced down at it, seeing the words without really believing them before pushing it back to Pete.

"Maybe. But you know better than everyone how fast things change. I'll believe it when I see it."

"Yeah, I'm with Dale. As nice as it would be just to cut down on our runs, I'm not going to hold my breath." Jay drained his mug then leaned forward. "So, what are we doing for dinner?"

"Oh for shit's sake, Jay, knock it off. Can you stop worrying about your stomach for five minutes? Please? You're getting on my nerves."

"What Mikey said." Pete gathered up the reports then slid them to side. "Are we still going to the hockey game next weekend?"

Dale nodded. "Yeah. As far as I know, anyway."

"What do you mean, as far as you know?"

"Just what I said. I talked to Lauren last week and she said it would be no problem for Kenny to get the tickets." Dale hadn't wanted to ask her, thought that maybe it was taking advantage of her relationship with Kenny Haskell, one of the defensemen for the Baltimore Banners. But Kenny himself had made the offer a few times so maybe it wasn't really taking advantage.

"Oh man, do you think he can get us seats on the ice? I've always wanted to sit there and pretend I was a VIP." Pete rubbed his hands together, looking like a little kid on Christmas morning. Dale still had trouble thinking of him as their lieutenant. Early last year he'd been a blue shirt just like them, while they were all dealing with a new Captain who had made their lives miserable. He'd even done his best to get rid of Mikey, for reasons Dale still didn't quite understand. But the Captain had been promoted to Chief and was now serving time in an office at headquarters, where he could do minimal damage. Pete had been in the last group to be promoted to Lieutenant and—by some twist of fate—the powers-that-be had kept him here at Station 14. It worked out well, even if they sometimes had trouble remembering that Pete was no longer a blue shirt like the rest of them.

"I have no idea where the seats are, I just know we should have the tickets with no problems."

"Well can't you call and ask?"

"No I'm not going to call and ask. That would be rude."

"No it wouldn't. She's your sister. All I'm saying is just call and ask where the seats are. I'm dying of curiosity."

"You're worse than a kid. Fine, I'll call her later. But I don't want to hear you bitch if they're not on the ice."

"Bitch? Me? Never." Pete laughed then turned to Jay. "As for dinner, I have no idea. Jimmy's in charge of it tonight."

"Are you freaking serious? Great, we're never going to eat because they're probably going to be on the road all night. Why the hell would you let the medic crew handle it?"

Dale's phone rang, the noise muffled because it was in his pocket. He pulled it out and glanced at the screen. It was Lauren. He pushed away from the table and walked out of the kitchen, the bickering fading as he moved to the engine room. "Are your ears burning?"

"No. Should they be?"

"Maybe. Pete was just asking about the tickets for the game next week. Was Kenny able to get them?"

"Of course he was. And he made arrangements for everyone to go to the locker room after the game, too."

"He didn't have to do that."

"He knows, but for some reason I still can't figure out, he likes you." Her laughter came through the phone, clear then muted. He heard some more background noise, deep and low, and figured she was with Kenny now and that they were talking. At least, that's what he hoped they were doing.

Dale moved deeper into the engine room, toward the back where a few chairs were set up. He pushed one close to the concrete wall and sat in it, leaning back so the front legs were off the floor.

"Kenny says hi."

"Tell him hi back."

"And he says you guys are getting the VIP treatment."

"Lauren, he doesn't have to—"

"And he says to shut up and deal with it." Dale heard a deeper rumbling, then more laughter before Lauren came back on the phone. "Okay, he didn't say that last part, I did."

"Yeah, that sounds more like it. So what's up?"

"Why do you think something's up?"

"Because you called."

"Maybe I just wanted to talk to you."

"Yeah, okay. Now out with it. What's up?"

"Nothing. I just wanted to make sure you knew Lindsay's trial date got moved back. It's going to be the end of April now."

Sour bile twisted Dale's gut. He squeezed his eyes shut and took a deep breath through clenched teeth, trying to settle his stomach. Trying to settle his nerves.

"You still there?"

One more deep breath then he opened his eyes. His grip on the phone was too tight and he made a conscious effort to ease it. "Yeah. I'm here."

"You are going, right?"

"I wasn't planning on it."

"Dale, you need to be there. She's our sister."

"No. She's *your* sister, not mine." His voice was tightly controlled, cold and distant. He heard Lauren sigh, pictured her pinching the bridge of her nose as she shook her head.

"It doesn't work that way and you know it."

"Lauren, I'm not getting into this right now."

"Fine. Just tell me you'll be there and I'll let it go."

"Lauren—"

"No. I'm not backing down on this. I'm going to be there. Mom and Dad are going to be there. You need to be there, too."

"Why? Tell me why. So we can pretend we're all one big happy family and that what she did doesn't matter?"

"That's not why and you know it." Lauren's voice had turned chilly, a little stubborn. Well, let her get upset. He wasn't budging on this, no matter what she did.

"I don't know anything of the sort."

"Because she's our sister, Dale. You can be mad all you want, but she's still our sister. We have to be there to support her."

"Bullshit." He leaned forward in the chair, the legs hitting the concrete floor with a hollow thud. "She tried to kill you, Lauren."

"Not deliberately—"

"I don't give a flying fuck if it was deliberate or not. She poisoned you. It doesn't matter why. You could have died. How can you even think of supporting her after what she did?"

"Because—" Lauren paused, clearing her throat. It didn't matter because Dale still heard the emotion in her voice, heard the thickness wrapping around her words. "Because she's family. And you need to be there. I'm asking you to be there. For me."

"Dammit Lauren—"

"I need to go. I'll talk to you later."

Dale stared at the phone for several long minutes after she disconnected the call. Emotions raged within him, dark and swirling, threatening to overwhelm him. Fuck. He didn't want to deal with this now. He didn't want to deal with it at all. And damn Lauren for putting him in this position, for saying she needed him to be there. Why couldn't she understand how he felt?

He jammed the phone in his pocket then stormed across the engine room, pushing past Mikey as she was coming out of the kitchen. She grabbed his arm, stopping him.

"Everything okay?"

"Yeah. Fine. Fucking fabulous."

She raised her brows, her hand still wrapped around his arm. "Yeah, I can see that. Where you off to?"

"I'm going downstairs to work out." He glanced down at her hand then back up at her. "Do you mind?"

"Need someone to spot you?"

"No, I don't."

She dropped his arm and stepped back, her hands

held up in mock surrender. "Suit yourself. I just thought you might want to go a few rounds with the punching bag and might need someone to hold it for you."

Dale stared at her, knowing what she was trying to do. He'd invite her down, throw a few punches, then end up listening to her talk. Ask questions. Give advice.

Or maybe just let him vent.

Yeah, like that would work. There wasn't enough time in the world for him to vent, to get the poison of his thoughts out of his system.

But maybe just hitting the bag would help. Maybe that would be enough to get him to calm down, to at least clear his mind, if only for a few hours.

He finally nodded then turned toward the basement stairs. "Fine, you can spot me. But I'm not talking about it."

He headed down the stairs, Mikey following him. And he could have sworn he heard her laugh and call him a liar.

Chapter Six

Lauren grabbed the dishes from the table and carried them into the kitchen. The sound of silverware scraping against china was high-pitched, too loud.

"I can get them, you know." Dale called out but his words were drowned out by the sound of water running and the garbage disposal kicking on. He sighed and looked over at Kenny, who was seated across from him at the dining room table.

They had come to his place for dinner, showing up with less than thirty minutes' warning with pizza and beer. Dale had tried to tell Lauren no, tried to tell her he wasn't in the mood for company. She didn't listen. She never listened.

"She's still mad at me, huh?"

Kenny shrugged. He had a bruise along his jaw and a butterfly bandage on the bridge of his nose, and who knew how many other cuts and bruises that Dale couldn't see. All of them were courtesy of the Banners' game last night, and probably the game before then, too. The Banners had tonight off then headed to

Chicago for a game tomorrow night, which made their visit even more suspicious. The couple should be at home, cuddling or whatever, not showing up here with pizza.

Kenny took a long swallow of beer and glanced over his shoulder before leaning closer to Dale. He spoke in a low tone, like he didn't want Lauren to hear him. "I'm not sure 'mad' is the right word. But yeah, she's upset."

"Great." Dale sipped his own beer, his brows lowered in a frown.

"Listen, it's not my place to get in the middle of this but I agree with you. Lauren knows that."

Dale waited, knowing Kenny had more to say. "But?"

"But—" Kenny shook his head. "I'm going to be there for Lauren. Because that's what she wants. And that's what this all comes down to: being there for Lauren."

"For you. You're supposed to be there for her. That's the way relationships work. It's not the same for me."

"Why not? I'd think it would apply to you even more because you're her brother."

"Well it doesn't, because—"

"Because you're being an ass." Lauren's voice carried into the dining room, loud and clear over the noise she was making. Dale clenched his jaw and shot a dirty look in the direction of the kitchen.

"Damn. I hate when she does that." He raised his voice so she could hear him. Not like he needed to, since she was hearing them just fine. "Why don't you save yourself the trouble of eavesdropping and just come back in here?"

The garbage disposal kicked off. "No, I'm good."

"You're a pain in the ass, is what you are."

"You still love me." Lauren stood in the doorway of the kitchen, leaning against the doorframe, a small towel slung over her shoulder. Tall, lean, with an athlete's body. Her dark hair was a little longer, falling just below her shoulders, the subtle waves framing her slender face. Amusement glittered in her dark eyes, eyes so much like his own. But beneath the amusement he saw something else: worry, anxiety. Disappointment.

Dale sighed and looked away, not willing to face the emotion he saw so clearly. "I really don't feel like talking about this, Lauren. You know that."

"Why?"

"Why? Really? How can you even ask me that? Because I don't want to, that's why."

"That's not an excuse."

"Tough, because that's all you're getting."

"It's a cop-out."

"The hell it is."

"Yeah, it is. Just listen to yourself—"

"Guys! Enough, please." Kenny held his hands out, like he was some kind of referee breaking up a fight. Dale stared at him for a long second then sat back in the chair, stretching his legs out. He didn't bother looking at Lauren. He didn't have to. He knew his sister too well, knew she was watching him with those wide eyes, studying him too intently, her chin tilted up in stubbornness.

Waiting for the right moment, waiting for him to show weakness so she could pounce on it and use it to her advantage.

She'd always been able to do that, ever since they

were kids and she wanted to do whatever it was he was doing and he would try to say no, try to convince her to do something else. Fishing, running, camping. Football. Hockey. It didn't matter. If he was doing it, she wanted to do it, just to prove she could.

And sometimes to prove she was better at it than some of his friends, just because she could. Determined and stubborn, she would never take no for an answer. Not when she was younger, not as a teenager. And not even now, when she was a grown woman.

He had a moment's sympathy for Kenny and almost asked the man if he knew what he was getting into. One look at Kenny and he shook his head, the words dying before they even came to life. There was no doubt in Dale's mind that Kenny knew exactly what he was getting into. And even if he didn't...well, that wasn't Dale's business. What was his business was the sensation of a set of eyes boring into him.

"Would you stop staring at me?"

"Guilty conscience?"

"I'm not going, Lauren. End of discussion."

"Yup. Guilty conscience. And you're going." She turned back into the kitchen, getting the last word in before he could tell her no.

Not that it really mattered because she wouldn't listen to him anyway. He swore under his breath then shot a dirty look at Kenny when he heard the man chuckling.

"Yeah, real funny. Keep it up and I'll break your nose again."

"Not like I haven't gotten used to it this season."

"Hm." Dale raised the beer bottle to his mouth, ready to take a long swallow. Loud music blared to life with an ear-numbing shriek. He jerked in surprise, spilling beer over his hand and down the front of his shirt. Kenny jumped, his head spinning to the side as he stared at the wall. Lauren must have jumped, too...and dropped something, from the sound coming from the kitchen.

"Dammit. Not tonight. I don't need this shit tonight." Dale pushed out of his chair and stormed across to the living room, ready to bang on the wall with his fist.

"What the hell is that?"

"It's my damn *neighbor*." He shouted the last word, hitting the wall hard enough that the picture next to him shook and tilted to the side. He waited then hit the wall again, not stopping until the music quieted.

He could still hear it, but at least it wasn't quite as loud. Kenny and Lauren were both staring at him, their expressions ranging from shock to outright disbelief.

Lauren shook her head, the corners of her mouth tilting in a sympathetic smile. "Wow. Now I know why you call him the neighbor from hell."

"Her."

"What?"

"My neighbor from hell is a *her*. Smurfette."

"Your neighbor's name is Smurfette?"

"Nah. That's just what I call her." Dale fought the grin that wanted to break out on his face. "Her real name is...shit. She told me. What the hell is it? It doesn't matter. She's Smurfette."

"Really?" Lauren tilted her head to the side, watching him, something dangerous sparkling in her eyes. "So what's her story?"

"There is no story. And don't even think about it. You are so way off base, it's not even funny."

"I didn't say anything!"

"You didn't have to. I know that look."

"What look?"

"That look." Dale pointed at her, frowning. "Like you're up to no good."

Lauren was getting ready to argue, he could tell from the gleam in her eyes and the crooked smile on her face. But a knock on the door, hard and insistent, stopped her. Dale bit back a groan. He knew that knock, knew without a doubt who was at the door.

And he wondered who was the lesser of two evils: his sister, or Smurfette.

The knock sounded again, louder this time. Then he heard a muffled squeal and he had to choke back his laughter, somehow knowing that Smurfette had hit the door hard enough to hurt her hand.

Lauren was still watching him, curiosity gleaming in her eyes. "Aren't you going to get that?"

"No."

"Seriously?"

"Seriously."

Smurfette knocked again, not quite as hard as before but still hard enough for the sound to echo through his apartment. Dale's eyes locked with Lauren's, both of them silently daring the other. It was just a question of who would break first and give in.

Lauren took a quick step forward. Dale swore under his breath then turned toward the door before his sister could reach it. He didn't know why, only knew that he didn't want his sister seeing Smurfette. Was it some kind of survival instinct? Or something more basic than that? He wasn't sure and was afraid to look too closely.

He opened the door a few inches, making sure to

place his body in the opening between the hall and his living room, blocking Lauren's line of sight. Sure enough, Smurfette was standing in the hall, her hair floating around her in a halo of fire as her blue eyes sparked with anger and impatience. Bright splashes of green and yellow and orange smeared her cheek, her left arm and both hands.

"You knocked one of my paintings over!"

"Yeah? Well, you made me spill my beer."

"Beer? Beer! You're worried about beer? You nearly destroyed my painting!" Her voice rose in pitch, each word louder than the other as she waved her hands in his face. She stepped closer and Dale leaned back, trying to avoid the paint on her hands. He wasn't fast enough; her left hand grazed his jaw, the touch wet and slimy against his skin. She didn't even seem to notice, just kept advancing on him, waving those paint-smeared hands in his face.

"Why? Why do you always do this to me? Why can't you just knock on my door like a normal, civilized, well-mannered, decent human being instead of a Neanderthal? Why?"

"Wow. Smurfette, calm down. It's not that big of a deal." But apparently it was, judging by the way she kept waving her hands, by the volume of her voice. And shit, were those tears in her eyes? No, it couldn't be. She was wound up, yeah. Angry, even. She couldn't have tears in her eyes and be angry at the same time, could she?

Dale fought the urge to look over his shoulder, knowing that Lauren and Kenny were both watching. The last thing he needed was for Lauren to come to the door and ask what was going on, for her to see Smurfette. Christ, he'd never live it down. And then she'd want to invite Smurfette in, probably want to talk to her.

No. No way in hell could he let that happen.

He stepped forward, forcing Smurfette to take a step back. Well, if she was a normal person, she would have stepped back. But Smurfette was anything but normal, he had known that from the very beginning, even before he'd met her. She didn't budge, didn't even blink when Dale's body pressed against hers. And she certainly didn't step back like he expected, so instead of air, he was feeling the soft curves of flesh that she hid beneath the flowing skirt and loose blouse.

The memory of the other day came to life with a heated intensity. Her body, draped over his shoulder; his hands, curled around the softness of her legs. Her fingers, digging into the flesh of his back as she kicked her legs, making him wonder if she'd dig her nails into him if he was stretched on top of her, over her, in her.

And fuck, what the hell was he doing? He'd done his best to push those images, that memory, from his mind. It had been a fluke, completely unlike him, completely out of character. Not that he didn't think that way, but about Smurfette? Hell no. She was the neighbor from hell. He needed his head examined if he was thinking like that about the woman in front of him.

And yeah, he apparently needed his head examined, because the thoughts weren't going away. She was standing in front of him, her eyes shimmering with moisture, her creamy skin turning a deep pink from anger and who knew what else, her hands still waving frantically in the air. She was still talking, he knew because her mouth was moving, but he didn't hear a word she was saying. He just kept thinking that with the way their bodies were pressed together, that it had to be obvious to her what his little brain was thinking, but she was oblivious.

Totally and completely oblivious.

"Dale? Who is it?" Lauren spoke from behind, nudging him in the back as she tried to look over his shoulder. He shifted, doing his best to block her view and push her away at the same time.

"Nobody. Go away."

Smurfette finally stopped talking, her mouth snapping shut with a small click as her eyes rounded in surprise. Something that looked suspiciously close to horror—with maybe a tinge of embarrassment—filled the ocean blue of her eyes, turning them a stormy gray. She raised her hand to her mouth and stepped back.

"OhmyGodI'msosorry." The words came out so fast that they ran together as one single word. Her chest rose with a deep breath, the loose material stretching across her full breasts. And shit, she wasn't wearing a bra.

Holy shit. Why in the hell had he noticed that? He shouldn't have noticed, shouldn't have even been looking.

Lauren finally pushed him out of the way, ducking her head under his arm and moving so she was standing in front of him. Dale clenched his jaw, his back stiffening when he heard Kenny chuckle behind him.

"Hi. I'm Lauren. And you are?"

Smurfette's gaze darted to him, her horror still clear. She shook her head and took a small step back, the toes of her bare feet peeking out from the hem of her skirt. She glanced over her shoulder, no doubt thinking she could bolt back to her apartment and disappear, then slid her gaze to Lauren.

"I'm so sorry. I didn't realize you had company. I'm sorry. I'll just go back—" Smurfette turned and almost lunged toward her door, seeking escape. Her hand closed over the knob and turned, but nothing happened. Dale watched, biting back a smile as she kept trying to turn the handle with no luck.

"Lock yourself out again?"

She turned and glared at him, the expression almost comical. Then she frowned, shaking her head. "I don't understand. I didn't think it was locked. I could have sworn—"

"Don't worry about it. You can come join us, we'll figure something out." Lauren made the offer before Dale could stop her. Damn his sister. What did she think she was doing?

He was afraid he knew exactly what she was doing.

"No, I couldn't. That would be so rude. I don't want to interrupt your—" Smurfette paused, her eyes darting back and forth between Lauren and him. "Your date."

"Date?" Lauren laughed, the sound too loud. Damn her, why couldn't she have just let Smurfette think what she was thinking? "Trust me, this isn't a date. I'm Dale's sister."

Smurfette looked over at him. "Dale? Your name is Dale?"

Great, now she knew his name, too. Not that it was a big deal, but he kind of liked the idea that she didn't know who he was.

Lauren kicked him in the foot and gave him a dirty look, then smiled at Smurfette. "Yeah, his name is Dale. And I'm Lauren. Why don't you come inside and get cleaned up and we can figure out how to get you back into your apartment." Lauren grabbed her elbow, careful to avoid the drying paint that covered Smurfette as she led her past Dale and into his apartment. She kicked him again when she pushed by him. Literally pushed, hard enough that he stumbled back against the door.

"What was that for?" He would have had better luck getting an answer from the wall because Lauren ignored him. This was so not what he needed. Not only was Smurfette now in his apartment, his sister was attaching herself to the woman. He didn't know what was going on in Lauren's head, but the gleam in her eye and bright smile could only mean one thing: trouble.

Dale shut the door with a little more force than necessary. Smurfette jumped and glanced over at him but Lauren merely smiled. "Dale, go get a towel or something."

"Really, that's not necessary. I don't want to impose—"

"You're not imposing. It's the least my brother can do for knocking your painting over. It was one you were working on, right? It must be, for you to be covered in paint. And I'm sorry, but I didn't catch your name?"

Smurfette's eyes widened, no doubt completely caught off-guard by Lauren. Dale couldn't help but sympathize because he was a little caught off-guard, too. What the hell was Lauren up to?

"Uh, Melanie. Melanie Reeves."

"Nice to meet you, Melanie. Here, have a seat and Dale will be right back with those towels." Lauren leveled a frown in his direction. "Won't you, Dale?"

He frowned back at her then moved past them into the kitchen, grabbing two towels from the drawer and hurrying back into the dining room. No way did he want to leave them alone any longer than necessary. He tossed the towels at Lauren, smothering a laugh when they smacked her in the face. She gave him a dirty look then turned her back on him.

Kenny yanked on the waistband of his jeans, hard enough that Dale almost fell into the chair next to him. "Smooth. Real smooth. You're lucky she didn't throw them back at you."

"You're not helping." Dale muttered the words, trying to keep his voice low. Why, he didn't know, since Lauren and Smurfette were mere feet away.

"So. You're an artist?"

"Uh, yes. I am. A painter."

"Cool. I've never met an artist before. Have you, guys?" Lauren glanced over her shoulder, her eyes narrowed as she shot them both a look. Dale had no idea what she was doing, what she was up to, and he was tired of playing games.

"Lauren, enough." He stood up and grabbed the towel from her hands then passed it to Smurfette. She took the towel from him, her eyes wide and uncertain as their gazes locked. "Is your kitchen door still unlocked?"

"Yes."

"Even though I told you to lock it. Why am I not surprised? Come on, you can wait in the hall. I'll go jump the balcony again." He reached for her hand but Lauren was faster, knocking it away.

"Jump her balcony? Again?"

"Yeah. This isn't the first time Smurfette's locked herself out."

"It was just the one time. I was doing fine. I would have been fine. You didn't have to rescue me—"

"You were stretched between the two railings like

someone on the rack, fretting that you were going to die."

Smurfette straightened, her posture regal and defiant. "I most certainly was not."

Dale snorted. "Yeah, okay. You're not fooling anyone. I was there, remember? Now, come on." He reached for her hand again but once more, Lauren stopped him.

"Since you know how to get into her place, you go take care of that. Take Kenny with you and Melanie will stay here with me."

An icy blast of something that might have been fear ripped through Dale. Lauren's words were low on the list of words he didn't want to hear. Not just low; probably dead last. Especially with the calculating gleam in her eyes. He wanted to pull her to her feet and drag her back to the bedroom and yell at her until she told him what she was up to. Not that that would do any good because Dale was positive she wouldn't answer him, no matter how much he yelled.

"Lauren—"

"Or we could sit here and continue our discussion about our sister."

Dale bit back a curse, his jaw clenched so hard that a sharp pain shot along the side of his face. Damn her. Why was she even doing this? He couldn't believe that Lauren would stoop to blackmail, even about Lindsay. And it's not like the threat really meant anything, not when he knew they'd end up having another discussion anyway. And another, and another, until Dale finally gave in.

He ground his teeth together then headed for the door, pausing to look back at Kenny. "You coming?"

"You really need me—"

"Yes he does. Now go." Lauren gave him some indecipherable look that Kenny must have understood because he followed Dale out the door and down the stairs, out into the damp night air.

"What the hell is my sister up to?"

"I have no idea."

"I don't like the idea of her upstairs with Smurfette. By themselves." Dale moved to the balcony, looking up at it.

"Why do you call her that?"

"Did you see the paint all over her?"

"Yeah."

"The first time I met her, the paint was blue." Dale grinned. "Reminded me of Smurfette."

"I'm going to pretend I didn't even hear that."

"Oh, come on. Smurfette was cute. Her voice was annoying as hell, but she was still cute."

"Now you're just scaring me."

Dale grinned again then jumped up, his hands closing around the spindles. He kicked out with his legs then swung them over the railing, landing with a soft thud. He looked down at Kenny, still smiling. "You coming?"

"How about I just meet you upstairs? It's not like you need me to help open the door."

"Fine. I'll just Lauren you wimped out."

"What is this, some kind of payback for something?"

"If I have to do this, so do you. Come on, get up here." Dale stepped out of the way, watching as Kenny climbed the balcony in much the same way he did. Then he turned and opened the door, stepping into the large eat-in kitchen, Kenny right behind him. The room looked just like it did the other time he'd been in here. Warm and cozy, with a colorful hooked rug covering the tile floor. The walls were painted a warm shade of yellow with splashes of bright red in the curtains and bold prints hanging on the wall. Even the canisters on the counter were red, a hodge podge collection of apples and roosters that shouldn't really go together but did.

"Interesting decorating choices."

"Wait until you see the rest of the place." Dale led the way out of the kitchen, smiling when he heard Kenny stumble to a stop behind him.

"Holy shit."

"Told you."

A small loveseat was tucked into the corner of what should have been the dining room, next to a compact stereo and a rack full of music CDs. The rest of the apartment—part of the dining room area and the entire living room—was empty of real furniture. At least, functional furniture, unless you counted the small table next to the door. There was a small bench along the far wall, shelving storage units on either side of the sliding glass doors, and a long table shoved against the wall adjacent to the kitchen. The rest of the space was empty.

But it was anything but plain, not with the multitude of colors surrounding them. Bright splashes, dark splashes. Greens, blues, reds, yellows, oranges. Even blacks and grays. Color was everywhere, like a rainbow on steroids had exploded into a million different pieces and landed on every available surface.

There was color on the canvases scattered around the room and on the walls, propped in the corner and on easels here and there. Puddles of color on the canvas drop cloth that covered the floor. Color smeared on the long table and even on the storage units filled with brushes and paints and jars and who knew what else.

"Holy shit," Kenny repeated, amazement and disbelief clear in his lowered voice. He moved into the room, studying several pieces, a thoughtful expression on his face. He looked back at Dale and grinned. "These are actually pretty good."

"You can't be serious." *Good* wasn't the word that came to mind when he looked at them. He didn't know what word came to mind. Hectic. Scattered. Unfocused.

Bright. Definitely bright.

"Yeah. These are really good."

"How would you even know that?"

"I took a couple of art classes in college."

"Please don't tell me you were into painting nudes."

"No. I studied art, not painted it. Art history, art appreciation. Shit like that. It was actually pretty cool. And I'm telling you, these are pretty good."

"I'll take your word for it." Dale moved toward the door, making sure it was unlocked before he opened it. "Come on, I want to get back. I don't like the idea of Lauren being alone with Smurfette."

"Wait, hang on." Kenny moved across the room, his head tilted to the side as he studied one painting in particular. The colors were bright yet somehow muted, the brush strokes bold and defiant—except for the smear running down the middle.

That must be the painting she had been working on, the one he had somehow caused to fall over. Guilt swept through him, cold and sharp, followed by a bitter sense of loss as he studied the painting. The emotions made no sense. Maybe he had been responsible for knocking the painting over. Maybe he had hit the wall too hard.

And it was just as likely that she hadn't had the canvas propped up right, that she had somehow knocked it over herself.

Maybe. The excuse didn't sit well with him, not when it was just that: a lame excuse. He cleared his throat to get Kenny's attention. "You ready?"

"Yeah." The other man straightened then closed the distance between them. "That's a shame, I really like that one. There's something very powerful about it, even with the smear. I might offer to buy it from her anyway."

"You can't be serious."

"Why not?" Kenny looked at him, truly puzzled. Dale didn't bother to answer. He couldn't, not when he was trying to figure out why the thought of Kenny owning anything of Smurfette's sat like a slab of concrete in his gut.

Ridiculous.

He held the door open for Kenny then tested the knob once more, just to make sure it was really unlocked, before closing it. Ten seconds later they were back in his own apartment. The sight that greeted them made him stumble to a stop, his gut twisting again.

Lauren and Smurfette were sitting next to each other on the sofa, laughing at something. The sound of her laughter was music, high and tinkling, almost like crystal. Dale blinked, silently swearing when the smile on Smurfette's face faded and disappeared when she turned and saw him standing there.

He cleared his throat and tried to look away, forcing his gaze to focus on something just behind her.

"Alright Smurfette, you can go home. Your door's unlocked again."

"Melanie's staying for a little longer, until we finish our wine." Lauren held up her full glass. Where in the hell had she found wine? Dale didn't drink it, didn't have any in the house.

No, that was wrong. There had been a bottle in the back of the cabinet, left over from the last time Lauren and Kenny had been by. Leave it to Lauren to find it and bring it out, to offer it to Smurfette. Dale just hoped she was a fast drinker.

"Guess what, guys? Melanie has never been to a hockey game. She's never even seen one before."

"Why am I not surprised?" Dale muttered the words as he moved past them to the dining room, looking for his beer. From the look on Lauren's face, he must have been louder than he realized. She frowned at him, but only for a second because her expression cleared, her eyes sparkling with amusement.

She raised her glass and touched it against Smurfette's then took a small sip. Dale grabbed his own beer, ready to drain it.

"So she's coming with us this weekend."

Dale paused, the bottle halfway to his mouth. He stared at Lauren, thinking he must have missed something. "Who's coming where?"

"Melanie. She's coming to the game with us this weekend. I told her she could drive with you."

Dale stared at Lauren, his mouth hanging open in shock. Then, very slowly and very deliberately, he tilted the bottle and drained it, placed it on the table, and stalked into the kitchen.

This called for something stronger than beer. A lot stronger.

Chapter Seven

Melanie heard the knock, knew instantly who it was. Him. Her neighbor. Dale. She knew not just because it was close to the time they were supposed to leave but also because of the knock itself. Hard. Demanding. Full of authority. It was just so...so...*him*.

And was she really going to a hockey game? Was she really? Not just with *him*, but with his sister and her boyfriend and 18,000 other complete strangers. What had ever possessed her to say yes to something so barbaric and out of character?

Melanie frowned. Now that she thought about it, actually consciously thought about it, she didn't think she ever really said yes. His sister had said something, that led to her saying something else about something, and suddenly Melanie heard that she was going to a hockey game. She hadn't even agreed, or even disagreed. She wished she could say it was because she had been so surprised and caught off-guard but that wasn't the case. No, if she was honest, she had to admit—to herself, at least—that the reason she hadn't said anything was because of *him*. Because he had looked so surprised and so speechless and so discombobulated and so…frantic. Yes, he had actually looked frantic, like a wild animal caught in a trap he couldn't escape from.

And now here he was, knocking on her door. To take her to a hockey game. She was actually really going to a hockey game. Together. With *him*.

Not *him*. He had a name. Dale. She needed to start thinking of him as Dale and not *him*. But oh sweets, she was afraid to. It was much safer to think of him as…well, *him*.

The knock sounded again, a little harder, a little more forceful. He—Dale—was probably getting impatient. Well, let him. He was early and she wasn't quite ready yet so he could just wait.

Except she was ready. She was dressed, she had her small bag hanging across her body, with her wallet and keys. She didn't need anything else. All she needed to do was walk across the room and open the door and that would be that.

Melanie took a deep breath for courage then moved to the door, pulling it open just as he was about to knock again. His hand kept moving forward, meeting air, and he stumbled, catching his balance a second before his body would have tumbled against hers. Melanie took a hasty step back, her heart pounding. Why? From excitement? Ridiculous. Why would she be excited?

Maybe he—Dale—was attractive. Okay, yes. He was attractive, no maybe about it. Tall. Hair the color of light coffee mixed with shades of peanut, not too short, not too long, a little shaggy on the top. Deep brown eyes, the color of strong-brewed tea, like dark sepia with just a few flecks of gold that captured the light. A strong face, like a warrior's. Not pretty but definitely captivating, with strong lines and planes.

He was well-built, with broad shoulders and broad chest, sculpted abdominals that she had seen up close that very first time they met. A trim waist and lean hips and strong legs. Not muscle bound, not like the pictures of bodybuilders and even some models she had seen. His muscles were honest. Though how muscles could be honest, she didn't know. She just somehow knew that his build wasn't really from working out, but from actually working.

She wasn't sure if that should comfort her—or scare her.

He was dressed casually in worn faded jeans and a long sleeve t-shirt with some kind of eagle logo on it. The sleeves were pushed up to his elbows, revealing the light spattering of hair on his muscled forearms.

"Are you done staring?"

Melanie started then took a quick step back, her gaze travelling up his body to meet his eyes. Small lines crinkled at the corners. Laugh lines, to match the amused gleam in his eyes and the crooked grin that teased the edges of his mouth. Melanie frowned and tilted her chin up.

"I was not staring."

"Sure you weren't, Smurfette." His gaze travelled from her head to her feet and back up again. It was a clinical glance, not an appreciative one, and Melanie fought the urge to be insulted by it.

"Is that what you're wearing?"

She glanced down at herself, not sure of his comment. Long skirt, loose blouse, comfortable sandals. She frowned. "What's wrong with what I'm wearing?"

"Nothing. It's just a little dressy. Don't you have jeans or something?"

"No."

He—*Dale*—opened his mouth to say something then quickly closed it. His brows lowered over his eyes and he frowned and Melanie didn't understand why.

"You really don't have any jeans?"

"No." Why did he look so surprised at that? She thought he might say something else but he just shook his head and stepped back, letting her out into the hallway. She was ready to pull the door closed when he stopped her.

"Wait. Are you sure you have your keys?"

"Yes, I'm sure."

"You sure you're sure?"

"Oh sweets! I am not an idiot. Yes, I have my keys." She rattled the small bag resting against her hip, the metallic jingling of keys unmistakable.

"Just checking."

She pulled the door closed then followed him downstairs and out to the parking lot. He turned left while she turned right.

"Smurfette, where are you going?"

"To my car."

"But we're driving together, remember?"

"Of course I remember. My car's over here."

"But my car is this way."

"I don't want to go in your car. I want to go in mine." And that was exactly what she was going to do. If he didn't like that, well, too bad for him. It was bad enough she had no control over the overall coming evening, being forced to go to a barbaric sports event with people she didn't know. She didn't want to be forced to rely on someone else—a virtual stranger—for her way home. Melanie was going in her car, so she could leave if she wanted to. If he didn't like it, he could drive himself.

She almost thought he was going to do just that. In fact, a small part of her wished she would. To her amazement, he changed directions and followed her across the parking lot, muttering under his breath when she stopped at her car and unlocked the doors. He stood on the other side, his arm resting against the white metal of the hood, his brows lowered in another frown.

Did the man not know how to do anything but frown?

"I don't think I'm going to fit into this thing."

"Don't be silly. Of course you will. My paintings fit with no problem, so will you." She opened her door and climbed in, smiling at the new car smell that greeted her. The Fiat 500L had been her gift to herself several months ago and she still loved it. She had wanted one of the smaller models, one with two doors, but her mom had wisely suggested she get the larger one so she could transport her art work. Her mom, of course, had been completely correct.

Melanie inhaled deeply then started the engine, listening to its whispered hum as the car came to life. The door opened and Dale folded himself into the passenger seat. Melanie couldn't help but grinning at the picture. "The seat does go back, you know."

"Not far enough it doesn't." He muttered the words in a harsh whisper then adjusted the seat. He shifted his legs around, twisting and turning in the seat, still grumbling as he reached for the seatbelt. Melanie put the car in gear and took off, almost laughing at his gasp of surprise. He leaned forward and grabbed the dashboard.

"Holy shit, Smurfette. Take it easy. I'd like to get there in one piece."

This time she did laugh. She pulled into the street with the sharp sound of rubber squealing against asphalt, maneuvering the small car through the residential neighborhood until she reached the main street. Traffic was a little too heavy for her liking and she sighed in disappointment. She'd still be able to zip around traffic once they hit I83, but it wouldn't be as fun as it usually was, not since rush hour had just started.

Her passenger would probably appreciate that, considering he was wedged into the seat, his legs locked in front of him, one hand against the dashboard and the other gripping the door. Melanie laughed again then leaned forward to turn on the stereo. The soundtrack from her favorite musical this month blared through the speakers, the deep tenor of Colm Wilkinson filling the car.

A car darted in front of her and she hit the brakes. Dale jerked forward and the car behind them blew the horn, the sound a long wail that could be heard over the music. Melanie glanced in the rearview then smiled and waved at the driver behind her. The horn blared again as the driver waved back with his middle finger.

"Well that wasn't very nice." Melanie checked her side mirror then pressed her foot against the gas pedal, shooting out into the break in traffic. The music came to an abrupt stop as her passenger turned the stereo off.

"Holy shit. Jesus Christ. You're a madwoman. A menace. You shouldn't be driving."

"That's not a very nice thing to say."

"Why? It's the truth! How did you even manage to get your license?"

"I meant the other thing you said. Your language."

"What? Holy shit? It seemed appropriate. And Christ, would you slow down? I'd like to not die tonight, especially in my first-due area."

"Not that. The other thing."

"What other thing?"

"What you said." Melanie glanced over at him and lowered her voice. "JC."

"What?" He frowned, a look of pure confusion twisting his features into something almost comical. His lips moved, like he was talking to himself, then his expression changed. "JC? You mean Jesus Christ?"

"Yes, that. You shouldn't say that, it's not nice."

"You have got to be fucking kidding me. Are you serious? What are you, super-religious or something?"

"No, I don't identify with any organized religion. But it's still rude to use any of the deities' names that way and you shouldn't do it."

Silence greeted her and she wondered if maybe her words had given her passenger something to think about. His muttered cursing told her she had been wrong.

"Out of everything that has come out of my mouth, that's what you have a problem with? You're insane. Nutso. Crazy."

"No. Most of your vocabulary is questionable, but I don't expect anything different from someone like you."

"Someone like me? What the hell is that supposed to mean?"

"It means what it means. Someone like you. A—"

"Neanderthal?"

"Yes, exactly." Melanie glanced over at him and smiled, expecting him to smile back. He was glowering instead. "Did I say something wrong?"

Oh sweets, she probably did. He just kept looking at her, his hands braced against the inside of the car, a ferocious scowl on his face. Not ferocious. Feral. Dangerous. And Melanie realized that he could be dangerous. He could be a murderous madman. She didn't know him, not at all. Why had she been so careless and agreed to go with him? He could take her anywhere. To a remote dirt road to kill her. To an abandoned warehouse to mutilate her body. To—wait, no he couldn't. She was driving. He couldn't take her anywhere, not unless he forced her to drive somewhere and he couldn't do that because she was driving.

Unless he had a weapon of some sort. Unless he—

She needed to stop. Just stop. She was overreacting, letting her imagination run wild as she usually did. Her father always cautioned her about those things, just as he cautioned her about choosing her words wisely and thinking before she spoke.

Imagination was a wonderful gift, as long as it was used wisely. Like with her art. Imagining the man sitting next to her to be a murderous madman wasn't a wise use of her imagination. And calling him a Neanderthal probably wasn't choosing her words wisely.

She took a deep breath and swerved in and out of the traffic. True, her passenger was still seething. He was putting off dangerous colors of scarlet and ebony, which perfectly matched the dangerous look on his face. But he wasn't a danger to her. Melanie was certain of that.

Mostly.

"I upset you, didn't I? I apologize. I didn't mean to." She glanced over at him, saw that his expression hadn't really changed yet. Well, maybe it had a little. He didn't look like was quite as anxious to throw her from the car any longer.

"So what's with the Neanderthal thing? Why do you keep calling me that?"

"Why do you keep calling me Smurfette?"

"There's a big difference between a cute little cartoon character and an overgrown primitive ape-man."

Cute? Had he said cute? Did that mean he thought *she* was cute? Sweets, she needed to stop being so silly and focus on what else he said. "I don't watch cartoons so I don't know what you're talking about. And you're not primitive. Not really. I mean, you don't drag your knuckles on the ground and carry a big club or beat your hairy chest and yell."

"My chest is not hairy."

"Yes, I noticed." And oh! Why had she just said that? Why had she admitted she had noticed? Not only noticed, but remembered? Heat filled her face, no doubt turning her skin an awful shade of red that clashed with her hair. She glanced over at him and her face flamed even hotter when she noticed his small grin.

"So then why Neanderthal?"

Why couldn't he just leave well enough alone? And why did he care? She didn't want to tell him, didn't want to admit to the little shiver of pure feminine delight that shot through her when she first met him. Yes, he had been rude—kind of—but it was much more than that and definitely more basic.

She had been filled with a certainty that he had been a protector. Strong and capable and willing to go to any length to take care and protect those around him. Such a silly, silly observation, one that had come out the wrong way when she called him a Neanderthal. Just one more example of her not thinking before speaking. And there was no way she would ever tell him that. Never.

Never ever.

Melanie looked away, frowning, focusing hard on the traffic stopped at the light at the end of I83. "Which way do we go from here? I'm not sure where we're going."

"You need to get in the right lane. Without hitting anyone, please."

She shot him a dirty look then glanced in the side view mirror, waiting for a break in the heavy traffic. A spot opened up and she gunned it, darting out with a squeal of rubber. He grabbed the dashboard again and stared at her.

"Je—" He stopped, his jaw clenched, then looked away. Turned and looked back at her. "Would you please stop doing that? I know we're out of my district now but that doesn't mean I want someone else to pick us up when you kill us."

"I'm not going to kill us. I'm a perfectly safe driver." Melanie slammed the brakes as the car in front her stopped, jerking them both forward. She refused to look at her passenger. "And why do you keep saying things like that?"

"Like what?"

"Like 'district' and 'first-due'. You said that earlier. I don't know what that means."

"It means just what I said. We're in the city now,

out of my district."

"District for what?"

"For the fire department."

"What fire department?"

He blinked, a slow lowering of his lids that did nothing to hide the exasperation shining so clearly in his eyes. "The fire department where I work." His words were slow and clipped, like he was struggling to find patience. She looked at him, surprised.

"You work?"

"What the—? Yes I work. What the hell? What did you think I did?"

Melanie shrugged. "I'm not really sure. You're always home. At least, home when normal—I mean, other—people are usually working. And you're in and out at all hours. I didn't think you worked."

"Well I do. I'm a firefighter. A driver."

"You mean a chauffeur?"

"No, I mean a damn driver. I drive the engine to calls, work the pump, get the water onto the red stuff. A driver." He snorted, shaking his head. "A chauffeur. You have got to be kidding me. Do me a favor, don't say that to any of the guys tonight."

"What guys?"

"The guys from work. Go down two blocks and make a left."

Melanie jerked the steering wheel and shot into the left lane. "Why would I say anything to the people who work with you? Are we going to your firehouse later?"

"No, you'll see them at the game."

"I will?"

Dale turned in his seat, his gaze steady and just a little confused. "Yeah. That's who we're going to the game with. It's a shift outing. Who the hell did you think was going to be there?"

"I don't know that I gave it any thought, to be honest. Your sister and her boyfriend—"

"I'd hope so, since he plays for the Banners."

Melanie ignored him, even though she wanted to ask a million questions. He played hockey? Professionally? He didn't seem like a professional athlete. At least, not like she imagined. He had seemed nice, although he had looked to be a little accident prone, with all his cuts and bruises.

"Who else?"

"Hm?"

"Who else did you think was going to be there?"

"Well you, obviously. I think your sister possibly said some other friends but I'm not totally sure because I wasn't paying as much attention as I should because I—"

"Enough, I get it. This is where you want to turn."

Melanie nodded then aimed the car through the intersection. Horns blared around them and she didn't understand why, just like she didn't understand the sudden paling of her passenger's face.

He straightened in the seat then gave her an odd look. "You, uh, you didn't think this was like a date or something, did you?"

"What? OhmyGod, of course not! No, not at all. The thought never crossed my mind. I wouldn't have agreed to go if that was the case."

"Because going on a date with me is that repulsive?"

"Of course not! I never said that. I would never even think that—"

"So you'd enjoy going on a date with me." He said

it like he was stating fact, not asking a question. Her eyes widened and she shook her head, strands of hair getting caught in her mouth. She swiped at them with her hand and shook her head again.

"That's not what I said!"

"Not in so many words—"

"Not in any words!"

"—but that's what you meant."

"It is not! It is totally not. Not even close. How could you even think that—"

"Turn right up at the light then look for the parking garage on your left."

Melanie tightened her hands around the steering wheel, wondering for a brief fleeting second how they would feel tightened around his neck. Horror filled her at the thought. She had never contemplated murder before. Never! The man was intolerable, totally intolerable, forcing her to think things she had never thought before, to feel things she didn't want to feel. Just look at what he'd done to her painting, what emotions he'd forced her to unleash on those poor blank canvases.

"Left. I said left. Right there. No, stop. Holy shit."

Melanie slammed on the brakes, turned the steering wheel, then pressed her foot against the gas pedal and darted in front of the oncoming traffic. The little car lurched, bouncing as it went over the concrete bump at the entrance of the garage. She hit the brakes again, the fender stopping inches from the black and yellow bar that blocked the way.

She calmly lowered her window and leaned out, grabbing the ticket that popped out from the dispenser. The gate opened and she hit the gas, propelling the car forward. Her passenger was strangely silent, not saying anything, not even when she parked and got out of the car and walked around to the passenger side, waiting for him.

Minutes went by and she still waited, wondering why he wasn't getting out. Maybe this wasn't the right place after all. Maybe she had made the wrong turn. If she had, that was all his fault for giving her incorrect directions. Maybe he didn't really know where they were going, maybe—

The door finally opened and he climbed out. Slowly. Almost menacing. He straightened his legs, slowly standing to his full height. And he was close. Too close. And he seemed taller somehow, bigger. It didn't make sense, she had been this close to him before, so why did he suddenly seem so dangerous? So...so—her mind went blank, words failing her. All she knew was that tingles shot through her, sparkling between them in shades of gold and silver and opal that shimmered in the air, muting his own dangerously vibrant reds and oranges.

"Give me your hand."

Melanie automatically put both hands behind her back and shook her head.

"Smurfette, give me your hand."

His voice, deep and husky and oh-so-controlled, was commanding. Compelling. She was offering her hand before she even realized what she was doing, cursing herself while she did it.

"Your other hand."

She held that one out as well, wondering what he was going to do. Was he going to hold it? Take her hand in his as they walked to wherever they were going? Another little thrill shimmered in the air, anticipation filling her. He reached out, his skin warm, his hand so much larger and darker and stronger than hers. The breath hitched in her chest as she waited, wondering—

Until he pulled the keys from her grip and shoved them into the front pocket of his jeans.

"Those are my keys."

"I know."

"But you can't take them! I won't be able to drive back home!"

"That's the whole point, Smurfette. You're not driving."

"What? But I don't—"

He stepped closer, amusement and warning mixing in his eyes as he stared down at her. "You're a menace to every single person on the road. You're not driving. Period."

"That is so not true! I'm perfectly capable—"

"Bullshit! You're not driving, end of discussion."

"You can't just—"

"I just did. Now come on." His hand closed around her elbow, leading her toward a bank of elevators on the other side of the garage.

"That is so high-handed. So autocratic. So pre-historic. So medieval. So...so barbaric."

He stopped and looked down at her, a shadow passing through his eyes. "So now I'm a barbarian, huh?"

Melanie opened her mouth to say no, to tell him that wasn't what she meant, but he didn't give her the chance. And she couldn't help but wonder if he was upset for some reason.

No, she must be mistaken. He couldn't be upset. That was silly.

Wasn't it?

Chapter Eight

"So that's your neighbor from hell, huh?" Jimmy stood next to him, balancing a plate of food on top of a plastic cup of beer while he ate. Dale glanced in the direction he was looking, his eyes falling on Smurfette—Melanie. They were in the lower level of the arena, downstairs in the exclusive VIP Lounge. The game started in forty minutes, which gave them plenty of time to eat and drink.

Smurfette was standing off to the side, an empty plastic cup of wine in her hand, looking lost and alone and out of place. Sympathy surged through him and he pushed it away as he grabbed a meatball from Jimmy's plate.

"Yup. That's her." He popped the meatball into his mouth and put the empty toothpick back on the plate. Jimmy gave him a dirty look and moved to Dale's other side, guarding his food.

"She's cute."

"She's a lunatic." A lunatic driver who was a menace on the road, one with no verbal filter whatsoever. If that wasn't bad enough, Dale honestly thought she had no idea she was insulting him. Not normal, everyday insults. No, her insults were cloaked in fancy-speak, delivered in a slightly husky voice from a mouth that was too full and luscious. You were so taken with her mouth that the words didn't register right away. And when they did register, you had to stop and think about what they meant before realizing you had been insulted.

Hell, if he was going to be insulted, he'd much rather it be done plainly, with no room for doubt. *Someone like him.* What the hell was that supposed to mean, anyway?

He knew exactly what it meant. Medieval. Prehistoric. A Barbarian.

Why the hell was he so pissed, anyway? It didn't make sense. It wasn't any different from when she called him Neanderthal. In fact, she had called him a Neanderthal more than once. For some reason, that didn't bother him. In fact, he had thought it was kind of cute. Not so much that she was calling him a Neanderthal, but the expression on her face when she said it. Like some part of her liked it. How was being called a barbarian any different? Dale wasn't sure how but it was. And it bothered him.

"Well, she's a cute lunatic." Jimmy popped a meatball into his mouth. "You make a move on her yet?"

"Fuck no. Not my type." And wasn't that the truth. He preferred his women warm, willing, and without a sharp tongue. Unless they planned on using that tongue for something besides insults.

"Cool. I'm going to go over and say hi." Jimmy turned, already moving toward Smurfette. Dale reached out and grabbed his shoulder, jerking him back. Jimmy swore under his breath as the plate toppled from the cup, nearly falling. He caught it at the last minute, but not before several of the meatballs hit his arm, smearing his sleeve with gravy.

"Dammit. What the hell did you do that for?"

"Leave her alone."

"Why? I thought you said you weren't going to make a play for her."

"I'm not."

"Then she's fair game. I mean, look at that mouth. And all that hair. Can you just imagine how that hair would feel as it wrapped around you—"

Dale curled his hand into a fist and hit Jimmy on the arm. Hard. Hard enough that beer sloshed over the rim of the cup. He ignored his look of surprise and stepped closer, standing nose-to-nose with the paramedic. "You leave her the fuck alone."

"Jesus Christ. What the hell, man?"

"And watch your language. It's inappropriate."

"It's inappropriate? Shit, since when do you care? And what the hell has gotten into you, anyway? Are you getting sick or something?"

Dale pinned him with a steely glare, silently warning Jimmy to shut the hell up. But the man had a point. What the hell was wrong with him?

Nothing was wrong with him. He just didn't feel like watching Jimmy make a play on his neighbor, that was all. Something told him that Smurfette was probably on the naïve side when it came to men and he didn't want Jimmy coming on to her, leading her on, using her.

Yeah, sure. That's all it was.

Dale broke eye contact with Jimmy and took a

long swallow of beer, his eyes darting across the room to where Smurfette was standing. He nearly choked.

She wasn't alone anymore. Lauren was with her, along with Mikey. The sight of the three of them huddled together made his gut tighten in fear. And now they were laughing, the sound catching the attention of several guys in the room. Dale's protective instincts kicked in and he started to move in that direction, only to stop when all three women turned and looked at him.

Not looked. Glared.

Smurfette's eyes caught his, their gazes locked as she leaned closer to Lauren and said something. Dale would have given anything at that moment for the ability to read lips, because he had a feeling they were talking about him. His suspicion was confirmed when Lauren stared at him, frowning.

Well shit. What the hell was that all about? And when the hell did Smurfette get another glass of wine? That must be her third, at least.

Lauren said something to the other two then stepped away, heading straight for him. Dale ducked behind Jimmy, frantically searching for a way to escape. Over there, by the bar. Maybe he could get lost in the crowd, hide so Lauren wouldn't see him—

"Don't even try it." Lauren stepped in front of him, blocking his escape. Her hands were fisted on her hips, her dark brows pulled low over her eyes. "Like I didn't see you hide behind Jimmy? You're losing your touch, big brother."

"I wasn't hiding. I'm getting another beer." He stepped around her and muttered under his breath when she walked with him.

"Good. I'll go with you."

"You don't need to. I can get my own."

"So what's your problem?"

"I don't have a problem." He made it to the bar and tried to squeeze through the people in order to get close enough to place his order. One of the bartenders saw him and made his way over. Dale pointed to his choice of draft then held up two fingers.

"I hope one of them is for me."

"Get your own. Ouch. What the hell was that for?" Dale rubbed the back of his arm where Lauren had just pinched him. Damn her. How did she always know exactly where to pinch?

"For being a jerk. Why were you so rude to Melanie?"

"I wasn't rude. Who said I was rude?" He reached for the fresh cups of beer but Lauren got to them first. He frowned, then motioned to the bartender for two more as he pulled a bill from his wallet. The drinks and food were free, but he always made sure to tip the staff.

Lauren took the bill from his hand and leaned forward, making sure the bartender saw it. Then she smiled at him. "Can I get two glasses of red wine, too? Thanks."

"You're drinking beer and wine?"

Lauren looked at him like he was losing his mind. "No. The wine's not mine."

"Then who's it for? Not Mikey, I know she doesn't drink anymore." She didn't, not since reconnecting with her high school love, who happened to be a recovering alcoholic with more than ten years' sobriety under his belt.

"They're for Melanie."

"Both of them? How many has she had so far? We haven't been here that long."

"Why do you care? She'll have plenty of time to drink water during the game. And it's not like she's driving anyway, since you were a barbarian and stole her keys."

"Is that what she said? That I stole them?"

"Didn't you?"

"That's not the point. The woman is a menace. She shouldn't be driving. She damn near killed me at least three times."

"So you had to act like a barbarian?"

"I did not act like a barbarian! Dammit. This whole thing was a huge mistake." Dale took one of the fresh beers the bartender had just placed in front of him and drank it in three long swallows. He refused to look at Lauren, refused to acknowledge the censure in her gaze.

"What was a mistake?"

"This. Tonight. The whole thing. Why did you even invite her? She doesn't fit in. It doesn't take a genius to figure that out."

"Since when do you care if someone fits in or not? And are you going to stand there and tell me you don't like her?"

"Was that why you invited her? In some lame-ass attempt at matchmaking?"

Lauren stepped closer, almost eye-to-eye with him. "I invited her because I thought you liked her. Because she made you smile. Because you acted more like your normal self the night she was there than you have in the last six months. Probably longer."

Dale stepped back, surprised at her low words, surprised at the emotion in her voice. He looked away, his gaze scanning the room without really seeing anything. Fuck. Had it been that noticeable? He didn't think so. Just because Lauren noticed didn't mean anything. She was his sister, she knew his moods and quirks better than anyone else.

He looked back at her, not quite able to meet her eyes. "I'm fine."

"You're so full of shit." She lowered her voice and leaned closer, resting her hand on his arm. Could she feel the tension in the bunched muscles there? Probably. "Dale, I'm worried about you. You've been too distant, too removed these last few months. Like you're blaming yourself for what happened. Blaming yourself for everything Lindsay's done, for what she's become. It's not your fault. It's not anyone's fault."

"Yeah? Prove it. How many times did you tell me I should be more understanding? That I was her big brother, that I should be trying to help her. And I didn't. I turned my back on her and look what happened. She's in jail because she almost killed you."

"Dale, that's not your fault. And I was wrong for saying that stuff. You were the one who was right. Maybe if I had listened to you, if I had stepped back sooner and forced her to take responsibility, none of this would have happened. Maybe this is all my fault. Did you ever think about that?" Her voice cracked and she looked away, blinking her eyes before taking a sip of beer. Emotion, sharp and bitter, cut through him, peeling him open in places he had thought permanently closed, in places he didn't want open.

Especially not here. Not now.

He took a sip of his own beer and nudged her, tried to smile. It fell flat. "It's not your fault. And I appreciate what you tried to do, but don't. I don't need you meddling."

"So you're really going to tell me you're not

interested in Melanie? Not even a little tiny bit?"

"No." He forced the lie through clenched teeth and hoped Lauren wouldn't notice. Maybe she did, maybe she didn't. He couldn't really tell because she suddenly smiled, a large smile that matched the calculating gleam in her eyes.

"Good, because I'm pretty sure Jimmy is."

"What?"

Lauren motioned at something over his shoulder and he turned to look. Smurfette was still across the room, Mikey nowhere in sight. But she wasn't alone. Jimmy was standing next to her, his arm braced on the wall above her head, leaning in close as he said something to her. He was too close, his mouth damn near against her ear. Smurfette looked up at him, her long hair falling behind her as she tilted her head back and laughed at whatever he had said.

"I'm going to fucking kill him."

Chapter Nine

Dale glanced at the score board, looking to see how much time remained. Ten minutes left in the third. If the last ten minutes were anything like the first fifty, it was going to feel like a very long, excruciating hour.

Not that the game was dragging. It wasn't. In fact, any other time, he'd be on his feet, pounding the glass, screaming and cheering with everyone else. They had prime seats, close to center ice right on the glass. It was a sell-out crowd and the Banners were on fire tonight, skating fast and shooting often. So was LA, which made the game even more exciting. Right now, the Banners were up by one, but that could change in a matter of seconds.

No, it wasn't the game that was dragging. It was the company around him that was making him miserable and wishing the night would end. He wasn't sure how Kenny had managed it but his shift had pretty much the entire front row—which was great for watching the game, but not so great for conversation unless you were talking to the person on either side of you. Adam sat to his left, alternately watching the game or doing something on his phone.

And Smurfette was on his right. Had that been Lauren's doing, or just a fluke? It didn't matter. And at the beginning of the night, that would have been exactly what he wanted. That had changed while they were in the VIP Lounge, when she had started talking to Jimmy.

When Jimmy had latched onto her, smiling and flirting and charming. It shouldn't matter, it shouldn't upset him.

But it did, and he didn't know why.

Bullshit. He knew exactly why. Jealousy. Pure and simple. And it pissed him off.

Smurfette had made it clear what she thought of him when she called him a barbarian. Had made it clear she wasn't interested in someone like him. It didn't matter that they had been flirting a little on the drive down. It didn't matter that she had blushed when he teased her about going on a date, or that he had been pretty sure she was open to the idea.

None of that mattered anymore, not when it was so obvious that she was flirting with Jimmy, falling for his charm. He wanted to tell her not to fall for it, to warn her that Jimmy flirted with anything that breathed.

Screw that. If she wanted to be one of Jimmy's conquests, then that was on her. She was an adult, she could make her own decisions.

That's what he kept telling himself. For some reason, he had trouble accepting it, no matter how many times he repeated it. It didn't help that he was pretty sure Smurfette was drunk. Not falling-down-drunk, not obnoxious-drunk. That would be too much to expect.

No, it was just his luck that Smurfette was a cute drunk. And she was a toucher.

Like right now. She was leaning to her right, away from him, giggling at something Jimmy was saying. But her left hand was hanging over the edge of her seat and brushing against his thigh. Or his arm. Once she had even grabbed his hand then had the nerve to turn and look at him in surprise, like he'd been the one to grab her hand instead of the other way around. And her left leg kept brushing against his, too, the material of her long skirt tangling around the hem of his jeans.

Dale was pretty certain she was the only person here wearing a long skirt.

He looked back at the ice, saw a knot of players barreling toward them as they chased the puck sliding along the boards. Bodies slammed against the glass in front of them, hitting hard enough that the panes shook. Cheers and yells erupted as the face of one of the LA players was flattened against the glass, held in place by Kenny.

Dale shifted, ready to jump to his feet with everyone else, when something dug into his thigh, dangerously close to his crotch. He sucked in a breath and reached down for Smurfette's hand to remove it. Instead of letting him move her hand, her fingers curled around his, holding on. She turned toward him, her eyes wide with excitement and glazed with alcohol, a dazed smile on her face.

"That poor man!"

"No, he's from the other team. That was a good hit."

"It was?"

"Yeah, it was."

"Still. That poor man. I hope he's not hurt."

"Smurfette—" She wasn't listening anymore, at least not to him. She was leaning to the other side, a smile on her face as Jimmy said something to her.

But she was still holding his hand, her grip tighter than he expected. What the hell? He loosened his fingers and gave his hand a little shake. Her fingers tightened around his with a little squeeze.

He looked down at their joined hands, his dark, hers pale. Her fingers were slender but strong, the strength surprising. It shouldn't. This wasn't the first time she'd dug her fingers into him. Hadn't she'd done the same thing two weeks ago, when he had to get her down from the balcony? He remembered the feel of her hands twisting in his shirt, of her fingers digging into his back as they searched for a hold.

And shit, he didn't need to be remembering that right now. Didn't need to be remembering his body's reaction as he wondered what else those hands could do if she was beneath him, her legs wrapped around—

The horn blared and eighteen thousand people surged to their feet as the winning score flashed across the giant screen. The Banners had won.

And Smurfette was still holding his hand. Not just holding it. She was actually leaning against him, her soft curves pressed against his arm, her leg flush with his. But she was still talking to Jimmy. What the hell?

Dale leaned closer, torn between telling her to let go—or ramming his fist into Jimmy's face.

"Don't worry, Jimmy. You'll meet a nice girl before you know it, one who can appreciate your true depths." Smurfette reached out and patted him on the chest with her free hand. Jimmy laughed then leaned down and pressed a kiss against her forehead.

"I'll take your word for it, Mel." Jimmy looked over at Dale, smiled, then turned and started following everyone else out of the aisle. Dale stared after him, wondering if the shock he felt was clear on his face.

Mel? Had he just called Smurfette *Mel?* What the hell? And they'd been talking about women? Had Smurfette been giving Jimmy relationship advice this whole time? No way. It wasn't possible. He looked down at the woman next to him, surprised that she had her tilted back, her eyes shining as she watched him. Her lips spread in a smile and she leaned forward and for one split-second Dale actually thought she was going to kiss him.

And then Adam nudged him from behind, throwing him off-balance. He caught himself at the last minute, bracing his free hand against the boards so he wouldn't fall on top of Smurfette. That didn't stop him from bumping into her, nearly knocking her over.

"Shit." He righted himself then put his hand on her shoulder, his eyes quickly scanning her to make sure she was okay. "Are you alright?"

"Of course silly." She laughed—giggled—then slipped her hand from his and made her way out of the aisle. Dale frowned then looked over his shoulder at Adam.

"What the hell was that for?"

"Sorry. The guy behind me was pushing." Adam jerked his thumb over his own shoulder, pointing at the people behind him. Dale shook his head then hurried to catch up with everyone else. He reached the end of the aisle just as Smurfette reached the first step. Her arm stretched out, her hand searching for the railing that ran down the middle of the steps. She missed the railing and nearly stumbled, her feet tangling in the hem of her skirts.

Dale grabbed her, his hands wrapping around her waist just before she fell. She laughed and tossed her head back, her body flush against his. Dale tried to readjust his hands as she moved and they slipped up, resting just under the swell of her breasts.

And shit. She wasn't wearing a bra.

"Oopsie." She laughed again and turned toward him, her arms resting on his shoulders, her body almost limp against his. "The railing moved."

"Yeah, I don't think so. Come on, let's go." He got her turned around so she was facing in the right direction, tried to get her to walk up the stairs. She swayed then looked down, a frown marring her face.

"The steps are moving, too." She giggled and grabbed the railing, her body swaying to the side, away from him. Dale reached for her, wrapping one arm around her waist and pulling her arm over his shoulders.

"Come on, Smurfette. Up you go."

"I am. You are. No, we are. Up. Right?"

Dale laughed, leading her. "Yeah. Up. There you go."

"Need a hand?"

Dale looked back at Adam, noticed the other man smiling. It wasn't funny. Or at least, it shouldn't be. Yeah, sure it wasn't. That was why Dale was having trouble not laughing himself.

"Just stay behind us and make sure she doesn't fall backward. Or that nobody bumps into us." There wasn't much chance of that, since they had been in the first row and everyone was ahead of them, crowding the steps to the concourse.

They reached the top of the steps a few minutes

later, Smurfette clinging to him, a dreamy smile on her face as she hummed something under her breath. She kept swinging her arm back and forth, keeping time to whatever she was humming. Dale looked down then did a double-take. What the hell was that in her hands?

"Smurfette, why are you carrying your shoes?"

She stopped her humming and looked up at him, a slightly dazed look in her eyes. "Hm?"

"Your shoes. You need to put them back on."

"Oh. Okay." She dropped them to the floor then pulled up her skirt, baring shapely calves and the firm flesh of creamy thighs. Dale grabbed her hands, stopping her before she raised the skirt even more and gave everyone a show. A bigger show. The guys were already watching her as it was. He didn't want them seeing more than what they already had.

"Easy Smurfette. We don't need to know what color underwear you have on."

She stopped trying to shove her foot into the upside down sandal and looked up at him, her head tilted to the side. Then she smiled, her expression serene and comforting. "Don't worry, I won't. I'm not wearing any."

Conversation screeched to a halt. Dale knew that was impossible, knew he must only be imagining the heavy silence that surrounded them. They were standing by the wall of the concourse, surrounded by thousands of fans celebrating the winning game as they pushed their way to the exits. There had to be noise. Shouts and screams and laughter.

All Dale heard was silence.

He looked around, saw his coworkers standing in a semi-circle around them. Pete and Adam. Dave, Jay, Jimmy. Mikey and Lauren. All of them wore varying expressions, from amusement to interest to laughing disbelief. Dale swallowed his groan and leaned down to pick up the sandals, holding them in one hand as he grabbed hold of her arm to stop her from swaying.

She looked around, the serene smile fading from her face, replaced by a worried frown. She leaned in closer to him and placed her hand on his chest. "That wasn't the propri—appro—the right thing to say, was it? I'm sorry. I try not to do that but I don't always remember."

"No, don't worry about it. All good."

"Good." She smiled again then blinked, the blue of her eyes deepening, shining with humor. "I had fun. This was fun. You were fun."

"Uh, good. Glad to hear it." Dale chuckled then looked over at Lauren. "I don't think—"

"Yeah, I figured that. Do you need any help?"

"No, we're good. I'll get her home and get her to bed, let her sleep it off." Dale put his arm around Smurfette's waist, said goodbye to everyone, then led her through the concourse. No way was she in any shape to make it downstairs for the small tour Kenny had arranged.

At least she was a manageable happy drunk, smiling and humming as he belted her into the car and drove home. The humming became softer, more intermittent once they hit the expressway, finally fading as her head fell back against the seat.

Dale looked over, something soft and warm and protective going through him as he watched her. It didn't make sense. How could he go through such a wide range of emotions in such a short time? Amusement, attraction, anger, jealousy. Back to amusement, then surprise, and now this protectiveness. What was it about the woman snoring so softly next to him?

He didn't know. Hell, he didn't know if he wanted to know. It wasn't right, couldn't be normal. She was his neighbor-from-hell who listened to weird music and painted weird paintings and rambled when she talked. A fiery free-spirit who danced to drums only she could hear.

His Smurfette.

He parked the car in front of their building and shut the engine then looked over at her, just watching. Weak light filtered in through the windows, catching in her hair and turning it to the color of smoldering embers, dark fire. Her face was flawless, her skin clear. Was it as smooth as it looked? Would her skin be cool under the touch of his hand? Or would it be warm, hot, a reflection of the mass of fiery curls that tumbled around her face and shoulder and down her back?

The urge to touch her, to run his hand along her cheek, was strong. Strong enough to scare him, to make his hands tremble. How could she make him feel, just by being there next to him? Dangerous. Too dangerous. He bit back a curse and climbed out of the car, slamming the door harder than necessary. It didn't matter because she didn't move, not even when he opened her door and gently pushed her shoulder.

"Smurfette. Wake up. We're home." He nudged her again. She shifted, her head turning toward him. Her eyes fluttered open, focused on his face for a split-second, then closed again as a small smile spread across her face.

"Come on, Sleeping Beauty. Time to go inside."

She murmured something but still didn't move. Dale sighed then reached in and grabbed her sandals and put them in her lap. He undid the seatbelt then eased one hand under her legs and the other behind her back. Gently, taking care not to jostle her, he lifted her out of the car and straightened, holding her close against him. She murmured something again and wrapped her arms around his neck, her head resting against his shoulder. Trusting.

Dale swallowed, refusing to acknowledge the tenderness that swept through him. He carried her inside and upstairs, readjusting his hold on her as he got her apartment door opened.

Bright light seared his eyes when he hit the switch with his elbow, making him pause. He blinked, then moved down the hallway to the bedroom, pausing for just a second when he entered.

More color, but much softer. Her room was a rainbow of soft pastels, from the hooked rug to the walls, from the thick comforter of the queen-sized poster bed to the sheer panels of its flowing canopy. Completely different from the vibrant explosion of color in the kitchen and living room but still uniquely her.

Dale moved over to the bed and leaned forward, ready to ease her onto the thick mattress. She stirred and tightened her arms around him, her eyes fluttering open.

And staying open.

Her gaze held his, the blue so deep he thought he might drown in them. Then she smiled, a sweet smile that sucker-punched him and left him struggling to catch his breath.

"You're taking care of me."

He didn't know how to react to the words. Was she surprised? Or something else? He couldn't tell, especially not after what she'd said earlier. He grunted then lowered her to the bed. "Did you think I'd just leave you there?"

"No. I knew you wouldn't."

Dale grunted again, probably sounding like the barbarian she thought him to be, then tried to move away. She tightened her arms around him, holding him in place.

"Kiss me."

Dale heard the words, saw her lift her face, felt the heat of her mouth close to his. So close. His heart slammed into his chest as he froze, indecision warring with desire warring with common sense. And then her mouth was on his, her lips warm and soft. She sighed, a tiny little moan deep in her throat. Her tongue darted out, touching the seam of his lips, slow and hesitant.

She sighed again and pressed herself closer, one hand caressing his cheek. Sweet, so sweet. Dale couldn't breathe, was afraid to move.

Such a small kiss, innocent and hesitant and surprisingly decadent. Blood roared through his veins, heated with desire, burning. It took every ounce of control—control he didn't even know he had—to hold himself still. Not to react. Not to take control and stretch out on top of her. Not to shove her skirt to her waist and plunge inside her.

Not to lose himself.

She tried to deepen the kiss, to press herself even closer, making it harder for him to keep hold of his tightly-reined control. He groaned and curled his hands into fists, afraid that if he touched her, he'd forget himself.

Would forgetting himself be so awful? In this case, yes. She had been drinking. What she was doing…it wasn't her. It was the alcohol. He'd be damned, in more ways than one, if he took advantage. He'd be nothing more than the barbarian she had accused him of being.

Smurfette pulled away with a breathy sigh, one mixed with just a hint of frustration. Her eyes fluttered open and she frowned at him, her brows tilted down, a little crease furrowing her brow. Was she actually pouting? Shit, she was. And the expression only made her look cute, which convinced Dale he really must be losing his mind.

"You're supposed to kiss me back."

"Smurfette, if I kiss you back, I'm not going to stop there."

Her eyes widened, the ocean blue becoming darker as her pupils dilated. A small smile teased the corners of her lush mouth. The look tightened something in him, something primitive and basic and too needy.

"That's what I want."

Her words nearly pushed him over the edge, almost made him throw his intentions out the door. His eyes searched hers as tension and anticipation settled around them, heavy. Heady. Primal.

One kiss. Just one kiss. Certainly he could control himself long enough for one kiss. One taste of her delicious mouth.

Dale captured her face in his hands and tilted her head back, his mouth claiming hers. This wasn't a tentative touching of the lips, a shy taste of the forbidden. His tongue swept out, parting her lips and delving into the hot recess of her mouth. Tasting. Learning. Conquering.

But was it conquering when she so sweetly surrendered? When she sighed and twisted her hands into his shirt, leaning into him?

He deepened the kiss, need and passion soaring through him as he lost himself in her taste, in his touch. Her hands uncurled from his shirt as she dragged them down his chest, along his sides.

Down to the front of his jeans, where she cupped the hard length of his throbbing erection. His last shred of decency and control roared to life, unwilling to be swept away in the insanity of the moment. He groaned and pulled away, grabbed her hand and moved it to the mattress. Could she feel the way his fingers trembled? Could she hear the steady pounding of his heart and the harsh rasp of his breathing?

"Melanie, stop."

"But—" He placed a finger over her swollen mouth and shook his head.

"No buts. I'm not going to take advantage of you. When I do finally have you, I'm going to know it's really you and not the wine." He moved his finger and placed a quick kiss against her lips, ignoring the look of shock and disappointment in her eyes. He pushed away from the bed and stood, adjusting himself. Then he pulled back the fluffy comforter and patted the mattress. "Time to sleep. Come on, under the covers."

Smurfette frowned but crawled under them without saying a word. She wiggled on the mattress, getting comfortable, then looked up at him, an odd light in her eyes.

"You called me Melanie."

He couldn't help his brief smile at her look, like she was almost upset that he had used her real name. "Must have been a slip. Now go to sleep. I'll check on you in the morning."

She tilted her head and he wondered what she was

going to say now. Then she nodded and flopped onto her back, her eyes closed. A second later, she was softly snoring, her chest rising and falling with the deep steady breaths of sleep. Dale watched her, surprised at the mix of amusement and tenderness flowing through him. He shook his head, calling himself every kind of fool, and pulled the covers over her. Then he walked out of the room, out of her apartment, carefully closing the door behind him before entering his own.

An apartment that suddenly seemed lifeless, colorless, empty.

He shook his head and pushed the thoughts away, adjusting himself once more as he made his way back to his cold lonely bed.

Chapter Ten

Her head pounded, reminding her of the beat of ancient African warrior drums she had once heard at a demonstration years ago. Only the rhythm was off and the pounding was aching, painful. Decidedly unpleasant, much like the stickiness that coated her mouth and tongue, leaving it dry and icky.

Melanie rolled to her back and carefully opened her eyes. She shouldn't have had so much wine last night. But she had felt so oddly out of place among the laughing noisy crowd. And so oddly out of sorts, knowing she had somehow upset Dale.

And oh sweets! No! Had she really—? Melanie brought her hands to her face and groaned, the harsh sound filled with regret and humiliation as the memory sharpened.

Yes, she had. Melanie had practically thrown herself at him, clinging to him, begging to be kissed. Well of course she had. The thought had been in her mind ever since the day he'd rescued her from the balcony. She had wondered about it, more than curious, and the wine had given her the courage to follow through, to kiss him and touch him.

And he'd turned her down.

How would she ever face him again? Maybe he would pretend it had never happened, pretend she hadn't made a fool of herself. He had been a gentleman about it. Maybe he wouldn't say anything. Except...

She frowned, trying to remember. He had said something, something that had caused excitement to dance along her spine. A promise. Or was it? Why couldn't she remember? She remembered everything else—well, almost; she remembered the embarrassing parts. Why couldn't she remember what he'd said? She thought it might be important, might be something she needed to remember...

The harder she thought, the more her head pounded. Maybe if she stopped trying to remember, it would come back to her. Yes, that's exactly what she would do. Maybe then, her head wouldn't hurt so much.

She rubbed her hands along her face then rolled out of bed with a little groan. Her skirt was twisted around her waist and she impatiently fixed it before stumbling to the bathroom. She refused to look in the mirror, afraid of what she would see.

Tea. Strong green tea with lots of sugar. And maybe some toast, with a little sugar and cinnamon sprinkled on it. She would eat her toast and drink her tea and then get back to work. The angle of the light told her she had slept much later than usual. Thankfully she was ahead of schedule and her most recent painting should be finished today. She could take them to Anna's gallery tomorrow. What would she think of them? Would she like them? Melanie hoped so. They were different than her previous works, different even from the one she was putting on auction. Dark and light and hope and confusion.

Melanie wasn't sure why her style was changing, was almost worried about it. The colors she saw now were so different, almost suffocating her until she got them out and put them on canvas. Like she was trying to tell the world something, trying to tell herself something.

If only she knew what it was.

Thinking about it only made the pounding in her head worse so she pushed everything from her mind and made her way to the kitchen, squinting against the bright light coming through the patio doors.

She was just ready to sit down at her small kitchen table, the tea and toast waiting for her, when she heard the knock at her front door. No, not knock. Pounding. The noise bounced around in her head, echoing the pounding that was already there. Melanie put a hand to her head and moaned, from the pain in her head as well as the realization of who was at the door.

Maybe if she ignored him, he would go away. Maybe he would think she was busy, or that she wasn't home. She didn't want to see him.

No, that was a lie. She did want to see him. She just didn't want to face him.

He banged on the door again, harder. Sweets, could the man do nothing quietly? Did he always have to be so forceful?

The memory of being cradled in his arms as he carried her up the stairs wavered in her mind. Why did she have to remember that, right now? A shiver raced through her, pebbling the skin of her arms, and she hugged herself.

Muttering under her breath, she took a quick sip of the tea, nearly burning her tongue, then shuffled out of the kitchen. She opened the door a cautious few inches, peering up at him through heavy lids. He was dressed in faded jeans and a maroon polo shirt. The sleeves clung to his sculpted biceps and pulled tight across his chest. He looked wide awake and refreshed. And too dangerous for her current state of mind.

His gaze moved from the top of her head to the toes of her feet then back up again, finally resting on her eyes. He blinked and the corners of his mouth twitched. He blinked again, his lips quivering. Melanie narrowed her eyes and frowned.

"What?" Sweets, was that her voice? Quiet and husky, a little scratchy and worn. His lips quivered again, finally stretching into a broad grin that made her swallow back a groan.

"I'd ask how you were feeling but I guess I don't need to."

Her frown deepened and she moved to close the door on him. He was faster than she was because he stepped around her and came inside, heading straight to her kitchen, something in his hands. She glanced at him, looked into the empty hall, then closed the door.

"Well, at least you're eating something, that's good. I would have skipped the cinnamon and sugar, though." He barely looked at her when she moved into the kitchen. He was standing at the counter, mixing something together. She almost asked what he was doing then decided it wasn't worth it. She would just sit down and drink her tea and eat her toast and ignore him, pretend he wasn't there.

It was like ignoring a sleek panther crouched inches away, ready to pounce.

Where had that thought come from? A panther? Melanie took a sip of tea then nibbled her toast, frowning. The man in her kitchen was nothing like a panther. Yes, he was dangerous, in ways she couldn't put into words, only recognized by instinct. Not a panther, though. A panther was sleek and powerful and would move in silently for the attack before you could see it. Her neighbor was...well, definitely powerful. She had noticed that the very first time she had met him, had been aware of it almost instantly on some deeper level where her self-preservation lived. Sleek? No. He was too rugged to be sleek, too roughly hewn and chiseled to be considered sleek.

Silent? No, she was certain anyone would see him ready to attack. The man in her kitchen would want that, would want his prey to know it was being hunted. He'd want to play with it, to make the conquering a challenge.

And goodness, what was she doing? No more cheap wine, and certainly not in excess. It only made her mind meander into meaningless tangents that were completely out of character for her.

"Drink this."

"What?" She looked up, surprised to see him standing next to her, big and strong and capable. He held a glass of some unappetizing concoction in one hand, and two small pills in the other.

"What is it?"

"Just drink it. You'll feel better."

Melanie leaned back in the chair, trying to put distance between them. It didn't work because he merely leaned forward, getting closer. "It's just aspirin and a hangover cure, that's all. Now come on, drink it. You'll feel better."

Melanie scrunched her nose in distaste and shook her head. "I don't want to."

"You don't want to feel better?"

"No, I don't want to drink it."

He chuckled, the sound deep and somehow comforting. He placed the glass in her hand, his hand over hers so she wouldn't drop it. "Same thing. This and the aspirin will make you feel better. Come on, bottoms up."

Melanie glanced at the liquid in the cup then took a hesitant sniff. It didn't smell too bad. Maybe. Kind of like tomatoes and something else, something just a little salty and spicy. She looked up at him, still frowning, then took the pills from his hand and popped them into her mouth. She raised the glass and took a sip, swallowing the aspirin. Another sip, then one more.

The taste finally hit her. Bitter and sour and vile and…she shivered, not wanting to drink anymore. But he was still holding the glass, speaking soft words of encouragement, tilting it against her mouth so she had to either drink it or wear it.

She finished the last of it then sputtered and gagged. A deep breath helped settle her stomach. That, and a long swallow of the tepid tea. She wiped her mouth with the back of her hand then glared at him. Her mood wasn't helped when she noticed the small smile on his face and the laughter in his eyes.

"That was…that was vile. Hideous."

"Hair of the dog, Smurfette. Trust me, you'll feel better in no time. Now why don't you go jump in the shower? That'll help, too."

"No. I don't want to." Maybe she sounded like a small child. She didn't care. The only thing she cared about was getting that awful taste out of her mouth.

She drained the tea then pushed away from the table, opening the refrigerator to pull out the pitcher of flavored water. Cucumber and mint. Surely that would help. It would probably even help her head.

She poured a glass and took several long swallows, watching him over the rim. He was leaning against the counter, his arms folded across that broad chest, a crooked grin on his face as he watched her.

"Feel better?"

Melanie placed the empty glass in the sink and shook her head. "No. It was vile. I think you're trying to poison me."

The change in him was instant. Shocking. And frightening. One second he had been standing there, relaxed and comfortable with amusement dancing in his eyes. And then...then he looked like a completely different man. A stranger. He straightened, rising to his full height, his arms by his sides and his hands clenched into fists. His face hardened, his jaw turning rigid and his mouth compressing into a thin pale line. And his eyes...the look in them frightened her. Hard. Cold. Distant and unforgiving. The darkness she had sensed in him from the very beginning exploded around him, drowning out the vibrancy of his other colors until there was nothing left but an empty void of pure blackness.

A different man stood in front of her, one she didn't recognize. One she would cross the street to avoid if she had been out walking. Melanie pressed a hand against her stomach and took a hasty step back, wondering what had happened, wondering at her sanity because she wasn't running from the apartment, screaming for help.

In the time it took her to blink, the darkness receded. Still there, but not as dangerous, not as encompassing. His hands uncurled and the hardness in his face eased. He looked away and shook his head, took a deep breath and looked back at her. For a brief second she thought she saw pain, raw and anguishing, in the depths of his eyes. But only for a second because he blinked, shielding any emotion she might have seen.

He stepped toward her, his eyes holding her prisoner as he came even closer. The heat from his body brushed against hers, filling her mind with images of flames, burning, searing, hotter than any inferno imaginable.

He opened his mouth and she waited, wondering what he would say, wondering at the flash of pain she saw in his eyes. Then he closed his mouth and shook his head and turned and walked out of the kitchen. The sound of the door closing, just a soft click, echoed through her apartment. A second later she heard a louder sound: his own apartment door, slamming shut.

Her body suddenly came to life and she hurried out of the kitchen, her hand on the door knob before she realized what she was doing.

What *was* she doing? Had she really been ready to go after him? But why?

She must truly be insane, to even think about going after him after glimpsing the danger that dwelled within. Insane to think he wasn't a danger to her. Insane to feel certain, deep down inside her, that he would never hurt her.

Not to feel. To know.

Melanie pulled her hand away from the knob, surprised that her fingers were trembling, surprised that her heart was beating so loud, so fast. She took a deep breath and closed her eyes, seeing the look of anger and pain and guilt that had flashed in his eyes.

She took another deep breath and gave her head a little shake, then made her way to the bathroom. A shower, maybe a long hot soak. She needed to clear her head, to put the man next door firmly from her mind.

For her own peace of mind.

Chapter Eleven

Angry. Frustrated. Bold.

The colors built, one upon the other. Light and dark. Bright and subtle. Each stroke contradicting the one before it. Each emotion clear and conflicting, staring back at her from the canvas.

Melanie stepped back, her chest heaving with each sharp breath. Her hand dropped to her side, the brush clenched between her sore, stained fingers. She blinked and wiped the tears from her cheek then laughed, the sound almost pitiful. Lonely.

She looked down at the brush, at the twisted and frayed bristles, and laughed again. Just a whisper of sound. Of disbelief and dismay. It was one of her favorite brushes and she had destroyed it, each angry stroke demanding more and more until it had nothing left to give.

Melanie tossed the brush to the work table then pushed the hair off her face with the back of her wrist. A streak of wetness chilled her forehead, just above her brow. No doubt a smear of paint. No matter how careful she was, she was always covered in paint when she was working. One quick glance at her skirt let her know now was no different. Blotches of vermilion and smears of onyx and cadmium orange covered the gauzy material, clashing with the blues and yellows that stained the skirt from the last time she had worn it.

She shrugged then grabbed a small towel, using it to wipe her hands until she could properly clear them. Then she took a deep breath and turned back to study the canvas.

It was...different. Again. Poignant and angry and afraid. The colors lashed out, screaming for release, begging for forgiveness. How odd that she should think of forgiveness when she looked at it, when the thought had never entered her mind while she'd been painting.

But then, she never consciously thought while she was painting. She felt. She saw and smelled and tasted. But she never thought. Her work was pure emotion, a reflection of hopes and dreams unrealized, an extension of fears and wishes and regrets and promises.

But this piece—and the pieces she had been painting for the last several weeks—were different. The emotion was there, but she was very much afraid it wasn't her emotion.

It was *his*.

Why did she have such a hard time with his name? She knew his name. Dale. A simple name for a complex man she didn't quite understand. A man she was afraid to understand.

A man she was dangerously attracted to. A man she had practically thrown herself at last night.

Yes, she really should stop thinking of him

as…*him.*

He was Dale. A man who made her want things even as he frustrated her to no end. Like now, with the music blaring through the walls. Nothing like her music, soft and melodic and soothing. Inspirational. His music was hard and loud and almost angry, seething with energy.

Maybe that was the explanation for the fresh painting. Maybe she was channeling the energy from the AC/DC songs she was hearing instead of the man who was obviously blaring them inside his apartment.

If only she believed that.

Now that she was done painting, she became aware of the dull headache throbbing behind her eyes. She had no doubt that part of it was left over from her uncharacteristic overindulgence the night before. And part of it was certainly from the driving bass of the music that hummed through the walls.

Odd that she hadn't bothered to play her own music while she was painting. She hadn't needed to. Except now, she wanted the music to stop. Now that she was done painting, she needed quiet. Time to relax, to rest, to regain the energy she so often expended when she worked.

She thought about banging the wall, much like he did whenever she played her own music too loud. No. That would only result in hurting her hand. But her irritation grew with each passing second, escalating until she thought she'd go mad with it. She wanted the music to stop.

She needed it to stop.

Frustration made her storm out of the apartment, the door slamming behind her as she moved two steps to the left. She curled her hand into a fist and banged on the metal door, over and over, not caring if the neighbors heard.

What neighbors? It was late in the afternoon on a Friday. All the other neighbors were probably working, except for sweet Mrs. Lillian who loved downstairs and across the hall. Nobody else could hear.

Including, apparently, Dale.

Melanie groaned in impatience, the sound more like a growl. She banged the door again then pulled her foot back, wanting to kick the door in frustration. She stopped herself at the last minute, probably saving herself from the indignation of a broken toe.

The music screeched to a halt. The sound of heavy footsteps came from the other side, muffled but loud nonetheless. The door finally swung open with a ruthless force that made her jump.

Dale stood before her, his expression fierce, his scowl dark. She jumped again, but not because of his scowl. It was because of what he was wearing.

Or wasn't wearing.

He stood before her in nothing but a pair of loose gym shorts and shoes. The shorts hung low around his lean hips and her eyes drifted down, following the dark line of hair that moved from just below his navel before disappearing into the elastic waistband of the shorts.

She blinked, her mouth watering. She blinked again and forced herself to stop staring, forced herself to look into his eyes. Except her own eyes seemed to have their own agenda, travelling slowly upward, studying each inch of bare skin pulled tight across hard sculpted muscle. A fine sheen of sweat covered all that bare skin. She noticed the way his broad chest rose and fell, the way his flat nipples puckered as she watched.

She curled her hands into fists and shoved them behind her back, very much afraid of the urge to run her palms all over his slick skin.

"What do you want, Smurfette?" His voice was a low growl, deep and rough. She swallowed again and forced her gaze to his, her heart tripping in her chest at the look in his smoldering eyes.

"I—" She stopped, not quite sure what to say. She glanced to her left, at the door leading to her apartment. To safety and sanity.

She didn't want safety and sanity.

"Don't even tell me the music was too loud."

She looked back at him, expecting to see that playful grin teasing his mouth. But there was no grin. His expression was hard, his jaw clenched and his brows lowered over those heated eyes that made her pulse race.

She should leave. Just turn around and go back to her own apartment and leave him to the blackness she could sense swirling just beneath his hard exterior.

Instead of leaving, she straightened her shoulders and raised her chin and did what he would do: she pushed right past him and walked into his apartment. He muttered something, too low for her to hear, then slammed the door.

He walked past her, down the hallway, his voice a low growl. "What do you want, Smurfette?"

Sweets! He was infuriating! How could he ask her a question and walk away at the same time? Like he wasn't even interested in the answer. She stomped her foot then moved after him, following him into the small spare bedroom. Well, not *into*. She stopped just inside the doorway, her gaze sweeping around the room.

Workout equipment filled the room. A weight bench and a treadmill and over there, in the corner, a huge bag suspended from some kind of metal support. A punching bag. Her eyes narrowed as an overwhelming desire to go hit the bag filled her. It would be better than hitting *him*. Well, maybe not.

He sat on the edge of the bench, leaning over to grab a hand weight. She didn't know much about weights but it looked heavy, even if he was raising it up and down with his elbow braced on his knee. She watched the muscles of his arm bulk and stretch, bulk and stretch. It was mesmerizing. Almost hypnotic. Almost…

Oh, he was so infuriating! He was ignoring her, not even looking at her, like he didn't even realize she was standing there, watching him. She stomped her foot again and crossed her arms in front of her, her hands digging into her own soft biceps.

"Why were you mad earlier?" Melanie didn't realize she was going to ask the question until it came out of her mouth. But now that it was out there, she realized she wanted to know. Needed to know. His anger and emotion, his unexpected reaction from earlier—she needed to understand it.

He didn't answer her, just kept lifting and lowering the hand weight, the metal making a heavy clunking sound each time he raised it. One, twice. He let out a deep breath then moved the weight to the other arm, holding it in a loose grip as he finally looked over at her.

"I'm not talking about it."

"Why not?"

"Because I'm not, now drop it." He looked away and resumed his exercise, leaving her frustrated and angry. She stormed over to the big bag in the corner then looked over her shoulder. He was still doing his arm lifts or whatever they were called, but his eyes were on her. Watching, wary. Maybe a little curious.

"What is this thing called?"

"A punching bag."

"So it's okay to hit?"

A brief smile flashed across his face, just a small one that died too quickly. "Yeah but I wouldn't. You'd only hurt yourself."

Now he was making fun of her! Well, she'd show him. She curled her hand into a fist, pulled back her arm, then swung it out in a wide arc. Her hand connected with the bag…and bounced right off. She gasped as pain shot through her hand, up her arm, into her shoulder. He had lied! The bag must be filled with concrete, hard and unforgiving. She hopped up and down, cradling her sore hand against her chest as she tried her best not to whimper in pain.

Metal clashed behind her, followed by a thud and heavy steps. "What the hell did I tell you, Smurfette? I told you not to do it. Why didn't you listen?"

Hands closed over her shoulders, turning her around. She opened her eyes, her gaze resting on the bare chest just inches from her. He reached for her injured hand, cradling it in his large one as he bent his head to examine it. His touch was gentle, light and reassuring. And dangerous. So dangerous.

"Wiggle your fingers."

"No. It hurts."

He looked up, amusement flashing in his eyes. He was close, too close. "No shit. Why didn't you listen to me?"

"I don't have to. You're not the boss of me."

"Spoken like a true six year old."

"That's not fair!" Even if it was true. So what if she sounded like a pouting child? It hurt. That allowed for some pouting. And pouting was better than what she wanted to do, which was run her hands all over his slick skin.

And how could she even be thinking like that, when her hand tingled with pain? She was mad at him. Mad at his easy dismissal of her, mad because he wouldn't answer her question. Mad because of what he made her feel and think and want.

He stood there in front of her, the heat from his body searing her, his eyes alight with amusement. Her hand was still cradled in his, held between them, his touch so gentle, like a lover's.

"You confuse me."

"*I* confuse *you*?" He made a little sound, almost like a snort. "Welcome to my hell, Smurfette."

"What's that supposed to mean?"

"It means you've confused me from the very first time we met, when you tried to paint me blue."

"I did not!"

"Like hell. Or haven't you noticed that streak of paint that's still on my door?"

She narrowed her eyes, ready to argue, then stopped herself. She tugged her hand, trying to free it from his grip, but he wouldn't let her. And the way he was looking at her...she didn't know what to make of it. It was like he was studying her, trying to figure her out. Or trying to make sense of what he saw. She didn't like it, didn't like how it made her feel. Like he was trying to decide if he wanted to kiss her—or toss her out the door.

"Why didn't you kiss me last night?" She hadn't

meant to ask the question, hadn't even realized she wanted to know. His hand tightened around hers for a brief second then loosened and she thought he might let her hand go. But he didn't. And he didn't move away, either.

"I did."

"No you didn't. Not really. It was just that one little kiss and then you left."

He released her hand and stepped back. Air washed over her, cool now that he wasn't standing so close. He watched her for a few seconds, his gaze unreadable. Then he shook his head, like he couldn't believe the words that had just come from her mouth. "You were drunk."

"No I wasn't." His brows raised in silent contradiction and she sighed. "Well, maybe a little."

"No maybe about it."

"I'm not drunk now." And gracious, did she have to sound so needy? So eager? But maybe she only thought she sounded that way, because he didn't seem to notice. Well, that wasn't quite true. His eyes darkened and she saw the way his pulse beat heavy in his neck. But he stepped away from her, not toward her, so maybe he didn't really understand what she was saying.

Fair enough, because she didn't quite understand it herself.

"You need to put some ice on that hand."

"I don't want ice." Yes, she was pouting. Even she could hear it in her voice. He looked at her again with a flash of amusement.

"Then what do you want?" His voice was anything but amused. The deep tone was husky, maybe a little harsh. The brown of his eyes deepened, their color darkening to the richness of fertile soil as he watched her. The air suddenly thickened, becoming heavy and warm, as warm as the blood rushing through her limbs, making her body tingle. She couldn't look away, not when his eyes held her in place, not when she saw the same question repeated in their dark depths.

The same, but different. Waiting for an answer. All she had to do was give it.

"I want…" Her voice faded with her confidence. She swallowed, her tongue darting out to lick lips that were suddenly dry. "I want you kiss it and make it better."

The corners of his mouth curled up in a smile that was part amusement, part wryness. He closed the distance between them and grabbed her hand, brought it to his both before dropping a quick kiss on her tender knuckles. Her fingers tightened around his hand, holding him in place when he would have dropped it and stepped away.

"What do you want, Smurfette?"

Frustration boiled inside her. How could one person—one man—cause so many conflicting emotions? Desire, bewilderment, curiosity. Confusion. Frustration. She narrowed her eyes and squeezed her fingers more tightly around his.

"Melanie. My name is Mel. A. Nie."

"I know what your name is." His eyes flashed with humor and she knew he was going to say it, could see it in the laughter in his eyes. "Smurfette."

She pulled her hand from his and stomped her foot. "Ohhh. You're impossible."

She stomped her foot once more, knowing it was childish but beyond caring. Then she stepped around him, just wanting to go home. To go back to her place and do her best to put him out of her mind before he truly drove her insane.

But she didn't get far. He grabbed her arm and spun her around, pulling her to him so fast that she stumbled and would have fallen. Did fall—flush against his chest, held in place by the strong arm wrapped around her. His mouth closed over hers before she could gasp in surprise, making her gasp for another reason. His tongue swept past the barrier of her lips, meeting hers. Dancing, tasting. Slow, so deliciously slow, like he had all the time in the world.

Melanie clung to him, one hand braced on his shoulder, the other pressed between them with her palm flattened against his chest. The steady beat of his heart danced against her palm. Hard. Solid. She sighed and pressed herself even closer, his arm tightening around her, supporting her as her legs went weak.

His hand cupped the back of her head, his fingers threading in the tangle of her hair. He tilted her head back and pulled his mouth from hers, trailing hot kisses along her jaw and neck. His teeth nipped the corded muscle at the base of her neck, by her shoulder, sending a thousand sparks of desire shooting through her. The sparks liquefied, pooling in her limbs, settling low in her belly and between her legs.

She tilted her hips and rocked against the rigid length of his erection, pressed so bold and hard against her. Dale groaned, a low growl deep in his throat, and claimed her mouth once more.

A kiss. It was supposed to be nothing more than a kiss. But it was so much more, its shimmering color exploding behind her closed lids. Rich. Vibrant. Powerful. Colors she'd never before seen, never before imagined.

She moaned and leaned into him, dragged her hand along the slick feverish skin of his chest and stomach. Hot and hard. Soft and velvety. His body was a contradiction of sensation against her palm as she dragged her hand even lower, as she traced the silky softness of that irresistible line of hair low on his stomach. Her fingers brushed against the smooth edge of the nylon waistband of his shorts. She hesitated only a second then dipped her fingers inside.

His hand closed around her wrist, stopping her, holding her hand in place. He broke the kiss and looked down at her, desire burning like smoldering embers in the depths of his eyes.

She held her breath, desire and anticipation welling inside her and warring with anxiety. Would he push her away? Come to his senses and tell her to go home?

He reached up with one hand and brushed the hair away from her face, tucking it behind her ear. His thumb grazed her cheek, the touch gentle. He rubbed the pad of his thumb over her lip and she leaned forward, nipping it between her teeth. She heard his moan, felt it low in her belly as desire flashed in his eyes.

Then he kissed her again, his mouth seeking possession, demanding surrender. His grip on her wrist eased and she wiggled her fingers, trying to slide her hand lower.

The kiss deepened, changing, becoming something more. Melanie sighed, the sound lost in the kiss as he grabbed her by the waist and lifted her. She reached for his shoulders, her fingers digging into his bare skin as he carried her.

He was carrying her!

She was weightless, floating, anchored to reality only by the feel of his hands around her waist. By the deep possession of his kiss, as if he was starving and she was his only means of survival.

Cool air brushed her skin as he pulled her skirt up, the material bunched in his hand. She felt the rasp of his knuckles against the back of her thigh. Higher as his hand explored, higher until he palmed the roundness of her bare ass.

He tore his mouth from hers with a growl, his brows lowered over his eyes as he stared at her. "Is this how you always dress?"

Melanie frowned, not sure why he would ask her such a silly question. "Yes, but—"

He interrupted her with a kiss, hard and quick. "Good. Don't change it."

She still didn't understand but then he kissed her again and she didn't care, didn't even remember the question. The only thing that mattered, the only thing that held her enthralled, was the feel of Dale's mouth on hers. Hard, insistent. The heat of his body against hers. Hard, promising. And the feel of the mattress under her back as he gently laid her on his bed.

Another thrill shot through her, electrifying and so alive. Dale's mouth moved away from hers and she sighed. The sigh was replaced with a small gasp of surprise as he kissed his way down her throat, his hand still under her skirt, his fingers lightly brushing the tops of her thighs.

Close. So close.

She tilted her hips, seeking to bring his touch closer, needing him to fill the emptiness and ease the tender ache between her legs. But he moved his hand, freeing it from the flowing material of the skirt bunched around her waist. She moaned again, in disappointment, felt him smile against the sensitive flesh of her neck.

His hand wandered up, catching the hem of her shirt and easing it up her body until cool air washed across her bare chest. He cupped the weight of one breast in his hand, his palm deliciously rough against her skin. She gasped as his thumb scraped across her nipple, gasped again when he pinched her. Not hard, not soft. Just right.

And then his hands were gone, the heat of his body gone. He pushed to his knees beside her, looking down with an odd gentleness in his eyes. She pulled her lower lip between her teeth, wondering what he saw, realizing how vulnerable she was. Stretched out on his bed, her skirt pushed to her waist, her blouse pushed up to her neck. Fully dressed but completely exposed. Embarrassment and a sudden shyness gripped her and she moved to grab her clothes, to push them back in place. His hands shot out, stopping her, his grip a contradiction of rough and gentle.

He didn't say anything; he didn't need to. The look in his eyes said it all. Desire, need, primitive male appreciation. The look empowered her, made her bold. Made her want.

She tugged one hand from his grasp and reached out, trailing the short length of her nail across his chest, down the hard planes of his stomach. Lower, to that soft line of hair that disappeared into the waistband of his shorts.

Dale grinned, a crooked grin that seemed strained somehow. He eased away, dislodging her hand, and reached for her shirt, pushing it over her head and tossing it to the floor. Then he was between her legs, his hands tucked into the waistband of her skirt, pulling it off her legs and tossing it behind him. He smiled again, one full of promise, and lowered his mouth to her legs.

Melanie gasped, her eyes drifting shut. The world around her disappeared, leaving nothing but bright shards of pleasure as Dale kissed her, touched her. Her ankle, her calf. The sensitive skin behind her knee and along the inside of her thigh. Higher, higher still until—

Yes. A thousand times yes. His mouth closed over her, hot and wet, his tongue licking, probing. But instead of easing the ache, it only made it worse. Made her yearn for more.

Her hands floated around her, finally resting on his head, the touch anchoring her. She dug her heels into the mattress and raised her hips, her legs spreading wider, opening herself to him. To his mouth, his touch, his magic.

A wave caught her, swept her up, rising higher and higher toward the promise of shimmering light. She felt her body reaching for it, felt herself hovering, waiting. Breathless. Unable to breathe.

Her hands dropped to his shoulders, her fingers digging into the hard muscle. He murmured something, the words lost, then gently slid a finger inside her. Probing, sliding. In and out, in and out. So slow. She heard a whimper, the sound almost frantic, then realized it was her. The noise was coming from her.

But she didn't care. Not when what she needed, what she craved, hovered just over the swell of the wave. She whimpered again and slid her hand along the back of his head, across his cheek and down. The tip of her finger met his tongue, tangled with the moist tip of it as he licked her. She eased her finger down, touching herself, rubbing as he licked, then spreading herself open for him.

He said something again, his voice deep and gruff and filled with...Melanie wasn't sure but it made her stop, made her ease her finger away. His hand wrapped around her wrist, stopping her.

"Oh no you don't." He guided her hand and placed her finger back where it was, finding just the right spot. "Let me watch."

Her eyes fluttered open, surprised at the need in his voice. He was stretched out between her legs, one hand resting against the top of her thigh, the other between her legs, his finger still sliding in and out of her. His eyes were half-closed, dark and deep and alight with an inner flame that seared her.

The look in his eyes almost scared her. Too strong, too potent, too hot. She tried to look away but she couldn't, the hold of his gaze was too strong. And then it didn't matter because he leaned forward and pressed his mouth against her, just above the spot where her finger rested.

Melanie closed her eyes, a soft sigh escaping her, blood roaring through her. She pressed her finger tighter against herself and moved it, sliding up and down, pressing hard as Dale kissed and licked and slid a second finger inside her.

The wave crested again, higher, bringing her closer to those elusive colors. Bright, vibrant, new. Shades and mixtures she had never seen before. Closer, so close—

And then she was there, reaching for them, awash with them as the earth shattered around her. Intense, bright, living. Promising and giving and taking. And beautiful, so beautiful her mind's eye was nearly blinded by the shining brightness.

She was vaguely aware of Dale moving, of him reaching beside her for something. Aware of the sound of something being torn open. And then he was back, his hands lifting her legs, guiding them over his shoulders as he pushed into her.

Hot, heavy, deep, filling her.

She reached for him, found only empty air and let her hands drop back to the mattress. The wave crested again, stronger, pushing her higher as even more colors exploded and fell around her.

Exquisite. Achingly beautiful. Each time one exploded, another took its place. Each one different, each one filling her with something she didn't understand.

Amazement. Awe. And need, a need that grew with each of his long strokes, harder and deeper. Her hands fisted in the comforter as she tilted her hips upward, meeting each deep thrust. Harsh breathing echoed around them. His. Hers. It didn't matter. The only thing that mattered was the feel of him, sending her higher, catapulting her into a world of exploding color.

She thought she may have screamed, but maybe it was just a whisper, the sound lost in the harsh growl of his release. Dale eased his hold on her legs and stretched out on top her, his hands clasping the sides of her face. Then his mouth was on hers, his tongue dancing with hers, dominating and reassuring as he thrust into her one more time, his growl lost in the recesses of her mouth.

Time stretched out, liquid and languid. The colors

around her dimmed, still vibrant but not quite as achingly sharp. Melanie sighed, her hands brushing along the hard planes of his back, his skin hot and alive.

She pressed a kiss to his cheek and sighed again as she let herself gently fade away.

Chapter Twelve

Dale propped his head in his hand and stared down at the dozing woman next to him. Her hair was a wild tangle of shimmering fire, spread across her pillow—and his. Late afternoon sun spilled through the bedroom windows, coating her pale skin in hues of pink. He reached out with one finger and gently traced the line of her collarbone. A small flicker of guilt seized him at the redness he saw, a sign of his touch, his kisses. The guilt evaporated, replaced by a sense of possessiveness. Dale almost laughed. He'd be better off not sharing that tidbit with her, since it would only convince her he really was a Neanderthal.

He curled his hand and let it drop between them, his eyes skimming the length of her body. Soft creamy skin, full breasts and feminine hips, luscious long legs.

His cock twitched, starting to harden, and he swallowed back a groan. As tempting as it was, he couldn't wake her again, not so soon after their last time together.

She had surprised him. Last night. This morning.

This afternoon when she barged into his apartment. He'd been brooding, pissed at himself for how he'd reacted to her words this morning, knowing they had been nothing more than that: innocent words. But they had surprised him, flattening him until he had trouble filling his lungs with air. Not at the words, but at the reminder of what had happened, what Lindsay had tried to do.

A reminder of his failure at being a big brother. A reminder of his own guilt and the part he may have played in it.

So he'd come over here, intending to work out until he collapsed in exhaustion, unable to feel anything. And then she had shown up, angry and frustrated and out of sorts and sending him spinning until he had no idea which way was up.

He hadn't meant to kiss her, even when she asked him to, even when she asked him why he didn't kiss her last night. A sense of desperation ripped through him when she walked by and he hadn't thought beyond the sudden irrational fear that if she left, he'd never see her again. Never get this chance again. So he didn't think beyond that, he just acted. And then he was kissing her and she was pressed against him, warm and soft in his arms.

Even then he hadn't expected it to go further than it did. Just a kiss, that was all he had hoped for. But the kiss had grown, becoming so much more, consuming him until he was lost.

And when he had her in bed...a shiver rippled his skin as his cock twitched again, in both memory and eager anticipation. Holy shit. He wasn't sure why but he had expected her to be shy, modest.

She was anything but.

A fire burned in her, selfless and giving. Eager, free, untethered. And when he came, when he surged inside her for that last time and lost himself, he had discovered he was soaring in a way he never thought possible. Not by himself, but with her. Together.

And fuck. He needed to stop thinking in terms like that. Talk about a fucking train wreck. Thinking like that was pure insanity. He had enough craziness in his life right now, he couldn't afford to add anything more to it.

But how in the hell was he supposed to know that an enchanting siren dwelled inside his sweet Smurfette?

He grinned again, remembering her frustration when he called her that. Remembering how her ocean blue eyes flared with impatience when she told him her name.

Melanie. Mel. A. Nie.

Yeah, like he'd be able to forget.

He leaned forward and dropped a kiss against her forehead, his hand curving around the soft globe of her ass then giving it a playful smack. Her lids fluttered open, her eyes filled with sleepy confusion as his gaze caught hers. Then a wistful smile teased her full lips, making him groan with want and need.

He rolled away and climbed out of bed, watching as her eyes drifted down to his semi-hard cock. And shit, if she kept looking at him like that, he'd jump back in bed and drive himself into her for a third time.

No. He didn't have time. *They* didn't have time.

"Come on, Smurfette. Time to get up. We're going to be late."

She pushed up on her elbows, seemingly unaware of her nakedness and what it was doing to him. Frustration flashed in her eyes, echoed by the small frown that furrowed a little line between her brows. The frown disappeared, replaced by confusion.

"Late?"

"Yeah." Dale glanced at the look, surprised at the time. "Real late. Shit. I didn't realize what time it was. If we leave in the next twenty minutes, we'll have time to grab a bite to eat."

Confusion was still clear on her face but she swung her legs over the side of the bed and slowly stood. Dale paused in front the closet, unable to tear his gaze away from her as she shuffled around the bed, searching for her clothes. And then she bent over, her back to him and her luscious ass high in the air as she reached for her skirt. His breath left him in a rush, a sharp hiss that she no doubt heard because she looked at him.

From between her spread legs.

Upside down, with her hair falling around her face and cascading on the carpet like a waterfall of molten lava.

His hand clenched around the edge of the closet door as he struggled for every ounce of willpower he had. He could not take her right now. He had more control than that. But fuck, all he wanted to do was march over there and grip her hips and drive his cock deep inside her from behind, holding her in place as she bent over.

"Is something wrong?" She finally straightened, watching him over her shoulder as she moved around the bed in search of her shirt. Dale swallowed and shook his head.

"No. All good." His voice was rough, catching in his throat. He forced himself to turn away, blindly grabbing clothes.

"Where are you going?"

"Not me. Us." He turned back around and frowned. She was dressed already, the skirt twisted a little. She pulled at it until it fell around her legs then looked at him. "There's a little bar north of Cockeysville we always go to. Duffy's. They have live music."

"Oh." She folded her hands in front of her, twisting them as she chewed on her lower lip. Dale paused, the clothes bunched in his fist.

"Don't you want to go?"

"No. I mean, I do. I just didn't think…" Her voice trailed off and she looked away. She didn't think what? Now he was confused. More than confused. He was worried. Had he done something? Said something he shouldn't have?

He closed the distance between them and pulled her into his arms, felt her body stiffen for the smallest second before she relaxed against him. "What didn't you think?"

She shrugged, her gaze focused on a spot near the base of his neck. "I didn't expect you to…I mean, you don't have to take me anywhere. I wasn't expecting anything."

What the hell? Was she telling him that she didn't want to go anywhere with him, that it had just been a quick—or not so quick—romp? Or was she telling him that she didn't think *he'd* want to take her anywhere because he thought it was just a romp? Neither option sat well with him.

"Smurfette, I'm not proposing marriage or even expecting anything. It's a night out. I'd like you to go because I think you'll have fun." Her frown deepened and he cursed to himself. Shit, he wasn't phrasing this right.

He pressed a kiss to her temple and cleared his throat. "I'm going out to meet some friends and listen to some great music and I'd like for you to go with me. And if we have time, I'd like to take you to dinner before we get there. Because I'm hungry and you probably are to. And because I'd like to take you."

There, that was better. Maybe. At least she wasn't frowning any longer. Of course, she wasn't exactly smiling, either. Then her face cleared and she gave him a small nod, like whatever had been going on in her head was finally settled. She stepped out of his arms.

"Okay. I'll go. Twenty minutes?"

Dale glanced at the clock again. It was more like fifteen now. But he just smiled at her and nodded. She smiled back then stepped past him, walking out of the bedroom without even looking back.

What the hell had that been about? He had no idea. Part of him was even afraid to look too deep into it, worried he'd overanalyze it and come up with scenarios that didn't even make sense. So he pushed the confusion and the questions to the back of his mind as best he could and jumped in the shower. Five minutes later, he was finished, dried and dressed and ready to go.

How much longer would it take Smurfette? He couldn't even guess. Was she one of those women who took forever in the shower, not finishing up until the water ran cold? Or would she take forever in front of the mirror, primping and preening, making sure her hair was just right and her makeup was perfect?

She didn't seem to be the kind of woman who spent hours in front of the mirror. She didn't need to. Her hair was perfect as it was, long and thick, with soft loose curls. And she didn't wear makeup. At least, he didn't think she did.

And what the hell was wrong with him? Was he really sitting here, pondering her bathroom rituals? He shook his head and grunted, calling himself a fool just as he heard a soft knock at the door.

He looked down at his watch. Damn, they still have five minutes. Not bad.

Smurfette stood in the hall, looking fresh and clean and wholesome. Not wholesome. Where in the hell had that word come from? Wrong word. Really fucking wrong.

Inviting. Yes, that was better.

She was dressed in another skirt and blouse, both of them in shades of blue that turned her eyes brighter. But her hair was pulled up in a thick twist, with loose tendrils falling down her neck and across her cheek. She pursed her lips and blew a curl from her face, then reached up to tuck a wayward strand behind her ear.

All he wanted to do was reach behind her and undo her hair, to revel in the feel of it as it fell around him.

Christ, what was with him? They just spent the afternoon in bed. He shouldn't be ready to throw her over his shoulder and take her back to his bedroom for another round or five.

He clenched his jaw and grabbed his keys, pulling the door closed behind him as he stepped into the hall.

"I can't find my keys."

"Why do you need your keys?"

"So I can drive."

He stopped on the bottom step and looked at her, trying not to let the horror show on his face. "You're not driving."

"But I like driving."

"You're not driving." He cupped his hand around her elbow and led her outside. "It's my turn."

"Oh." She stumbled to a halt and looked at him. "But I still need to find my keys."

"No you don't. They're on my kitchen counter."

"Why are they there?"

"Because I forgot to leave them at your place last night."

"Oh. Well at least I didn't lose them. I was afraid I'd lost them."

"No, you didn't lose them." He helped her into his car then ran around the other side and climbed in. Ten minutes later, they were seated at a nearby Mexican restaurant that boasted delicious food and fast service. Smurfette looked around her, her eyes wide as she took in everything. The crowded bar across the room, the brightly colored decorations and murals painted on the walls. Even the tables were painted in bright colors. She almost looked like she was in sensory overload—and basking in it.

It amazed him, how two people could see things so differently. As much as he loved the restaurant, he'd always found the bright décor to be jarring, almost an eyesore. But watching her look around, he imagined seeing it through her eyes. Were the fruit baskets piled in the mule's cart too bright, a caricature of their real color? Or were they merely a bigger-than-life depiction to convince the viewer he wanted the fruit? To make them seem more desirable?

And what about the mule, with its pointed ears and large eyes? Was he supposed to feel sorry for the animal? To relate to it somehow?

Yeah, he needed a drink.

But they both settled on ice tea and water, sipping between bites. Dale pushed his empty plate away and looked at Smurfette, who had barely eaten half of her overstuffed burrito and hardly any of the flavorful black beans.

"Don't you like it?"

"It's delicious." She pressed a hand to her stomach and smiled. "But there's so much of it, I can't finish."

"Then you can get it boxed up and eat it tomorrow." He signaled the waiter, motioning for the check and a box. The older man returned with both and Smurfette busied herself with boxing the leftovers as he paid the bill. Then they were back in his car, twilight long gone as he drove north up York Road, turning onto Shawan.

The car windows were partly down, allowing the cool night air to blow in on them. There was just a hint of chill in the air, a last bite as early Spring tried to shrug off Winter's last hold. He wondered if Smurfette brought a jacket then figured she probably wouldn't need one. Duffy's would be crowded, keeping her warm. And if she still got cold…well, he could manage the job of keeping her warm just fine.

"Where are we going?" Her voice was quiet, a little curious.

"A place called Duffy's on Falls Road. It's just a little bar, nothing fancy. Cold beer and frozen pizza if you get really hungry. And live music every other weekend."

Her eyes widened, a small smile teasing the corners of her full mouth. "Is it a honky tonk? I've never been to a honky tonk."

Dale chuckled, stopping for the light at the intersection of Shawan and Falls. "Not quite, no. Just a bar. The best honky tonks are in Nashville, anyway. At least, that's what I hear."

"Oh." She leaned back against the seat, looking out the window as the dark landscape whizzed by them.

"I think you'll like it. It's Nick's band and they're really good."

"Who's that?"

"Nick is Mikey's fiancé. You met her last night."

She nodded but didn't say anything and for a brief minute, Dale wondered if she really wanted to be there. To be with him. She would have said no if she didn't, right? Of course she would have.

Maybe.

He pulled into the gravel lot, easing his car to the end and nosing it in beside Jay's truck. The night was quiet, filled with the sounds of early insects brave enough to venture into the chilled air. Good, the band hadn't started yet.

He opened the door for Smurfette, taking her hand and helping her out. She gave him an odd look, her head tilted to the side, studying him. His eyes met hers, trying to figure out what she was thinking.

He'd probably have a better chance at figuring out which numbers would pop up in tomorrow night's lottery drawing.

They walked inside, music from the jukebox greeting them. Dale placed his hand in the middle of Smurfette's back, guiding her across the floor to their customary table in the corner. Dave was already there, along with his girlfriend CC. Pete had claimed the chair on the far end next to the wall and was straddling it backward, leaning across the table in deep conversation with Jimmy. Adam was on the other side, his attention on the phone in his hand, a frown on his face.

Dale introduced Smurfette to CC then greeted everyone by name, in case she didn't remember from last night. He slid a chair out for her then took the empty one next to her, reaching for the pitcher of beer and the stack of plastic cups in the middle of the table. He poured the first one and held it out for Smurfette. She shook her head, her lips pursed.

"No, thank you. I don't drink beer."

Dale hesitated, something about the way she answered catching him off-guard. He sat the cup in front of him then pushed away from the table. "Did you want something else? I can go get some wine—"

"No, thank you. I'm fine." Her voice was a little strained, her gaze not quite meeting his. Dale leaned forward, lowering his voice so he couldn't be overheard.

"Is everything okay? I can get you something else, it's not a big deal."

"No, I'm fine."

"Are you sure? You look like something's bothering you."

Her eyes darted around the table, settling on CC before moving back to him. She leaned closer, her hand resting on his arm. "You did it again."

"Did what?"

She looked around once more then frowned at him. "You didn't use my name."

"Yeah I did."

"No. You called me Smurfette. Again. That's not my name."

Was she serious? That was why she was upset? He looked into her eyes, really looked. The ocean blue had turned gray, the shade reminding him of an angry sea just before a storm. But it wasn't just her eyes. It was the way she held herself, her shoulders a little too tight even though she was leaning toward him. Even her hand was a little stiff, her fingers pressing into the skin of his arm.

He closed his hand around hers and leaned forward, pressing a quick kiss against her pursed lips. Then he banged the table with his fist, catching everyone's attention. Conversation around him drifted away, fading into the surrounding noise. One by one, heads turned, curious gazes fixing on him.

He looked around the table, his eyes finally landing on CC, and cleared his throat. "Guys, let me introduce Melanie."

Pete and Jimmy stared at him like he'd just started speaking a foreign language. Adam looked up from his phone, frowned, then went back to whatever he was doing. Even Dave and CC seemed a little confused, although CC, at least, was smiling, like she understood what he was doing and why.

Yeah, of course she would. Didn't women stick together?

"Better?"

She nodded, a bright smile on her face. Dale almost rolled his eyes but stopped himself at the last minute. He draped his arm across the back of her chair, his hand lightly brushing her shoulder as he leaned closer, keeping his voice low. "So why does that bother you?"

"What?"

This time he did roll his eyes. "Me calling you 'Smurfette'?"

"Because it's not my name and I can't tell if you're

making fun of me."

"Making fun—?" Is that what she really thought? He frowned, trying to understand why she would think that. He'd never meant to make fun of her. Yeah, maybe he liked to tease her, but he thought the name was cute. He was ready to tell her that, to explain it, when she started talking again, a small pout on her face.

"You don't like it when I call you a Neanderthal."

"There's a big difference. I'm not insulting you when I call you 'Smurfette'."

"And I wasn't insulting you when I called you Neanderthal."

"Really?" His voice was gruff, a little too harsh. "Sweetheart, you were nothing but insulting the first day we met. If I remember correctly, you even compared me to a gorilla. Told me I had no manners. And let's not forget last night, when you called me a barbarian. And primitive and prehistoric and authoritative and—"

"And you called me 'Smurfette'."

He felt his temper rising, creeping up his chest like a dormant animal slowly rising from a deep slumber. Dale pulled his arm away and slid the chair back, his jaw clenched. "For the last time, it's not an insult. It's nothing more than a damned nickname."

He stood up fast enough that the chair tilted backward. He caught it before it fell then stepped around it, resisting the urge to shove it away. Several pairs of eyes watched him as he walked away, heading to the bar. Screw them. Screw this. Screw the whole fucking night. Let them think whatever they wanted to think. He needed to get away, to cool down, just for a minute.

Jay greeted him at the bar, a silent question in his

cool gray eyes. Dale frowned then slid onto the empty barstool and asked for a glass of water. Not that water would do him any good, not unless he poured it over his head to cool off.

What the fuck was he doing? Why was he being such an ass? Arguing over a stupid fucking name. How could she not know he liked calling her Smurfette? How could she even think he was trying to insult her? Christ, anyone who had ever seen the stupid show would know he wasn't being insulting.

And it sure as hell didn't come close to being compared to a barbarian.

"We've got some empty boxes in the back if you want to hit something."

"I'm good." He grabbed the glass Jay slid across to him and took a long swallow, wishing it was something stronger. "And what do you mean, 'we'? You act like you actually work here."

Jay shrugged, a grin on his face. "I just like hanging with Angie."

Dale snorted. Yeah, sure. They were living together, spent all their free time together, and yet Jay still wanted to help out on the occasional nights Angie was tending bar.

Dale couldn't imagine being with someone all the time, not like they were. He glanced behind him to the small stage where the band was setting up and saw Mikey lean closer to Nicky, a smile on her face as she leaned in for a kiss. His eyes drifted over to their corner table, where Dave was sitting close to CC, his arm draped around her.

Fuck. How did they do it? Make things work like that? He couldn't even manage one night with someone without it blowing up in his face.

And all because of a stupid, silly name.

He really was an ass.

Jay propped his elbow on the table and leaned in. "So what's going on with you and your neighbor?"

"Not a damn thing." Except, apparently, for sex. Which, apparently, was nothing more than a one-time deal. Because, apparently, he was an ass.

"You sure about that?"

"Apparently. Why?"

"Because she just walked out."

"What?" Dale swung around on the stool just in time to see the door close behind Smurf—behind *Melanie*. "Fuck." He jumped off the stool and pushed his way through the growing crowd, the first strains of music filling the small space as the band started to play.

What the hell did she think she was doing? And where the hell did she think she was going? She didn't have a car, didn't have a way home. And it was too damn far to walk. Damn her.

No, damn him.

He pushed through the door, the cool night air slamming him in the face as he looked around. Sure enough, she was heading toward the road, not even hesitating as she turned left.

In the wrong direction.

"Melanie!" She must have heard him but she kept walking, not even hesitating. "Melanie!"

Still nothing. He shook his head and hurried to catch up, calling one more time. "Smurfette!"

She stopped, her back stiffening. What the hell? She'd stop for that, but not when he called her real name?

He caught up to her, stepping in front of her in case she decided to keep walking. "Why didn't you stop when I called you?"

"I did."

"No you didn't."

"I did! I'm stopped, aren't I?"

"I called you twice before that—" Dale snapped his mouth shut, stopping before the conversation got even more out of control. "Where are you going?"

"Home."

"Home's that way." He pointed behind her. She glanced over her shoulder, frowning, then lifted her chin a notch and turned and started walking again. Dale mumbled under his breath and caught up to her again, once more stepping in front of her.

"Why are you walking?"

"Because I want to go home."

"Why?"

She looked away, but not before he saw the shadows clouding her eyes. "Because this isn't as fun as I thought it would be and I'm tired and have a long day tomorrow at the gallery and I want to go home."

Regret and anger filled him.

Anger at himself, for ruining what should have been a fun night. All he had wanted was to take Smur—Melanie—out. To spend time with her, get to know her more. To have fun and listen to music and maybe even dance, to hold her close in his arms as they swayed to the soft strains of some rock ballad.

Regret because he knew he'd never get another chance. Regret because—no matter how much he might make fun of Mikey and Jay and Dave—he knew he'd never have what they did. What a kick in the ass that was, because he never even realized he might want what they have.

Yeah, well. What the hell. It wasn't meant to be.

He wasn't destined for anything like that and he knew it. That didn't mean he didn't regret what could have been a fun night. He opened his mouth, ready to tell her to head to the car, that he'd take her home. But she spoke before he could get the words out.

"Is this a date?"

Chapter Thirteen

Is this a date?

Where the hell had that question even come from? Totally out of nowhere, with nothing to do with anything they had been talking about. And what the hell kind of question was that, anyway? A date. No, it wasn't a date. Not really. Maybe. No. No, of course it wasn't. He wouldn't bring a date to hang out with his shift. Would he?

"Well? Is it?"

"It's—I—" He narrowed his eyes. "Do you want it to be?"

Her head tilted to the side, her own eyes narrowing. "I don't know."

Not quite the answer he'd been expecting, or even the one he hoped for. Asinine. He hadn't been hoping for anything except a relaxing night out, hanging with friends.

Dale ran a hand through his hair then dragged it down his face, feeling the rasp of stubble against his palm. Should he try to salvage the night or just take her home? He didn't know. He didn't even know what she wanted. Her face was carefully blank, her eyes giving nothing away.

"How about we just go back inside and listen to the music and try to have some fun? Just hang out and enjoy ourselves." It was a lame attempt at...something. He knew that. But that didn't stop him from hoping she'd say yes.

"Can I ask you something before we go back in?"

Dale almost said no, afraid of what might come out of her mouth. He nodded anyway, surprised that she suddenly looked away. She seemed to be studying the cracked asphalt and gravel beneath her sandals.

A minute stretched by and he wondered if she was going to say anything else. Or if she was just going to stand there, her hands twisting in front of her, and keep staring at her feet. She finally took a deep breath, her shoulders rising with the effort, and peered at him through her thick lashes.

"Why can't you call me by my name?"

"Why does that bother you so much?"

"I told you why. I can't tell if you're insulting me or not. Or if you even remember my name. And if you can't remember my name, then I don't want to go back inside."

Christ. Were they really going to have this conversation again? He didn't know why it upset her but it obviously did. That much was clear on her face. In the way her brows pulled low and in the tiny little furrow between her eyes. Didn't she understand it was just a silly nickname?

"I know your name. Melanie. Smurfette is just a nickname. That's all. I told you that before."

"But you didn't even say my name when we..."

She looked away, shuffled her feet and twisted her hands some more. Her voice lowered to a whisper. "Earlier. When we were together."

"Yes I—" He slammed his mouth shut. Fuck. Now he understood. Maybe it didn't make sense and maybe it was foolish—to him. But she was right, he hadn't used her name. Or maybe he had, but only that one time. He thought. Hell, maybe he really hadn't, at all. Had he called her Smurfette? He couldn't remember. Christ, it wasn't as if his brain had been in any condition to form rational thought, not when he had been completely lost, drowning in the sensation of her touch, her body, her heat.

He cleared his throat and stepped closer, tucked a finger under her chin and tilted her head up. "Melanie."

Her eyes widened just a fraction, the blue suddenly deeper in the shadows of the night. He said her name again, his voice just above a whisper. "Melanie."

Then he dipped his head and lowered his mouth to hers, the kiss soft and gentle. She sighed, her hand sliding up his chest. But she didn't push him away, just held her hand there, the warmth of her touch seeping through the woven material of his shirt.

He dipped his tongue inside her mouth, seeking, reassuring. And God, it would be so easy to lose himself. To let desire sweep him away once more. Not here. Not now. He pulled away, her soft moan mingling with his.

"Melanie." He said it one more time, the name coming out rough and needy. He cleared his throat and stepped away, tried to grin in an effort to hide just what the too-short kiss had done to him. "Are you ready to go inside now?"

She stepped away, a small smile on her face. Did

she look a little stunned as well? Or maybe that was just wishful thinking, because she nodded and turned around, heading back to the door. He hurried to catch up to her, calling himself every kind of fool as he followed her inside. He was overreacting from nothing but a kiss. It hadn't even come close to the kisses they shared earlier. Deep, passionate, hungry. Nothing like that.

Maybe it wasn't the kiss. Maybe it was the fact that it didn't seem to effect Melanie at all.

And maybe he just needed to sit down and have a drink and shut up and stop thinking. Now that the band was playing, that should be easy to do. Just like it should be easy to avoid conversation, since you had to shout to be heard.

"You okay?"

He glanced over at Mikey then took a seat, nodding. So much for avoiding conversation. "Yeah. Fine. Why?"

"You look a little dazed."

"No. I'm good. Just preoccupied." He reached for the pitcher of beer and poured a fresh cup, glancing over at Melanie. She was turned to the side, away from him, talking to Jimmy. Again.

He pushed away the surge of irrational jealousy. They were just talking, that was all.

Dave leaned forward, raising his voice. "About next week?"

"What?" Dale frowned before understanding sunk in. Next week. Hell. Why had Dave even brought that up? He took a long swallow of beer, brushed the back of his hand across his mouth, and shook his head. "No, something else."

"You sure about that?"

"What's next week?" Pete shouted the question across the table. Great. Now everyone was looking at him, their expressions ranging from curiosity to concern.

"His sister's trial date." Dave answered the question, not even looking at Dale. "Unless they reschedule it again."

Adam looked up from his phone, his blue eyes curious as he finally focused on the conversation around him. "I thought she was going to take a plea."

Dale shifted in the chair, aware that Smurfette was watching him too closely, more than curiosity in her gaze. He looked down at the cup in his hand and forced a smile to his face, trying to ignore the sudden knot in his gut. Why the hell had Dave even brought it up? Especially here? Now? Yeah, everyone at work knew about it. But the woman next to him didn't, and he didn't want her to know.

Embarrassment? Something else?

He looked around the table, noticed they were waiting for answer. Couldn't this have waited until day work? Instead of now, when everyone had to shout to be heard? "No plea. She's still convinced she didn't do anything wrong."

Of course she was. That was Lindsay. Innocent. Always innocent. Everything that happened was someone else's fault. Their parents' fault for not paying tuition after she got kicked out of college twice. Lauren's fault for expecting her to help with expenses when she moved in with her. His fault because he wouldn't defend her. His fault because he hadn't been there for her, because he'd been a shitty big brother.

Everyone's fault except Lindsay's.

A hand closed over his arm, the fingers long and

slender, the touch trying to be comforting. The muscles in his arm tensed and he had to stop himself from pulling away to dislodge Melanie's hand. "What happened?"

She may have meant the question to only be for his ears but her voice was too loud, carrying so that everyone at the table could hear it. Why wouldn't it be? It was too loud to talk, too loud to carry on a conversation in a normal voice. He couldn't fault her for that, couldn't fault her for asking a normal question born of nothing more than curiosity. That didn't mean he intended to answer her.

He shook his head, ready to tell her it wasn't anything, to tell her it didn't matter. But Jimmy leaned in and Dale could see he was ready to tell her everything.

"His youngest sister tried to—"

"Jimmy—"

"—kill Lauren."

The band stopped playing at that exact second, so that Jimmy's voice carried to the tables surrounding them. A few patrons turned to look their way, shrugged and turned back. Dale wasn't paying attention to them, though; he was focused solely on Smurfette.

Her eyes widened, a look of horror and disbelief flashing in the deep blue of her eyes. Her lips parted on a gasp of surprise. The horror and disbelief were quickly replaced by sympathy. Her hand tightened around his arm but her question was directed at Jimmy.

"That's awful! What happened?"

"She, uh…" Jimmy's voice faltered as he caught Dale's scowl. He shrugged and reached for his beer. "I'm, uh, not sure."

"She poisoned her. Or tried to, at least." Pete

answered the question, oblivious to Dale's glare, oblivious to the awkward tension that hovered over their table.

Mikey finally broke the silence, tossing a damp cardboard coaster in Pete's direction, hitting him square in the chest. "Smooth move, Pete. Smooth."

The music started up again, a slow rock ballad this time. But it was too late to save Dale from the embarrassment, from the shame that filled him. He stared into the full cup, willing the floor to open beneath him, willing himself to disappear.

What the hell must Melanie think? He didn't want to know. It was too easy to remember the horror that had flashed in her eyes. Too easy to imagine the contempt she must certainly feel, wondering what kind of man he was. Wondering what kind of brother he was, to have let something so terrible happen.

"I'd like to dance please."

He looked up, expecting to see Melanie leaning over to Jimmy. But her hand slid down his arm and closed over his, her fingers threading through his. She tugged and he finally looked at her, surprised to see she was standing up, pulling him with her.

She led him onto the crowded dance floor and stepped close, wrapping her arms around his waist. He stood still for a heart-stopping second then finally slid his arms behind her, afraid to hold her too close as she started swaying to the music.

"That's why you were so upset."

Dale finally met her eyes, surprised to see understanding in their depths. "Upset?"

"This morning. When I said you were trying to poison me."

His steps faltered. He hesitated, not sure what to

do, then slowly started dancing again. "I wasn't upset."

A smile, small and sad, briefly touched her lips. "You were. But now I understand why."

"There's nothing to understand."

She didn't say anything, just rested her head against his shoulder and snuggled closer as they moved in a small circle on the dance floor. Another couple jostled them from behind and he looked over his shoulder, ready to say something. Melanie's hand curled around his cheek, forcing him to look down at her. She pushed up on her toes and pressed a quick kiss against his mouth, her smile easing some of the tension knotting his insides. "Just dance with me."

"Melanie—"

She tilted her head, a tiny frown marring her smooth face. "You sound mad."

"I'm not mad."

"No. I mean when you say my name. It makes you sound mad."

"That doesn't make sense—"

"I think I like it better when you call me 'Smurfette'. You smile when you say it."

Damn if he didn't grin. He couldn't help it.

"What happened?"

His grin disappeared. "I don't want to talk about it."

"Okay." She rested her head against his shoulder once more, long enough for them to complete one slow circle in place. Then she looked up at him again. "You can talk to me if you want to."

"I don't want to."

"Okay." Thirty seconds went by before she raised her head for the third time. "But you can if you want to."

"Smurfette—"

"See? You're smiling."

The song ended but she didn't step out of his arms, even as other couples moved past them. Nick announced the band was taking a break and the jukebox kicked on, the music nothing more than background noise. Yet they still stood there, in the middle of the floor, their arms around each other. Dale thought that maybe she wanted to dance again. There were other couples on the floor, doing just that. But it wasn't a slow song, so she shouldn't be standing so close, wrapped in his arms, if she wanted to dance.

"Smurfette, what are you doing?"

"Holding you."

"Um, did you want to dance?"

She shook her head. Some of her hair fell from the loose knot at the back of head, long tendrils escaping to brush against her smooth neck.

"Did you want to go back to the table and get a drink?"

"No."

"Then what do you want?"

Her smile was sweet, radiant, powerful enough to knock the breath from him. She looked around then leaned close, her voice barely more than a whisper. "I want to go home with you again."

Chapter Fourteen

Melanie drifted through the crowd, absently smiling and nodding at the few people who went out of their way to catch her attention. She thought she may have even spoken to one or two, but had no real memory of what she said.

These things always made her uncomfortable. Too many people, too much schmoozing. Too much smiling and nodding and muttering vapid words, always hoping they were the correct ones. Always worrying that they weren't. It was the side of the business she absolutely hated. She'd much rather be home, listening to her music and painting, unaware of everything else around her. Home was where she was most comfortable, not here in Anna's gallery, moving among the crowd of unfamiliar faces. Here, she felt like she was on display, as much a part of the exhibits as her paintings.

But today...today was worse, somehow. The desire to leave, the urge to run out the door and disappear, was stronger than it had ever been. The music, a mellow concerto meant to soothe, was too loud, abrasive to her ears despite the low volume. It wasn't meant to be heard, to drown out conversation. The music was carefully chosen, the volume carefully controlled to be nothing more than a cultivated background.

Melanie wanted to go in the back and yank the cords from the wall to stop it.

Her fingers tightened around the delicate stem of the crystal flute. The champagne was lukewarm now, its fizz long gone. She hadn't even had a single sip. She moved to the corner and placed the full glass on the empty serving tray then discreetly tugged at the hem of her dress. It felt like her legs were on display, her skin exposed from just above her knees all the way down to her feet.

Heat filled her face and she wondered if she was blushing, then glanced around to see if anyone noticed. Maybe she could blame it on the warmth of the room, muggy with the heat of too many bodies.

Sweets! It wasn't like it really mattered if anyone noticed. It wasn't as if they would know she was blushing because she realized the irony of feeling exposed in the dress—when she had been much more exposed yesterday with Dale.

Yesterday…and last night.

She reached for the flat champagne and brought the glass to her mouth, taking a long swallow in hopes the liquid would cool her off. Just as she expected: flat and lukewarm. She grimaced and put the glass back, her gaze darting around the room without really seeing anything.

No, her mind was too preoccupied with memories. Of yesterday. Of last night. Of her date that wasn't really a date—she thought—with Dale. Of going back to his apartment afterward.

Of waking up this morning, wrapped in his arms, her body safely held against his. Bare flesh to bare flesh. Would he be mad, she wondered?

Probably.

She hadn't meant to sneak out, not really. Didn't even think she was sneaking. But she had seen the glowing numbers on his alarm clock and realized how late it was and he had looked so peaceful, so content. She couldn't bear to wake him up.

No, she hadn't been sneaking. But she had made sure she was quiet as she moved through his apartment, remembering to grab her keys before she left. Then she had hurried next door to shower and change and practically ran outside to reach her car, hurrying to get here on time. No, she hadn't been sneaking. But she still felt guilty and she didn't understand why.

"You seem distracted, dear." Anna's clear voice interrupted her thoughts and Melanie turned, glad she no longer had the glass in her hand because she would have surely dropped it in surprise.

"I'm sorry. I don't mean to be." Anna laughed and Melanie wondered if she had said something wrong. The woman reached out and placed a hand on her shoulder, the touch reassuring.

"I'm sure you don't. But you should mingle more, smile at the pretty people to encourage them to open their wallets. You know as well as I do that they like to feel as if they're buying a piece of the artist as well."

Melanie frowned, the words filling her with their usual coldness. She knew what Anna said was correct, but that didn't mean she was comfortable with it. She never had been. "Can't I just be one of those reclusive artists? A hermit, shrouded in mystery?"

Anna laughed again, the sound soft and throaty. She thought Melanie had meant the words as a joke, but she had been serious. More serious today than when she usually said them.

"Nonsense. Come, let me introduce you to your most recent fan. He's wealthy, a recent widower, and fancies himself a patron of the arts." Melanie inwardly groaned but plastered a smile on her face as Anna guided her through the crowd. If Anna noticed her hesitation, she didn't say anything because she kept talking.

"He's already expressed an interest in the auction. A very pointed interest."

Melanie stumbled, her heel catching on an uneven floor plank. She caught herself before she pitched forward onto her face and hoped nobody noticed.

But of course, someone had. The gentleman Anna had steered her toward. He was Melanie's height, with a slight build that made his clothes hang on his lean frame. Thinning sandy blonde hair, faded with gray, topped a long narrow face. His nose was perfectly straight, his lips too red for his coloring. Despite his smooth face, he was probably in his late fifties. A businessman, no doubt. Maybe a CEO or CFO, by the way he carried himself, even though there was nothing about him that Melanie would call impressive.

He stepped forward as Anna introduced them, his lips spreading in a closed smile as he reached for her hand and brought it to his mouth. Melanie's hand tightened and she barely caught herself before she pulled it away. His cologne was too strong, but she could still smell his breath. Sour and stale, like raw onion that had been left too long in the sun.

"Ms. Reeves, a pleasure. I've just discovered your work and must admit I'm a huge fan."

"Thank you." Melanie smiled and tugged her hand free from his hold. She clasped her hands together and held them in front of her, making sure her smile didn't falter. At least he seemed nice enough, and he had a nice voice. That didn't mean she wanted to engage in a lengthy conversation with him. With anyone, for that matter. She never knew what to say or how to answer the inevitable questions or even how to accept the compliments.

She just wanted to go home and paint.

No, she wanted to go home and see Dale.

The widower—*what was his name?*—kept talking, unaware that she wasn't paying the slightest attention. She smiled and nodded and made little humming noises here and there. At least he was wasn't asking her questions, wasn't expecting her to say anything. She nodded again at something he said and discreetly looked around for Anna. Where had she gone? She generally never left her alone this long with any of the gallery's visitors. Yes, she insisted that Melanie mingle, but she also knew how uncomfortable she was and would always rescue her before it became unbearable.

Or before Melanie said something she shouldn't.

Her gaze swept the room, skimming over a familiar face. She paused, looked back, squinting her eyes to make sure she wasn't imagining things. No, she wasn't. A smile spread across her face, the heavy weight of tension and discomfort evaporating in a splash of pale light. Her parents were here! But why? She hadn't even known they were coming.

She turned back to the CEO or CFO or whoever

he was and quickly excused herself, walking away as he was still talking. Anna would apologize for her, she was sure. It didn't matter anyway, not when her parents were here!

"Mom! Dad!" Melanie pushed by the last person standing between them. She saw them smile, felt her mother's arms wrap around her in a quick hug. Then her dad was beside them, hugging them both, his deep laughter warm and rich in her ear.

"You act like you haven't seen us in ages!" Her father stepped back, a broad smile shining through his dark beard. The lines at the corners of his eyes deepened, adding character and charm to his weathered face.

Melanie smiled back, her arm still around her mother's slim waist. "I'm just so surprised to see you. I didn't know you were coming." And maybe it was more than that. Maybe she had just needed to see them, to know her family was close while her mind was so far away, so preoccupied and worried and scattered.

Her mom stepped back, her blue eyes sparkling with humor and maternal pride as they travelled over Melanie. "You look lovely, sweetheart. So suave and sophisticated."

Melanie rolled her eyes at the laughter in her mother's voice then glanced down at the dress. Her mother, of all people, would know exactly how uncomfortable she was in the outfit, how unlike her the dress was. She wished she could look more like her mother, cool and comfortable in oatmeal linen slacks and a loose, flowing, salmon-colored blouse. Melanie may have inherited her talent and her looks from her mother, but she definitely had her father's sense of style.

She looked over at him, eyeing his loose pants and brightly-colored shirt and Birkenstocks with envy. Melanie wished she was wearing her own sandals. Better yet, she wished she could just kick off the low heels and walk around in her bare feet.

But that wouldn't be appropriate, not here.

"We wanted to surprise you and take you out for a late lunch."

"When you're done here, of course." Her father grinned, his gaze sweeping around the room and missing nothing. "Very nice crowd. Are they planning on any of your work selling today?"

"I've already sold two pieces." Melanie turned to see Anna approaching them. She extended her hand, accepting her father's as she glanced at Melanie with an expectant expression.

Introductions! How could she be so forgetful? She had mentioned Anna numerous times while talking with her parents, but this was the first time they were meeting. Melanie silently admonished herself then tried to cover her mistake with a small smile.

"I'm so sorry. Anna, these are my parents. Michelle and Michael Reeves. Mom, Dad, this is Anna James."

Anna and her mother quickly became engrossed in a conversation about her mom's own work. Her dad used the opportunity to move next to her, leaning in close, concern in his eyes. "You look tired Sweet Pea. Is everything alright?"

"Of course. Yes. Don't I look alright?"

"Lovely as always, just like your mother. But tired as well."

"Oh." Did she? She thought she had looked just fine earlier, when she was getting ready. But this was her dad; he had always had a talent for seeing what others didn't, especially when it came to his only child.

Melanie shrugged and glanced down. "I'm fine. I went out last night, that's all."

"You went out?" The teasing surprise in her father's voice made her smile. She didn't miss the underlying curiosity, though.

"I did. I had Mexican food and then we went to a little bar called..." She frowned, trying to remember. A funny name, or at least she thought so. "I can't remember. But it was a nice little place and they even had a live band."

"'We'?"

"My neighbor and his friends."

A frown creased her father's face. "Your neighbor? Do I need to need to break his legs? Blindfold him and dump him into the nearest hog pen?"

"Daddy!" Melanie laughed then looked around, hoping nobody had heard him. Her mom stepped closer and placed a hand on his arm, her smile radiant.

"Now Michael. You know you almost got caught the last time you did that."

A look of horror crossed Anna's face for the briefest second. The expression quickly disappeared, immediately followed by one of cool professionalism. Melanie smiled, ready to explain to Anna that he had only meant it as a joke. Surely she had to know that, but just in case—

"Ms. James just told me she scheduled an auction for one of your pieces. Why didn't you tell us, sweetheart? That's wonderful news."

"Oh. I—"

"Actually, I'm adding a second piece to it." Anna

turned to her and smiled. "One of the others you brought in last week. It's the smartest thing to do, especially after the buzz you've been generating today."

Melanie blinked, afraid she wasn't hearing correctly. Another piece? But which one? She remembered exactly which pieces she had brought in last week and couldn't imagine which one Anna was even talking about, couldn't believe that either of them would be worth anything. Not at auction. What was Anna seeing that she wasn't? Surely she must be mistaken, or only being nice because her parents were here.

"Sweetheart, that's wonderful! Oh, how I wish we could see them." The smile on her mother's face was warm, full of maternal pride that filled Melanie with equal parts pride and embarrassment.

"They're upstairs. If you'd like, I can take you up and show them to you."

Melanie shook her head, ready to tell Anna no, that wouldn't be necessary, but her father spoke right over her, saying they'd love to. Then Anna was leading them through the gallery to the back room and upstairs, away from the stifling heat and noise of the crowd. She unlocked the door to the office and turned on the light, stepping back to let her parents through.

And there they were, her latest creations propped against the far wall. Two canvases sat apart from the others, dark and vivid, the brush strokes bold and confusing, echoes of the frustration she had been feeling when she painted them.

Her parents stood back a little, studying the paintings with their artistic eyes. Melanie wanted to slink from the room, to run down the stairs and escape, afraid of what they'd think or say. The paintings were so different from what she usually did, something that even someone with an untrained eye could see. What would her parents, each of them an artist in their own right, think? What would they see?

Melanie was afraid to find out.

Her mother turned to her, a small smile on her face, a certainty of knowledge in her eyes. "Who is he, sweetheart?"

Melanie shook her head, in denial and refusal to answer. Maybe she could pretend she didn't understand her mother's question, could convince her parents they were seeing something that wasn't there.

"Who?"

Her mother's delicate brows arched over her eyes. She looked at the paintings once more than back at Melanie. "Why, the man who's causing you such turmoil and frustration, of course."

Chapter Fifteen

Dale stood at the door, his head cocked to the side, listening. Yes, those were definitely footsteps coming up the stairs. Were they Smurfette's? He pressed his ear to the door, his eyes closed as he tried to pick up on the different sides. The footsteps were coming closer, not continuing to the third floor. The faint rattle of keys, a soft thud and frustrated murmur as something hit the floor just outside his door.

Not his door, but Smurfette's. That had to be her, dropping her keys and muttering something to herself. He frowned, listening closer. Had he heard another set of footsteps? No, it must have just been the sound echoing in the hallway, or maybe just his imagination.

She was back later than he thought she'd be. He vaguely remembered her saying something about something somewhere—a gallery?— but he hadn't paid any attention to it last night. Actually, he completely forgot about it until he woke up this morning and realized Smurfette wasn't in his bed. There'd been a moment of frustration and disappointment until he remembered she had mentioned she had somewhere to be today. At first, his mind still hazy from sleep and left-over pleasure, he thought about getting up and going next door and asking if she wanted him to go with her. And then he rolled over and looked at the clock, staring at it for a long minute until his mind cleared enough to actually register the late hour.

Technically still morning, but definitely too late to go anywhere with Smurfette.

So he'd spent the day doing mostly nothing, waiting for her to get home. Maybe they could go to dinner again, or out to a movie. Something. And then he'd talk her back into his bed and spend the rest of the night licking and tasting every delicious curve of her body.

He glanced down at himself, a grin on his face, thinking this would be the perfect time to surprise her. A towel was slung low on his hips, his chest and hair still damp from the shower. Yes, this was the perfect time to surprise her. With luck, they could even skip going out and just get straight to the fun part. Even Smurfette would be able to see he had risen to the occasion, with the way the towel was tenting out in front of him. And if she couldn't…well, it would be an easy matter to accidentally-on-purpose let the towel fall away.

He pulled open the door and stepped into the hallway, a smile on his face as he reached for the loose knot holding the towel in place. "Hey Smurfette, how about we—fuck! Shit!"

Dale made a mad grab for the towel, catching it just before it fell to the floor. The rest his body froze like a wild animal caught in a bright spotlight a second before the poacher's fatal shot brought it down.

Smurfette stood in front of her door, the key partially inserted into the lock. Her mouth hung open in shock, a wave of red rushing up her neck to spread across her face. A man and a woman stood behind her, similar expressions on their faces. They were older, maybe early fifties, if that. And it only took one quick glance to realize they were her parents. The woman's resemblance to Smurfette was unmistakable. As unmistakable as the protective glare the man shot his way.

Dale straightened, the ends of the towel fisted in his right hand. A cool draft wound its way around his legs and up and he hoped to hell the towel was covering him. He wasn't about to look down to check.

"Uh.." He cleared his throat, wondering if his face was as red as Smurfette's. "Sorry. I didn't realize—I'll just go back inside. Sorry." He pushed on the door, opening it so he could slink his way back into his apartment. The woman's words stopped him.

She stepped closer to Smurfette, gently tapping her on the chin to close her mouth. Then she looked at her daughter and smiled, turning that same smile on him. "So is this him, sweetheart?"

Him? What the hell did she mean by that? He looked over at Smurfette, hoping to catch a glimpse of a clue or something, but she wasn't looking at him. Her gaze was glued to the floor, her hand tightly curled around the keys.

"Mom—"

"Well I can certainly understand how he'd inspire you to create such energetic work."

Dale blinked, not understanding. Not sure he wanted to understand. His gaze moved between the two women then darted to the man, to her father. Yeah, he was better off watching the women, if the guy's expression meant what he thought it meant.

And why the hell wouldn't it? He'd just come into the hall, ready to expose himself, practically shouting that he'd had sex with the man's daughter. Of course the man was ready to kill him. He was close to wanting to kill himself, figuring something quick would be far less painful than a prolonged death by embarrassment—or by whatever torture her father was clearly planning.

He took another step back, one leg inside the safety of his own place. "You're busy. I'll, uh, I'll just let you go—"

"Why don't you come join us?"

"I don't want to interrupt—"

"Nonsense. We'll see you in five minutes?" Her father may have said it as a question but there was no mistaking the silent demand in his eyes. His dark eyes held Dale's, assessing, sizing up.

"Yes sir." Dale hurried back into his apartment, slamming the door shut before anyone could say anything else.

Before he could dig his grave any deeper than he already had.

Fuck.

He let his head rest against the door, his heart pounding in his chest. How the fuck could he be so stupid? He'd known there had been more than one pair of footsteps. He'd known it! But he had convinced himself it was just a trick of his ears because he hadn't been thinking.

Well, he had. Just with the wrong fucking brain.

He pushed away from the door and hurried back

to his room, grabbing a pair of jeans from the dresser and pulling them on. What else? He couldn't wear a plain t-shirt. Something a little dressier, but not too dressy. He flipped through the shirts hanging in his closet, looking for just the right one. He needed to make a good first impression. Or rather, a better second one.

What the hell was he doing? Why the sudden frantic worry? He was acting like he was meeting his girlfriend's parents for the first time.

Sure, yeah. He *was* meeting Smurfette's parents. But it wasn't the same thing. It wasn't like they were a couple and she was introducing him to her family because their relationship had moved to the next level. There *was* no relationship. They were just...

What the hell were they? Neighbors, yeah, but besides that? He was attracted to her. They'd had sex—yesterday, and last night. But that was it. So what did that mean? They were just friends with benefits?

Hell, he wasn't even sure what they had could be called friendship. Yeah, he liked her. But he didn't really know her. Not really. It wasn't like they hung out and talked and all that shit.

So not friends with benefits. Neighbors with benefits?

Denial twisted in his gut, along with a bitterness at what the phrase meant. It was too casual, too cold and callous and distant. Whatever the hell was going on between him and Smurfette, it sure as hell wasn't cold and callous and distant. Not as far as he was concerned, anyway.

A loud bang shook his wall, pulling his attention to the present. He glanced at the clock, not bothering to hide his grin. So Smurfette had thought she could get his attention by banging on the wall, huh? Well, she was right.

He grabbed the shirt off the hanger, a pale green dress shirt. Maybe a little too fancy, but why not? He buttoned it and rolled the sleeves up as he walked out of the bedroom, sliding his feet into the pair of loafers he'd had on last night. Shit, no socks. Screw it, he could put socks on later. It wasn't like he was going to be over there that long, anyway. Just long enough to convince her father not to kick his ass, that was it.

Dale glanced in the mirror above the small table near the door, running a hand through his hair. It was getting a little too long on top, longer than he liked. Well, now wasn't the time to worry about it.

Thirty minutes later, he was wondering if he could use getting a haircut as an excuse to escape. He was sitting at the small table in Smurfette's kitchen—because there was no place else to really sit in her place—squirming under her father's impenetrable gaze and her mother's probing questions.

How long had they known each other?
How long had they been seeing each other?
What did he do for a living?
Did being a fireman pay well?
Wasn't he worried about getting hurt on the job?

Dale shifted and reached for the cup of tea, taking a sip to hide his discomfort and lubricate his throat. He hadn't had a chance to get a word in, unless it had been to answer one of the many questions being thrown at him non-stop. And Smurfette wasn't helping, either. She just sat there, perched on the edge of the stool she had dragged in from the living room, her gaze flitting around the room, landing on nothing in particular.

Especially not him.

What the hell was up with that?

He looked over at her, silently willing her to look at him. Maybe if he could see her eyes, he would be able to tell what she was thinking. She was almost as uncomfortable as he was, he knew that much. At least, he thought he knew. Or maybe he was just reading too much into her body language and seeing things that weren't there.

"That's an interesting tattoo I noticed, Dale. Was there a reason you chose that?"

He turned back to see Mrs. Reeves watching him, a small smile on her face as she glanced at his chest. Dale automatically reached for the shirt buttons, wondering if maybe he'd forgotten to button them. His hand dropped to his lap. No, his shirt was buttoned, at least enough to hide the tattoo. But she had gotten a clear look at his chest when he'd stepped into the hallway earlier, all but naked.

"Uh, yes. Ma'am." He took another swallow of tea, not quite able to meet her eyes. "I had it done after I graduated the Fire Academy. As a celebration of sorts. Ma'am."

And damn, could her father's look be any more intense? The man had barely looked away from him since he walked through the door. Smurfette had introduced him as laid-back and easy-going but Dale didn't believe it. Sure, maybe the man had a legitimate reason for giving Dale the death-glare, but he thought he'd ease up by now.

Even his own father hadn't given Kenny this much grief when he first met him and realized he was seeing Lauren. Had he?

"Mom, Dad, didn't you say something about a late lunch?" Smurfette finally spoke up, breaking the awkward tension that had settled around them. Dale breathed a sigh of relief, certain freedom was close within his reach. Just a few more minutes...

"Yes, of course, sweetheart. Although it would be dinner by now, wouldn't it?" Mrs. Reeves stood up, gently tugging her husband's arm. "Come on dear. You can finish glowering at Dale over dinner."

"But he's not—"

"I wasn't—" Dale snapped his mouth closed the same time as Smurfette and looked over at her, frowning. Her eyes briefly met his then darted away. He hadn't planned on going with them, didn't even think they would invite him. But did Smurfette really have to look so horrified at the thought of him going with them?

Why the hell did that even bother him? It shouldn't. Hell, he didn't *want* to go to dinner with them. Didn't want to be subjected to Mr. Reeves' glare any longer than he had been. But he didn't want Smurfette to look like the idea of him going with them curled her stomach, either.

"Well of course he's coming with us. We're just getting to know him." Mrs. Reeves smiled down at him, tugging on his arm until he had no choice but to stand and follow them out of the kitchen. He glanced over at Smurfette, wondering why she looked so miserable, why she wouldn't meet his eyes.

Maybe it was just because she was as uncomfortable as he was. He could understand that, after his stunt in the hallway when she came home. He eased a little closer, placing his hand against the small of her back. All he had wanted to do was lean down and whisper in her ear, reassure her it would be fine, that he'd behave. But she stiffened and stepped away, finally looking at him with a mix of panic and irritation in her blue eyes.

He dropped his hand and frowned, not missing the fact that her father had noticed the strained byplay.

What the hell?

Chapter Sixteen

The radio squawked to life, loud and sharp, bouncing off the block walls of the kitchen. Everyone paused, frozen like statues in a children's game, heads cocked to the side as they listened. The alarm sounded, a harsh buzzer that was louder than the radio.

"Dammit. It never fails. How do they know exactly when we're sitting down to eat?" Jimmy grabbed a cheeseburger from the platter, tucked a bottle of water under his arm, then hurried from the kitchen. Dave grabbed his own burger then followed, muttering under his breath.

"Have fun!" Pete laughed and pulled out a chair, reaching for the platter.

"Yeah? Don't be surprised if I call for a medic assist." The room filled with groans at Dave's parting words, everyone turning to look at Pete. He paused, a burger half-way to his mouth, and looked around.

"What?"

Jay answered for all of them. "You know he's probably going to call us now, right? Just because you were a smart ass."

"Well, at least we'll be finished lunch before he does."

The words had the same effect on everyone as the sound of a gun signaling the start of a race. Dale leaned across the table, knocking into Mikey as they both reached for a burger at the same time. She rolled her eyes and tossed one on his plate, then took her own.

He sat down as he took a bite, sliding the bowl of pasta salad closer to him when Adam pushed it his way. Another bite as he spooned a heaping portion of pasta onto his plate before sliding the bowl across to Jay.

It still amazed him that he didn't get heartburn after meals at work. There were days when it was a mad race, when they often took two bites in between a dozen calls, not caring that the food was cold when they finally got around to eating it. It didn't matter, as long as they got to eat.

Why could he eat like this and not get heartburn, but couldn't manage to survive one dinner out without having his gut twist into knots? Probably because he didn't feel like he was being interrogated here at work, didn't feel like he wasn't welcome.

He still couldn't figure out what had happened Saturday night at dinner. Smurfette had been distant the entire time, barely looking at him as her parents kept asking him questions. Her father seemed to finally warm-up to him about an hour into the meal. Although maybe *warm-up* was too extreme a phrase. It was more like he no longer wanted to rip Dale's head off his shoulders and use it as a bowling ball. But even after that, Smurfette had been quiet, still acting like she didn't want him there, like she hadn't wanted him to come along at all.

The real pisser was that he didn't get a chance to talk to her about it. About anything, really. Her parents had driven them back to the apartment but instead of dropping them off, they came back inside. Dale had excused himself, telling them he had to get to bed early because he worked the next day. And then he had waited up, listening for Smurfette's parents to leave, hoping that maybe she'd knock on his door.

That maybe she'd want to talk. Or something else. Definitely something else. But he'd fallen asleep, alone in his bed, waiting.

That had been two days ago and he still hadn't seen Smurfette. Even her apartment was quiet. Her car was in the parking lot so he knew she was home, even if he heard no sounds coming from her place. Was she avoiding him? Or was there something else going on? Maybe she was just busy working.

Her parents had mentioned something about an auction coming up, something that sounded pretty important. He had no idea what they were talking about, a fact that made even her mother frown when she realized it. Whatever it was, they both seemed proud, even if Smurfette seemed terrified for some reason. So maybe that was it, maybe she was just busy.

He'd go over tonight and knock on the door, and keep knocking until she answered. And if she wasn't home, he'd do the same thing tomorrow. All day, until he had to leave for night work. He just hoped she would be home tonight or tomorrow because if he didn't see her before his shift tomorrow night, it would be at least Thursday morning before he saw her again because he had to go to court for his sister on Wednesday.

One more thing he didn't want to think about. No,

he'd much rather think about Smurfette, even if she was confusing him right now. He didn't like the unease that filled him whenever he remembered the expressions on her face Saturday night. He'd feel better after they talked, after he found out what was bothering her.

Dale reached for his fork, digging into the pasta salad Pete had made, eager to taste it. He put the first bite in his mouth when the radio squawked to life again, immediately followed by the clanging of the bells.

"Dammit Pete!" Jay shoved back his chair, the noise repeated four more times as everyone followed suit. Dale leaned over his plate, shoved one more bite of pasta salad into his mouth, then ran out the door and into the engine room. He grabbed his gear and tossed it into the cab then climbed up behind the wheel and buckled himself in, waiting a few seconds before starting the engine. There was the deep rumble of the powerful engine coming to life, the smell of diesel exhaust, the throbbing vibration of the engine beneath him. He looked over his shoulder, making sure everyone was inside as Pete climbed into the officer's seat. Then he put the engine in gear and pulled out of the station, the siren beginning its low wail as he made a right at the end of the ramp.

Pete leaned across, confirming the address, then pushed the button for the air horn, parting traffic before them. Several minutes later, Dale stopped in front of a house and pulled the engine along the curb. The medic unit sat in the driveway, its back doors open, Dave and Jimmy nowhere in sight.

A young woman ran out of the house, long hair flying, tears streaming down her face as she flailed her arms. Dale and Pete climbed down from the engine at the same time, the heavy doors thudding closed together. Dale moved to the back compartment and pulled the wheel chocks, setting them in place before moving to the other side. The engine crew was already moving in, Adam stopping at the medic to grab some more gear before following.

A minute later, Adam poked his head out of the open door, waving to Dale. "We might need a little help in here."

Dale moved forward, wondering what was going on and why they would need help. It was a medic assist, it shouldn't be anything they couldn't handle—not with six of them already inside.

He understood why Adam had called him in as soon as he entered the house. His nose wrinkled against the sour smell of decay and rot from the piles of clothes and old food that spilled out from the kitchen. The crew was in the living room, shuffling back and forth as grunts and the sound of bare flesh smacking bare flesh filled the crowded room. The woman who had run out was in the far corner, still screaming, her hands twisting in the tangled knots of her hair.

"Help him! You need to help him!"

Somebody, maybe Jay, tried to tell her they were trying but his voice was lost in the noise. Dale moved closer, trying to take in the entire scene, trying not to let his gaze get lost in tunnel vision.

Now he understood why they called him in. The patient, a large man of maybe thirty and weighing at least three hundred pounds, was crouched in the middle of the room, swinging wildly with his large arms and beefy hands.

And he was completely naked.

Sweat covered his pallid skin, his eyes round and bulging with fury and fear. The man's gaze darted around, each movement of his eyes choppy and unfocused. Jimmy tried to grab one arm, to stop him or calm him down, Dale didn't know. But the man flung Jimmy to the side as if he was nothing more than a ragdoll then lunged for Dave.

Mikey shouted a warning then jumped on the man's back, trying to pull him away from Dave. The man shook her off then lunged forward again, swaying and staggering, off-balance. Dale hurried forward, reaching for the man the same time as everyone else. If they could get him calmed down, or at least subdued, the medic crew could treat him.

Or at least get him secured to the stretcher so he could be transported to the hospital.

It wasn't just the man's size that was hindering them. Yes, he was big, with apparent strength behind his size. But he was also sweaty.

And completely naked.

There was nothing to grab but damp limbs, which immediately slipped from their hold. Dale wasn't sure how much time had passed. It could have been sixty seconds or it could have been ten minutes. The police had arrived, two officers joining them in the overcrowded filthy room. As outnumbered as he was, as much as he had been fighting, the man had to be getting tired. There was nowhere left for him to go.

All they had to do was get a secure hold on him. As if realizing what was going to happen, the man bowed his arms and charged forward, resembling a desperate wrestler moving in for one last round. Dale moved forward, caught between Jay and Adam just as the man lunged toward them. Jay caught one arm and Adam caught the other, Dave and Mikey moving in behind him. Pete grabbed the restraints, heading toward them.

The man's arm slipped from Jay's hold, throwing all of them off-balance. Dale reached out, trying to grab the flailing arm as everyone tumbled to the floor. Dale's hand closed around something just as he landed on his side, the man sprawled partly across him, his pasty white ass dangerously close to his face.

And it wasn't the man's arm Dale held in his hand.

"What the—dammit!" Dale let go and freed his arm, his face twisted in appalled disgust. Jay and Dave were having a hard time smothering their laughter. Mikey didn't even try, just turned around and hurried outside, muttering about getting something from the medic. Even the cops were turning red from suppressed laughter.

Dale grimaced and hurried backward, freeing his legs from the man's heavy weight. Pete leaned down, his hand extended to help him up. He pulled it away at the last minute, his mouth twitching as he stepped back.

"Yeah, never mind. You can get up yourself."

"Christ, I hope not," Jimmy mumbled next to him. Dale frowned then pushed to his feet, pausing only long enough to wipe his hand over the back of Jimmy's shirt. Shit. He would never live this down, not for the next year, at least.

Once the excitement of finally getting the man under control died down, it only took a few minutes to get him on the stretcher and into the medic. Adam climbed into the back with Dave to help during transport to the hospital. The engine would follow, just in case they needed help getting the man out of the medic.

Dale glanced at his watch, grimacing when he saw the front of his shirt was stained with sweat and…he didn't want to think what else. With any luck, they wouldn't catch any calls after leaving the hospital and they'd make it back to the station so he could take a shower.

With alcohol. Lots of it.

Chapter Seventeen

The canvas mocked her, staring back at her, glaring in stark whiteness. Melanie glared back, her brows pulled down so low that her forehead ached. Part of her was tempted, sorely tempted, to grab one of the palette knives and start slashing. To just lash out and slice, shredding the canvas until nothing was left.

Sweets! Where had that urge come from? She'd been frustrated before. Worried and angered and full of questions and doubts. But never before had she wanted to do violence, not that way. With a brush, yes. With colors and strokes, absolutely. But never before with a knife.

She sighed and dropped the palette to the workshop table. It made a hollow sound as it hit the wooden surface, its cleanliness mocking her as much as the canvas.

She'd been standing there for so long that her calves ached, the muscles cramped from not moving or stretching. And what did she have to show for it? Nothing.

Complete nothing.

As much as she would love to blame *him*, her neighbor...she couldn't. It wasn't Dale's fault that her mind had been on him for the last two hours. It wasn't Dale's fault that her ears had been straining, listening for the tiniest noise, the tiniest indication that he was awake and walking around.

He was. Had been for the last—she glanced at the clock and frowned—forty three minutes. It was almost three o'clock. He'd be leaving for work soon and she had no idea when she might see him next. She knew he would be busy tomorrow with his sister—his youngest sister, the one she hadn't met. And she knew he was working tomorrow night as well.

Maybe Thursday morning, then, when he got home from his shift. Maybe.

Why was she being so silly? Why was she hiding? Because that's exactly what she was doing. She could at least admit that to herself, if not to anyone else. Not that there was anyone else to admit it to.

She had hid in her bedroom Sunday evening, the small television turned down so low she hardly heard it. But she had heard his knock. No, not just once. Several times, like he knew she was in there and wanted to get her attention. But she had stayed in her room, pretending she hadn't heard him.

She'd done the same thing Monday night, too. But he'd only knocked once, then, not long after he got home from work. He'd gone out after that, somewhere. Maybe with his friends from work? She didn't know.

And now it was Tuesday afternoon, the day almost gone, and he was getting ready to leave for work. And she still hadn't talked to him, hadn't even seen him except for that brief glance when she looked out her bedroom window last night when he left to go...somewhere.

She was such a coward. A lonely pathetic coward. And she couldn't even blame Dale for it, no matter how tempted she might be. It wasn't his fault. It wasn't even her mother's fault. Melanie had been the one to paint the images, had been the one to release her emotions on a blank canvas for all the world to see.

Even if she hadn't meant for anyone to really see it.

But her mother had seen, and had known immediately what those bold angry strokes and bright chaotic colors had meant. Hues of crimson and orange and yellow and smoky black. Her mother had seen, and somehow knew that a man had caused it.

Melanie's hand tightened around the brush as her mother's chosen word rushed to mind, unbidden and unwelcome. Not *caused*. *Inspired*. That was what her mother had said: *inspired*. Like the chaos that stared back at them could inspire anyone.

And when they came home from the gallery and Dale had opened the door, standing there in nothing but a stark white towel and a broad grin, her parents had known. Of course they had. What kind of man would prance around in a towel in front of a woman if they hadn't been together?

It didn't matter, though, not really. He could have been fully dressed and her mother would have still known. Her father too, to a certain extent. But he didn't see colors like she did. Like her mom did. And all it had taken was once glance to realize her mom had seen in Dale the same thing she had. Not just the colors and conflict and guilt and life. No, it was so much more than that. It was his essence. Strong. Powerful.

Overwhelming.

Yes, her parents knew, without a doubt.

So Melanie did what she did best: she hid. Even when her mother insisted he join them for dinner, when her father drew him into the conversation—or maybe just endlessly hounded him with questions—Melanie had started hiding. If she hid, she wouldn't have to admit…anything.

Her father knew that, too. He'd always been able to read her moods and fears and insecurities, ever since she was a little girl. And at the end of the night, after Dale had disappeared into his apartment and before her parents were ready to leave, her father had pulled her aside and told her what he always told her: don't hide from life. Embrace it.

But she didn't know how to, not really. She never had. Yes, she could pretend. She could smile and laugh and take pleasure from the tiniest of things. But she couldn't embrace it, not wholly. She'd always shied away from completely opening up and giving in because she was always so afraid of being shunned. Ever since she was a little girl, the one who saw colors and lived in a world full of images and sights that none of her classmates could see. She was the odd one, the one who was laughed at. So she had learned to keep that part of her hidden, expressing it on canvas instead. And she had become so good at hiding who she was, hiding away from the world, that she hadn't even realized what she was doing.

And then she had met her neighbor. Her infuriating, teasing, wonderful and conflicted neighbor who had no inkling of what he did to her. Who made her laugh and smile and called her by a silly nickname without making fun of her. Who took her out to a hockey game and to a honky tonk. Who made her come alive and not feel ashamed of what she felt when she was with him.

And all she wanted to do was hide again. Because she was afraid.

She tossed the brush to her workbench and made an angry swipe at her damp face. For once she didn't have to worry about smearing paint on her cheek or forehead. The realization angered her, almost as much as the realization of how big a coward she truly was.

A sound caught her attention, tugging her from her morose thoughts. A door opening then closing, the sound a little too loud, as if someone was slamming the door. A jingle of keys, a small cough.

Dale, leaving for work.

She hesitated only a second then leaped the two steps to her own door, pulling it open with a breathless rush of air. Dale was at the top step, dressed in dark blue uniform pants and a dark blue t-shirt. The sleeves hugged the muscles of his arms, the material pulling tight across his broad shoulders and back. A garment bag, the kind they gave you at the expensive stores, was slung over his left shoulder. He reached for the railing, getting ready to walk downstairs. He hesitated and looked back at her, barely more than a brief glance. But he didn't say anything, just gave her a curt nod of acknowledgement.

Melanie realized he wasn't going to say anything, nothing at all. Not even hello. She stepped into the hallway, her hand twisting the knob to make sure the door was unlocked before it closed behind her. She didn't think, just called his name, her voice sounding funny to her own ears. Rusty and hoarse, like she hadn't used it recently. He stopped again and turned, his hand still on the railing as he looked at her, his brows raised above his dark eyes. "Did you need something, Melanie?"

The sound of her name falling from his lips in a flat voice cut through her, slicing deep. It was wrong, so terribly wrong. She didn't want to be Melanie, not to this confusing man in front of her. She was Smurfette, not Melanie.

She shifted, her hands twisting in her skirt, bunching the material in her fists. She cleared her throat and tried to smile. "Are you heading into work?"

He looked down at himself then back up at her, not answering. Of course not. It was obvious he was going to work. Silly, stupid question. She knew he was, dressed as he was in his uniform. Why had she even bothered to ask?

"I need to get going."

"Wait!" Melanie moved closer to him, wanting to reach out and touch him, to keep him from leaving. She didn't want him to leave, not yet. "You, uh, you have your sister's thing tomorrow, don't you?"

A shadow passed through his eyes, his jaw clenching hard enough she thought she saw the muscle tick on the left side of his face. He took a deep breath and blew it out, his face clearing.

No, not clearing. Becoming blank, completely expressionless. "Yeah."

"Oh. I…good luck."

He laughed, the sound short and bitter. "Luck. Yeah, sure."

"Will you be home tomorrow?"

"Probably not." Now he sounded impatient, like he was in a hurry to get away from her. Melanie stepped closer, close enough she could make out the gold flecks in his eyes, feel the heat of his emotions rolling off him.

Heat, not cold.

"Will you be home on Thursday? I thought maybe we could—"

"Melanie, I need to go."

There it was again. Her name. Anger and impatience bubbled inside her, pushing away her fear. She made a sound, low in her throat, and stomped her foot. Then, before she could think, afraid she'd stop if she did, she closed the final few inches between them. He didn't move, just watched her with detached curiosity. So she grabbed him by the shirt, her hand fisting in the soft material, and leaned up on her bare toes.

And kissed him.

He didn't move. He didn't react at all. Melanie cracked one eye open, wondering why he wasn't kissing her back. She pressed herself closer and ran her tongue along the closed seam of his lips, holding her breath as she waited.

She breathed a small sigh when he moved, then moaned in disappointment when she realized he was moving away from her, not toward her. His fingers closed around her wrist and she thought he'd pull her hand away but he didn't.

"What are you doing?"

"I'm kissing you."

"Why?"

"Because—" She stopped, frowning. Had he really asked her why? Yes, he had. And now that she was looking closer—really looking—she saw that he was frowning, his brows pulled low over serious eyes. Watching her, studying her.

Then he moved, lightning fast. And before she

could blink, before she could catch her breath or ask herself what he was doing or even wonder at the odd dark light in his eyes, he leaned forward. His mouth crashed against hers. Hard, hot, wet. Unforgiving and demanding. Her heart slammed against her chest and she moaned, low in her throat. Melanie leaned in, her fist once more gripping his shirt. His hand cupped her cheek, the flesh of his palm warm and rough against her skin. He slid his hand past her ear, his fingers wrapping in the strands of her hair as he deepened the kiss even more.

And then he pulled away, abruptly, without warning. His eyes were even darker now, his brows still pulled together in a dark frown. His voice was rough when he spoke, low and husky with an odd edge she didn't understand.

"I have to go, Melanie."

He turned and hurried down the stairs, the sound of his steps loud in the empty hallway. She watched as he pushed through the door without looking back, was still watching minutes later, staring at the door long after it closed behind him.

How could he kiss her like that and then just walk away? How could he kiss her like that and still call her *Melanie*?

And then she realized: he hadn't kissed her out of passion or need or desire. No, his kiss had been something different. Almost...punishing? But why?

Heat filled her, rushing to her limbs, causing her hands to curl into fists. Something ragged and harsh filled her ears, the sound almost foreign. And her lungs burned, her chest rising and falling in a short choppy motion that confused her at first.

She was angry, she realized. Not upset, not merely

irritated but really, truly furious. Fuming. Enraged. She looked down at her clenched fists, noticed the way her fingers paled and the way her hands shook. A sudden, overwhelming urge to hit something seized her. To really hit something, over and over, until this strange feeling left.

She moaned, the sound growing louder, frightening her.

How could he do what he just did? How could he drive her to this brink of madness? To this urge to do violence? With something like shock, Melanie realized she had never been this angry before. Not angry enough to physically lash out.

She clamped her mouth against the strange sound coming from her throat and stormed back into her apartment, slamming the door behind her. It felt so good, the act of doing something, of hearing the loud noise, that she did it again. And again.

Then she turned to her workbench and grabbed several tubes of paint, squeezing sloppy ribbons of color onto the palette. She didn't pay attention to the colors, didn't care, just let emotion guide her as she mixed them.

Then let emotion take over as she grabbed a brush and attacked the canvas, her conscious mind blank as an odd possession claimed her soul.

Chapter Eighteen

"Where have you been?" Lauren's voice sliced through the hallway, a sharp echo against the marble floor and walls. Dale slid to a stop, the soles of his shoes squeaking. He glanced around, his eyes skimming over the small groups scattered here and there, then reached down and adjusted the sleeves of the dress shirt.

"We had a fire this morning and didn't get relieved until late." And then he had to rush through a shower, hoping he got most of the soot and grime and sweat off before getting dressed.

Lauren frowned, her lips pursed as she looked him over. She didn't say anything. How could she? It wasn't like he had control over their runs, or control on when they got back to the station. Never mind that she had suggested he take off last night, just in case this exact thing happened. That hadn't been an option he was willing to take and she knew it, just as she knew he really didn't want to be here.

He was here for her, that was it.

She shook her head and brushed his hands away, reaching up to straighten his tie. He noticed the slight trembling of her fingers, the paleness of her face and the way her skin seemed to tighten and pull around her eyes. It made her look vulnerable and delicate, a look so at odds with her inner strength.

"You okay?"

Lauren took a deep breath then dropped her hands, her eyes not quite meeting his. "I'm fine."

"She's a mess." Kenny stepped next to them, his arms sliding around Lauren's waist. She leaned back, resting against him, her eyes briefly closing. Dale didn't miss the way she seemed to breathe a little easier, the way her face smoothed out as some of the tension left her.

Equal parts jealousy and protectiveness surged through him. Protectiveness because Lauren was his sister, it was his job to protect her. Never mind that he liked Kenny and knew he was good for her, just like he knew Kenny would do anything for her. He'd already let one sister down; he wasn't going to make the same mistake with Lauren.

Except Lauren wasn't the sister who needed him.

And he wasn't jealous, not really. Lauren was happy, happier than he'd ever seen. Kenny was good for her, Dale had known that from the very beginning. But he couldn't help but wish he had the same thing they had, that maybe, one day, he'd find—

An image of fiery red hair and ocean blue eyes popped into his mind, followed by the memory of yesterday's searing hot kiss. He pushed both the image and the memory from his mind. He couldn't think about Smur—Melanie—now. Wouldn't think about the way he'd kissed her or why, like he was trying to punish her for something. He couldn't afford to think about it. Not here, not now.

Dale took a deep breath, trying to steady the tangle of knots in his gut, then looked around. "Where are Mom and Dad?"

"They're in a conference room somewhere with Lindsay and her attorney."

"Why?"

"They're trying to talk her into taking the plea bargain."

"Isn't it too late for that?"

Lauren chewed on her lower lip and shrugged. Kenny was the one who answered.

"Apparently not. And if she doesn't, Lauren might have to testify."

The tangled mess of knots in Dale's gut tightened. "What? I thought they said she wouldn't have to. That none of us would have to."

"I don't know. Things change, I guess."

"Then what about us? We were both there. I'd think they'd call us first."

"I don't know." Kenny's frustration and worry were clear in his voice and on his face. His arms tightened around Lauren's waist, holding her close as she looked at him over her shoulder.

"I'll be fine. I don't want to do it but if I have to…" Her voice trailed off and she shrugged, acting like it was no big deal. But Dale saw the worry on her face, saw the anxiety in her eyes. Maybe she thought she was fooling them, but Dale knew better. From the look on Kenny's face, so did he.

"This is such bullshit. Why is she being so stupid? Doesn't she realize she's not going to get off on this? She admitted it to a rink full of people. Hell, she admitted it to the cops! I don't understand—"

"Dale, lower your voice." Lauren placed a hand on his arm, squeezing. Could she feel the tension running through him? Feel the way his muscles bunched and tightened with it?

Yeah, probably.

He sucked in a deep breath of air and let it out slowly, trying to calm himself. But the anger and fear and worry and guilt clung to him, each fighting for dominance, their claws buried so deep in his chest he wondered why his heart was still beating.

"She still won't take responsibility for it, acting like it was a harmless prank." Kenny's voice was tightly controlled, his anger held back. Lauren sighed and looked at each of them.

"She didn't mean to—"

"Bullshit!" The word came out in a harsh whisper instead of a furious scream, but there was no mistaking his anger. "Stop making excuses for her, Lauren. Even now, after everything that's happened, you're making excuses. Why?"

"Because in her mind, it was just a prank. And because I refuse to accept the fact that she deliberately tried to kill me. If she knew what could have happened—"

"Stop making excuses for her! She's had plenty of time to think about what she did. Christ, she's spent the last six months in jail because of it! She knows what she did and she still won't accept responsibility!"

"Enough." Kenny edged in front of Lauren, his expression hard. A glint of danger and warning flashed in his eyes as he stared at Dale. The message was clear: Kenny might agree with Dale, but Lauren came first, no matter what.

Dale stepped back and ran a shaking hand through his hair. His hand was actually shaking! Hell, his whole body was shaking. From frustration and anger and a lethal mix of other emotions, too dark to examine.

It should have never gotten to this point. Never.

Yet here they were, and there was nothing any of them could do. Nothing at all. The time for action had come and gone long ago, back when Lindsay had first started acting out. Back when doing something could have made a difference.

Lauren stiffened, her face paling even more as she looked at something behind Dale. He turned, his gaze landing on his parents as they exited a room with Lindsay's attorney. His mother looked suddenly older, an expression of grief on the face that was so much like Lauren's—and in the eyes that were so much like Lindsay's. That same grief clung to his father, in the dejected slump of his broad shoulders and the detachment in his brown eyes—the eyes that Dale and Lauren had inherited. His father's hand was wrapped around her mother's, his grip tight. Dale briefly wondered who was supporting who. Did it matter? No, it didn't.

His parents approached them, defeat silently screaming on their faces. He looked over at the attorney, not daring to breathe as he waited for the words he knew was coming.

"She refuses to take the plea deal."

Lauren stepped beside him, her hand closing around his wrist. Dale didn't think she even realized she was doing it. She was so focused on the attorney that she probably didn't even feel the heavy weight of Kenny's large hand resting on her shoulder, offering his strength and support.

"So what does that mean? What happens now?" Lauren's voice shook, a quiver softening the edges of each word. The attorney looked at each of them and Dale thought he saw something like frustration in the man's eyes.

"We go to trial as scheduled. The prosecutor will present his case and he may or may not call each of you as a witness." His gaze rested on Lauren, softening for a brief second. "Of the three of you, I think he'd probably call you, Lauren. Yours would be the most damaging testimony. Your sister opted for a bench trial, against my recommendation. I could have played to a jury's sympathy, made it more personal in the hopes of an acquittal. With a judge, I doubt that will happen."

The muscle in Dale's jaw twitched, an ache throbbing just below his ear from clenching his teeth together so hard. He forced himself to relax, forced himself to take a steadying breath. "So this is it, then?"

"I'm afraid so. I don't expect it to take long. Your sister admitted what she did, and there's very little I can offer in the way of defense."

"And sentencing?"

"That will be up to the judge but considering the charges against her, I wouldn't say that five years is unlikely."

Their mother gasped, a short wail of grief and disbelief cut off too early. Dale looked over at her, at the tears in her eyes and pasty hue on her face. His gaze moved to his father, at the stony expression and clenched jaw, as if he refused to allow himself to feel any emotion. Only his damp eyes gave him away.

Dale shoved his hands into this pockets and turned back to the attorney, asking a question he should have already known the answer to. "And if she takes the deal?"

"A year. With time served, she'd be out in eight months."

Dale clenched his jaw again. Anger and confusion warred within him, fighting and scraping until he felt raw inside. Why wouldn't she take the deal? What the fuck was wrong with her?

"I want to talk to her." The words, cold and demanding, left his mouth before he knew he was going to say them. Lauren stiffened beside him again, her hand tightening around his arm. He looked over at her, saw the worry in her eyes. His stomach tightened and lurched and he had to swallow back the acid burning his throat. What the hell did Lauren think he was going to do? Did she really think he was going to make things worse? That he was going to go in there and lay into Lindsay?

Yes, that was exactly what she thought. He could see it, a reflection of fear so clear in her eyes. He pulled his arm away and looked back at the attorney. "I want to see Lindsay."

The man didn't say anything for a long minute. None of his thoughts were reflected on the smoothness of his face, in the cool emptiness of his eyes. He glanced down at his expensive watch then nodded. "We have a few minutes."

Dale followed him up the hall, back to the room his parents had just left moments before. The attorney opened the door then stood back, motioning for Dale to enter. Only then did he realize that the man had no intention of following him in. What the hell? Did he think Dale could accomplish something the rest of them couldn't? Or did he realize it was a hopeless battle and didn't want to waste his time?

Dale hesitated on the threshold, wondering what he was doing. He hadn't seen Lindsay since her bail hearing, hadn't wanted to see her. Why the sudden urge to see her now? Was it to talk some sense into her, or for some other reason?

He took a deep breath and stepped into the room. The door closed behind him with a quiet click and he almost jumped, then swore to himself as he looked around. It was nothing more than a conference room, with fluorescent lighting attached to aged and stained ceiling tiles. The walls were painted a sober industrial gray, the floor tiles a lighter shade of the same color.

He'd been expecting something different. Something a little fancier maybe, a little warmer. The room didn't even come close to what he'd pictured, like something from one of the many crime and court dramas on television now.

It looked more like the kitchen at work, minus the wall of windows and television set. Strictly designed for basic function and nothing more. A long table took up most of the room, surrounded by a handful of sturdy chairs. But Lindsay wasn't sitting at the table. She was standing in the corner, leaning against the wall, her arms folded across her.

Had he imagined the lost expression on her face? Or was that only what he wanted to see, behind her mask of defiance?

He moved over to the table and pulled a chair out but didn't sit in it. Instead, he leaned against the edge of the table and braced his foot on the seat of the chair. He faced his sister, his own arms crossed in front of him in a mirror image of Lindsay.

They stared at each other as time stretched around

them, vibrating with tension. She looked different. Thinner. The dress pants were too loose, the blouse a little too big as it hung from her shoulders. Her perpetual tan was gone, long ago faded to reveal paler skin. Even her hair was different. A little shorter, he thought, although maybe that was just from the way her hair was pulled back into a neat clip at the base of her neck. The color wasn't the same, though; the blonde wasn't as bright or vibrant and no longer looked as if it had been kissed by the sun.

But her attitude was the same, all pure Lindsay. Like it was just her against the world and everyone else be damned. As long as she got what she wanted, everyone else could go to hell.

She hadn't always been like that, though. When had it changed? When had the impish laughing child turned into the hard woman standing in front of him, meeting his glare head-on? He didn't know, couldn't remember. There was a seven-year age difference between them. Dale had been headstrong, determined, independent. He hadn't had the time or the inclination to worry about a baby sister who always seemed to get in the way when he was a teenager. Then he had moved out, started working for the fire department, focused on living his own life. And he had drifted even further apart from the sister he had nothing in common with. It wasn't like it was with Lauren, who shared his personality, his love of sports and action and adventure.

Had he even tried? He couldn't remember if he had or hadn't. And did it make a difference?

Lindsay finally looked away, her gaze dropping to the floor. Dale sighed and shifted against the hard edge of the table. "I remember this one time, when we went

INTO THE FLAMES

on vacation. Some camping trip Dad thought would be fun to drag us to. I don't even remember where we went, but it was hot. So hot you couldn't breathe. And we were sleeping in this huge tent, all five of us, because Dad was convinced that was what close families do."

Dale almost smiled, the memory so clear he could feel his lungs fill with heated moist air, damp with humidity. Where had they been? He couldn't remember, didn't think it mattered. "You were maybe six or seven, I think, and even more bored than the rest of us. It got so bad Mom made us all go on a hike, just to get out of her hair. Not far, just around the campground. It started raining and you got scared because you didn't like the thunder."

The memory grew clearer. A flash of lightning streaking across the gray sky; a boom of thunder, so loud it shook the ground. Lindsay and Lauren each held onto one of his hands, their grips loose and trusting in his larger one. The boy he had been knew he should lead them back to the campsite but he was held in place, mesmerized by the sounds of the storm, by the feel of the warm rain against his sweaty skin.

He closed his eyes for a brief second and tilted his head back, as if he could still feel the rain washing over him. Stupid. So stupid. He opened his eyes and looked at Lindsay, saw she was still staring at the floor.

"I remember you saying you wanted to go back to be with Mom and Dad. And then something happened, maybe it was just more thunder, I don't remember. But you screamed and took off running. I called out for you, Lauren and I both did, but you didn't stop. So we ran after you."

Muddy water splashing against their bare legs as

the rain pelted them. Another flash of lightning, a crazy streak that split the sky and seared his eyes. Branches slapping against their faces and overgrown weeds and brambles pulling at their legs. A shiver of panic, low in his gut, when he realized Lindsay wasn't in front of them, that they should have caught up to her already.

"Lauren tripped over a log and hurt her ankle. I was really worried by then, not knowing where you had gone, wondering where you had disappeared to. So I picked up Lauren and ran back to the campsite." He didn't have to close his eyes to see the memory. It was so clear, like it was happening right now. The rain pelting them, cold now as the wind picked up and the sky grew even darker. Panic and fear slicing through him, making him stumble as he ran with Lauren, struggling with her lanky weight. She had been scared, too; he could tell from the way her cold hands clung to his shoulders, by how silent she was. By the fact that she didn't argue with him, that she let him carry her. He hadn't been looking around them at that point, so completely focused on getting back with Lauren so he could get his dad, tell him what happened. He hadn't seen his youngest sister, huddled under the dead branches of a fallen tree, her wide eyes watching as they stumbled past her.

Dale blinked, his gaze focusing on the room around him, surprised to realize it wasn't raining. He looked at Lindsay, thought he saw...something...in her eyes. He sighed and brushed at a piece of imaginary lint on his pants, then flattened his palm against his leg.

"You never said anything, Lindsay. Never called out. Nothing at all. I never understood why."

"It wouldn't have mattered even if I had."

Dale's head shot up, his eyes narrowed at the tone

in her voice. Shaky, a little sad, but still with an edge to it. He frowned. "How can you say that?"

"Because you were more worried about Lauren. You always were."

"You're wrong, Lindsay. I was worried about you. We both were. We had no idea where you had gone, what happened to you." He hadn't thought about that trip in years, had completely forgotten about it. But the fear and panic in his chest were just as sharp and real now as they had been back then, all those years ago.

Lindsay laughed, the sound short and bitter. "Worried. Yeah. That's why you were carrying Lauren, telling her it would be okay."

"I was carrying her because that was the quickest way to get her back to the campsite. And I was telling her it was okay because I was trying to convince her we'd find you." Dale pushed away from the table and moved closer to Lindsay, holding her gaze with an iron will so she wouldn't look away.

"You don't get it, Lindsay. You never have. I would have carried you, too, just the way I carried Lauren. Hell, I would have carried you both at the same time. I'm your big brother. I would have taken care of you." Fuck, why was his voice breaking? He swallowed and shook his head, ran a hand down his face. But he didn't look away. He couldn't.

"I'm your big brother, Lindsay. And I'd still carry you. Today. Now. I'd still take care of you. But you have to let me. You have to let all of us."

Her eyes were steady on his, a whirlwind of emotions flashing through them so fast, Dale couldn't tell them apart. Then she looked away and pulled her arms more tightly across her chest, like she was hugging herself.

"What do you want, Dale? Why did you come in here?"

"You need to take the deal, Lindsay. If you don't, you're going to spend the next five years in prison."

"No. I might not spend any time—"

"Lindsay!" He reached out and cupped her cheek on one palm, turning her head so she had no choice but to face him. "That's not going to happen and you know it, not when you already admitted what happened. Your attorney already told you that. You need to take the deal. Please."

"Why? Why do you even care?"

"Because you're my sister, Lindsay. And because I still care." And he did, more than he had realized. More than he wanted to admit. It didn't matter how many times he had told himself he was beyond caring, or how many times he had tried to turn his back on her. Yes, Lindsay needed to grow up, to accept responsibility for her actions. That didn't make her any less his sister and it didn't mean he still couldn't care for her.

And it didn't mean he wanted to see the next five years of her life wasted.

The door opened behind them, followed by a discreet cough. Dale dropped his hand and looked over his shoulder as the attorney came in. "It's time. They need a decision."

Dale looked back at Lindsay, wondering if she could see the pleading in his eyes. "Take the deal, Lindsay."

She watched him for a few long seconds, her wide blue eyes filled with emotion he didn't understand. Then she blinked and moved past him, her shoulder brushing against his arm as she walked by without saying a word.

Chapter Nineteen

Melanie paced back and forth in the living room, her bare feet rustling the worn canvas that covered the floor. She veered around the small spot of wet paint, took three more steps, then turned and went the other way. Back and forth, each step agitated and impatient. Not even the soothing voice of Alfie Boe singing in the background could calm her.

She paused in front of the small stereo in the dining room, her fingers hovering just above the volume knob. Should she turn it up some more? No. If she did that, the music would be too loud for even her, and that would defeat the purpose of her plans. The music had been playing for over an hour, and she had to admit that even she was beginning to tire of it. It was different when she was painting. When she was painting, she was so lost in her own work that she was barely aware of the music.

But she wasn't painting now and the only reason she was playing the music so loud was to get his attention. Dale was home, she knew he was. She had heard him come up the stairs a few hours ago, his steps heavy as they passed by her door. She had stood there, holding her breath, wondering if he would stop—

But he didn't. Not even a slight pause. He just continued to his door and went inside, the sound of the door closing quiet and muted. Almost sad, somehow. Such a silly thought. Doors couldn't be sad.

But she couldn't shake the impression, and wondered if maybe it was Dale's sadness she was feeling. No, that couldn't be right either. She *saw* feelings, in pulsating swirls of whirling colors. She didn't *feel* feelings. Which meant she was imagining things. Again.

So she had moped around her apartment, straightening things, organizing her supplies, making a list of what she needed to replenish. And all the while, she kept listening, picking up each little noise and tiny bump coming from next door.

Wondering if she should just go over and knock and ask him what was wrong. Ask him what he meant by that kiss the other day.

No, she couldn't do that. That would be too desperate somehow. But if he came over *here*, then she could ask him. And that's when she decided to play the music. If she played it loud enough, he would bang on the walls. She would ignore him, or turn it up even louder so he'd bang on her door instead.

Except he didn't do any of those things. No wall banging, no door knocking. Nothing. Not a peep. Had he gone to sleep? Surely not. Unless—

Melanie frowned. Maybe he'd bought some of those special headphones, the ones that blocked all the noise. If he had done that, then it wouldn't matter how loud she played the music.

Which meant she was giving herself a headache for no reason at all.

"Well phooey." Melanie said the words but hardly heard them. She sighed then stomped over to the stereo, ready to turn it off as she chided herself for being so foolish. She barely heard the knock, wouldn't have heard it at all if she hadn't already turned the volume down.

She nudged the knob a bit more to the left, lowering the volume even more, then hurried across the room. The knock was too soft, too polite and civilized, to be Dale. Which meant it must be one of her other neighbors coming to complain. Sweets, wouldn't that just be the case? It was no less than what she deserved for trying to get his attention when he obviously had every intention of ignoring her.

She pulled open the door, an apology hovering on her lips when she was hit with a blast of color. Dark, swirling, leaden and muted. Powerful and depressing, so depressing, tears filled her eyes. She placed her free hand against her chest and struggled to pull in a deep breath, to keep the agonizing colors at bay before they could shred her emotions. She had one frightful second where she was afraid sweet Mrs. Lillian was coming to tell her that something had happened to Little Bits. Then she blinked, her breath rushing from her in a surprised gasp.

Dale was standing in front of her, dressed in nothing but a worn t-shirt and a loose pair of gym shorts. Shadows darkened his eyes, obliterating the gold flecks that usually danced in their depths. Stubble covered his jaw and his hair, usually so neat, looked unkempt, the longer strands at the top messy and mussed. She reached for him, acting solely on instinct, then let her hand drop to her side. She was still gripping the edge of the door, the cold metal digging into her palm.

"Melanie. Please." Bleak desolation filled his voice, matching the desperate swirl of colors threatening to drown out his vibrancy.

He'd said *please*, almost like he was begging. Why? Please, what? The music? Something else? She glanced behind her, blinking against the brightness filling her apartment, then looked back at him, at the grayness threatening to claim him.

"I—I'm sorry. I turned it down."

He didn't say anything, didn't even nod. He didn't move, didn't turn to go back to his own apartment. He just stood there, a wall of desolation.

Her hand tightened around the edge of the door even more. "Is—is everything okay?" She was afraid to ask the question, afraid of the answer. What could have happened to make him this way? To cause him such pain and desperation? He didn't answer but he didn't need to. Melanie knew, as certain as she knew her own name.

His sister. His youngest one. Something must have happened yesterday at her trial.

She hesitated for only a second then reached out for his hand. His fingers were cold against hers, as if the life was already seeping out of him. Drowning, lost in the swirl of bleak mist consuming him. She tugged, pulled him inside and closed the door.

Then stood there, not knowing what to do.

Tea. Tea would help, wouldn't it?

She led him to the kitchen and pulled a chair out but he didn't sit. He leaned against the wall instead, his head tilted back, his empty gaze focused on the ceiling.

Melanie hesitated then turned toward the stove, her hands shaking for no apparent reason. She would fix him some tea, try to get him to talk. Maybe if he talked, the awful grayness cloaking him would leave.

But he still held her hand. His fingers tightened around hers, pulling her back when she would have turned away. She stumbled and caught herself, only inches away from him. He was looking at her now, his dark eyes oddly intense, still shadowed but filled with something else as well.

Desire. Need.

Need for her? Or for something else?

It didn't matter. He reached up and cupped her cheek, his palm cool against her skin. His thumb brushed against her lower lip, stayed there as he stared into her eyes.

"Please." It wasn't a question or a demand. It was a plea, bare and ragged, full of a desperation that left her breathless and frightened. She didn't have to ask what he meant—she could see it. She could feel it, reaching out to her, grabbing her, claws of need digging into her.

Melanie thought she may have hesitated but couldn't be sure. And then it didn't matter. The only thing that mattered was the feel of Dale's body against hers, his hands roaming over her, threading in her hair with a desperation that left her breathless. But for all his desperation, his touch was gentle. His mouth, soft and warm against hers, nipped and tasted, seeking permission. Melanie groaned and pushed herself closer, her hands grabbing the hem of his shirt and lifting it. His skin heated under her touch, searing her palms as she ran her hands up his chest and pulled his shirt over his head.

His desperation, his need, was contagious. Desire, bright and sharp, filled her. But not just desire. A need of her own. A need to soothe, to comfort, to heal.

Dangerous. Giving into this was dangerous, Melanie could feel the certainty of that on some deeper level she never knew existed within her. She hesitated, hovering on the edge of a great abyss, knowing that if she stepped over it, if she allowed herself to fall into it willingly, there would be no coming back.

She closed her eyes and flung herself into it, felt herself falling. Felt herself flying.

She closed her mouth over his, the kiss hot, wet. Their tongues crashed together, each fighting for dominance. He groaned, the whispered sound mingling with her own. She pulled his lip between her teeth, nipped, felt him shudder against her. Then she pulled her mouth away and trailed kisses along his jaw, the stubble rough against her lips. Down along the column of his neck, her tongue tracing the corded muscle. Sleek, powerful, masculine.

She spread her hands wide and ran them along his chest. The pounding of his heart beat heavy against her palms, full of life and strength, sending a thrill through her. Did her own heart beat as heavy? A living, pulsing reminder of life and need and desire and hopes?

She thought it might, thought the pounding she heard might be her own heart, echoing his.

Melanie sighed and pressed her lips closer, tasting the warm saltiness of his skin as she dragged her mouth across his chest. Lower, down to his stomach. The muscles there contracted, his breath a harsh gasp in the still air around them.

Melanie dropped to her knees, her mouth and tongue licking and tasting. She wrapped her hands in the waistband of his shorts and dragged them down to his hips, lower. His erection sprung free, long and thick, hard and heavy, the wet tip brushing against her cheek.

She looked up, saw his head tilted back, his eyes closed and his mouth parted. Need, swift and sure, pulsed through her. Need…and power. White hot, blazing. She placed a kiss against the sensitive flesh of his inner thigh as she reached for him, her hand closing over the velvety smoothness.

His breath rushed out of him. Harsh, almost guttural. His hand fisted in her hair, his fingers gentle as she stroked him. Long, hard. From the thick base all the way to the glistening tip. Back and forth. Slow. So slow.

She ran her tongue across the smooth tip, licking at the bead of moisture, sighing as the tangy taste exploded against her tongue. Hunger spread through her, needy and urgent. She closed her mouth around him. Sucking, licking, feasting.

He held her closer, his hand tightening in her hair, his hips thrusting. Melanie sighed again, taking him deeper into her mouth. Sucking, stroking. Over and over as desire, wet and hot, pooled between her legs.

Her body thrummed, vibrating with need. Humming with power. She heard him mutter something, his voice nothing more than a growl, the words making no sense. His body tensed, his hands curling against her scalp. But instead of holding her closer, he pulled away with a harsh groan.

And then he was lifting her, his mouth hot and hard against hers. His tongue delved between her lips, demanding surrender. She felt his arms around her, felt him turn so her back was against the wall. He grabbed her skirt, bunched the material around her waist, exposing her.

And then his arm was behind her, supporting her bottom as he lifted her.

"Wrap your legs around me."

It was a demand, leaving no room for question, no room for anything but compliance. Melanie raised her legs, wrapping them around his waist. Her hands dug into his shoulders, her eyes on his. He must have seen her hesitation, her fear of being dropped, because he shook his head then pressed a quick kiss against her mouth. "I won't let you go."

She didn't want to read into the words, knew she shouldn't. But she wanted to, with a basic desire that went far beyond what her body was feeling. And then it didn't matter because he pushed into her, filling her.

Her eyes drifted shut, her head falling back against the wall as he drove into her, over and over. Hard and hot, each stroke deeper, each stroke giving more. Demanding more. She clung to him, her nails digging into his skin as her hips thrust forward, matching his rhythm.

Slow. Fast. Over and over until she didn't know where her body ended and his started. Short gasps ripped from her chest with each stroke, the sound of her harsh breathing echoing his. Her muscles tightened around him, squeezing, drawing him deeper inside. She bit down on her lower lip as sensation spiraled around her, pulling, tugging. Tighter, stronger, until there was nothing left but need and desire and warmth and brightness.

Tighter still, until everything exploded around her. Fracturing, flying, spinning out in a wide arc of color. Melanie gasped and called his name, over and over as her body shattered around him.

And still he plunged into her. Hard, deep, fast. Melanie clung to him, her eyes fluttering open as waves washed over her. His masculine beauty mesmerized her, all hard planes and strong lines.

His head tilted back, his jaw clenched. Dark lashes fluttered against his cheeks as his mouth parted on a low groan. He drove into her. Once, twice. His body tightened under her hands and he thrust inside her again. Again and again.

Until his own climax washed over him in a vibrant mix of red and cherry and rose that pulled her under once more. Its intensity frightened her, sent a shiver of anxiety through her, only to have it swept away by the sensations of his body inside hers. The sensation of her body's reaction to his.

He groaned, long and low, then leaned forward. His mouth captured hers, his tongue thrusting in a rhythm that matched the plunging of his hips. Hard, slow, deep. Slowing even more, drawing her in, holding her steady.

Anchoring her in a sea of swirling light and color that threatened to sweep her away.

Chapter Twenty

What the fuck was he doing?

Dale closed his eyes, wishing the blackness would come back and claim him. Better to be lost in the darkness of his earlier mood than lying here, dealing with the guilt of what he'd done.

And what the hell did that say about him? About what he was becoming?

Nothing he wanted to admit.

He blew out a heavy breath, the sound a rushed whisper of air in the stillness of the room. He should get up. Find his clothes. Get dressed and go back to his own place.

Where he could wallow in his misery and guilt with no witnesses and no fear of temptation.

Melanie stirred beside him, a sweet little sigh escaping her as she rolled over. She shifted, her hand brushing against his hip. His cock twitched and he ground his teeth together, willing his body to not react to just that little touch. Too late.

What the fuck had he done?

What he'd done was use her, use her body. He'd lost control and gave in, forgetting himself, forgetting everything but the feel of her sweet body as he drove into her, over and over.

More than once.

Without a condom.

He'd realized his mistake the second time, had tried to pull away. And then she'd told him she was on birth control. It shouldn't have made a difference. Hell, it didn't make a difference—he hadn't known at first, hadn't cared because he'd been so focused on himself instead of protection, responsibility. He should have stopped, even after she told him. Should have realized what he was doing and stopped. Apologized. Gone home.

But he didn't. He kept using her, driving into her like he could drive away his demons. He'd used her, like he could somehow find himself by losing himself in her body.

Just one more sin, one more shortcoming for which he'd have to eventually answer.

So why was he still here? In Melanie's bed, with her body stretched out alongside his as she slept? He needed to leave, get out of here.

Except she wasn't sleeping. He felt her move, felt the gentle touch of her hand stroke the sensitive skin of his inner thigh. Higher, her fingers skimming the heavy weight of his balls before tracing the hard length of his cock. His body tensed and he reached for her hand, his fingers closing around her wrist.

"Don't." He pulled her hand away, sitting up and swinging his legs over the side of the bed. Her body stiffened, her confusion and hurt a living thing, wrapping over him. Accusing, smothering. He sighed and ran a hand down his face, then dropped his head onto his fists. Did he have to sound so angry? So accusing? Like his failures were her fault?

"Melanie, I'm sorry. I shouldn't—" His voice was still too rough, too harsh. He took a deep breath and let it out. "I'm sorry."

"The darkness is back."

He stiffened, hearing the quiet words but not understanding them. The darkness? Was she talking about him? How could she not be, when the description was so fitting?

All the more reason for him to get up and leave.

He placed his hands along the edge of the mattress, his fingers digging into the softness. All he had to do was push himself off, stand up and move and leave. A cool hand rested against his back, the touch gentle and soothing. Dale closed his eyes, clenched his jaw.

"What happened yesterday?"

That was why he needed to leave, why he should have left a long time ago. Why he should have never come over here. He knew she'd ask, knew she would want to talk about it. And the way she asked should have surprised him. Worried him. Not *what was wrong* but *what happened yesterday*. Like she could see inside him, like she already knew.

"Nothing." He tried to shrug her hand off but it was too late. She was leaning against him, the soft weight of her breasts pressed against his back. Both hands were on him now, their touch gentle as she ran them down his arms. Her fingers spread and closed over his as she pressed a kiss against the back of his neck. Dale stiffened, afraid of her touch, afraid of his body's reaction to it.

"Melanie—"

"You're in pain. Let me help." She kissed his neck again, her hands moving back up his arms, over his chest. Over his heart. Dale stiffened and reached for her hands. Didn't she know how dangerous her offer was? How easy it would be for him to roll over on top of her, plunge into her welcoming heat, use her to forget?

Didn't she know what she asking of him? Didn't she realize he'd only lose more of himself if he did that? And yet it was so tempting. It would be so easy to do. To accept what she was offering, to take. And take.

And take.

"Melanie—" His voice trailed off, her name lost on a low moan as she tugged her hands from his and dragged them down across his body. One hand cupped around the length of his erection, stroking. Long, hard, sure. His head tilted back, his jaw clenched against the sensation of her cool hand around him. He couldn't—he should make her stop, tell her no.

He didn't have the strength to. He didn't *want* to, not when her touch was magical. Not when her touch made him forget.

She shifted behind him, moving until she was kneeling by his side. Her hair fell across his chest, the soft strands teasing his skin, burning him. She pushed against his shoulder, urging him back until he fell against the mattress, the tangled sheets cool under his skin.

And she kept stroking, up and down. Slow, so fucking slow. Her mouth closed around him, hot, wet. A groan escaped him, low and guttural, almost inhuman. He grabbed her head, wrapped his hand in the thick curls of her hair, holding her in place. He thrust his hips up, shoving himself deeper into her mouth. Wet, hot. So fucking hot.

Her nails dug into his thigh, her tongue swirling around his cock each time he thrust. Little moans floated in the air around them, soft whispers of desire as she sucked harder, faster. He clenched his jaw and raised up on his elbows, watching as her head moved up and down. Her hair fell around him like liquid fire, wrapping around his arm, teasing the flesh of his stomach and thighs. Burning, searing, torturing.

Fuck. He was so close, so fucking close. One deep thrust, that was all it would take. One deep thrust, forcing his cock to the back of her throat, exploding, spilling himself into her mouth.

No, not like that. Not now.

He bit back a curse, held himself still as she kept sucking. No, not like this.

Dale leaned down, grabbing her, pulling her away as he rolled to the side. She gasped, a throaty sigh of surprise and disappointment. He stood, facing her, pulling her to the edge of the mattress and spreading her legs. Her eyes widened as he stood there, staring down at her. At the tangle of hair spread around her face and shoulders. At her pale creamy skin, so soft and warm and alive. At the small strip of short fiery curls between her legs.

He ran his thumb along her clit, felt her legs shiver as he dipped the tip of his thumb inside her. Wet, so fucking wet. He pulled his thumb out, dragged it back up her clit, spreading her satiny moisture. He wanted inside her. Needed inside her. Now.

He grabbed her thighs, his hands dark against the creamy skin, and spread her legs further apart. Opening her, spreading her. Then he leaned forward and drove himself inside, heard her gasp of surprise as he buried himself.

Pulled out, thrust himself in once more. Slow, hard, her muscles clenching around his cock, trying to hold him in place. Squeezing, begging.

He threw his head back and groaned, holding himself still for a long minute. Fuck, she was so hot. Tight. Wet. Her pussy fitting around him like a silk glove. He pulled out, slow, until just the tip of his cock was inside her. Then he thrust his hips and drove into her, burying himself once more. Again and again, fast and hard.

She cried out, her hands closing around his, her grip tight. Dale forced his eyes open, looked down at her, his breath hitching in his chest at the beautiful sight. Her back was arched, her full breasts thrust upward, the tips of her dark peach nipples hard and erect. Her head was titled back, her neck stretched. Her teeth pulled at the fullness of her lower lip, her breath frozen in her chest. Beautiful, so fucking beautiful.

He pulled out, drove forward again. Once, twice. Her slick muscles clenching around his cock, holding him in place for one long exquisite second before exploding, quivering around him in short, sharp spasms. Her nails dug into his hands and she screamed his name, her hips thrusting against his.

He leaned forward, stretched out on top of her. He grabbed her hands, held them over her head, his grip hard as he kissed her. Claiming, possessing, his tongue thrusting into her mouth as he drove his hips into her, over and over.

His balls tightened, the deep ache growing as he plunged deeper inside her. He ripped his mouth from hers, tilted his head back. "Fuck. Smurfette—"

Her name died on his lips, replaced by a deep growl as everything coiled deep inside him, tighter and tighter until all control left, erupting in a firestorm of wildfire that danced along his skin. Burning, searing.

Consuming as he exploded inside her wet heat.

He collapsed on top of her, spent, sweaty. His chest heaved with each harsh breath, spots dancing across his closed lids as her muscles still quivered around him, gently slowing.

Seconds stretched into minutes, fluid yet meaningless. Air filled his lungs, filled with the scent of sex and fulfillment. Filled with Melanie's own scent, sweeter, inviting, magical.

He was still stretched out on top of her, his hands still holding hers in a tight grip above her head. He needed to move, he was too heavy for Melanie, he must be crushing her.

Melanie.

The horror of what he'd done, what he'd called her, hit him with the force of a collapsing wall. What the fuck had he done? He couldn't even call her by the right fucking name? How could he have done that?

He rolled to the side and pushed himself off the bed. He couldn't look at her, couldn't bear to see the horror that must surely be on her face. Or the disappointment and accusation that was surely in her eyes.

"I'm sorry." The apology sounded empty to his own ears. Too rough, too throaty. He heard the rustle of the sheets as she moved behind him but he couldn't look at her. Where were his clothes? He needed to find his clothes, get dressed, get the fuck out of here.

Were they in the kitchen? No, he'd grabbed them and brought them into the room earlier. So where the fuck were they? There, on the floor by the foot of the bed.

"Dale—"

He interrupted her, not ready to her the disappointment in her voice. "I'm sorry. I need to go."

He stepped into the shorts and yanked them on. The sheets rustled more as she moved and then he felt the cool touch of her hand against his lower back. He stiffened and clutched his shirt in one fist.

"Dale, I—"

He stepped away, shaking his head. "I need to go."

She called his name again but he ignored her, his steps fast and heavy as he moved through her apartment. Like he was running away, like he was trying to escape.

What the fuck had he done?

He pulled the door closed behind him, hurried into his own apartment and slammed the door. If only he could close out the demons so easily. But he couldn't, not when they were inside him. Not when guilt tore at him, shredding him with razor-sharp claws.

He'd used her. Hard. More than once. He'd used her to forget, to lose himself.

And he *had* lost himself. He'd lost more than he bargained for.

What the fuck had he done?

Chapter Twenty-One

A light breeze drifted past him, the early May evening air holding just a hint of chill. Not enough to make him get up and go get a jacket, though.

The only thing that could actually make Dale get up now was a call and so far, thankfully, they hadn't turned a wheel. The quiet suited him fine, gave him time to sit outside, away from everyone.

Away from the questions. Away from the glances or outright stares. Away from the meaningful talk that was only succeeding in driving him up a wall. He didn't need to talk, didn't need anyone's concern. Right now, all he needed was to be left alone.

He leaned back on the bench and stretched his legs out, tilting his head back to stare at the sky. The sun was hovering on the horizon, streaking the sky with a shades of oranges and pinks. The brighter colors mingled into the darker purple of twilight. It made him feel small, insignificant. Torn between light and dark, pulled in too many different directions, confused as to which way to go.

He blinked, watched the colors deepen as the sun sank even lower. Vibrant, bold. Somehow calming and confusing at the same time. And no matter how hard he tried not to, the colors made him think of Smurfette.

No. Melanie. Her name was Melanie.

Dale sighed and closed his eyes, shutting out the colors dancing across the sky. It didn't matter what he called her, because he hadn't seen her in six days. Not since he'd used her then ran from her apartment, bewildered and ashamed and horrified.

Not since the day after Lindsay's trial, when she refused to take the plea deal. When she surprised everyone and stood in front of the judge and changed her plea to guilty and been sentenced to three years.

Three fucking years. Why in the hell had she done that? She could have taken the plea and only served one year. One fucking year instead of three. What the hell had she been thinking? What had she been trying to prove?

Dale took a deep breath and pressed the heels of his hands against his eyes, pushing in hard. It didn't help, didn't matter. The image of Lindsay standing in front of the courtroom was still crystal clear, like he was seeing it live in person instead of as a memory.

Standing there, next to her attorney, looking lost and alone as the man told the judge his client wanted to change her plea. Dale had realized what was happening before Lauren or his parents and had jumped up, telling her no.

Her back had stiffened at first, so like Lindsay with her attitude. Then she had turned and looked at him, looked at all of them with tears in her eyes. But for the first time since Dale could remember, her eyes were clear of attitude, clear of manipulation or ulterior motives. And then she had looked at him and smiled, just the barest lifting of her lips before she turned back to the judge and pled guilty.

She turned around again, tears streaming down her face, and apologized to Lauren, to their parents. Lindsay finally admitted to everything she'd done and accepted responsibility for her actions. But why had she done it like that? Why hadn't she accepted the plea deal?

There had been no surprise on her face, no regret when the judge sentenced her. And just before they took her away, her arms cuffed behind her back, she had turned and looked at him one more time.

"It's okay, because I know you'll always be there to carry me, right?"

Lauren and his parents had asked him later what she meant but he couldn't tell them. He couldn't share their earlier conversation. Or maybe it was that he wouldn't share it. That moment, that memory, would forever be between Lindsay and him.

"Fuck." He took a deep breath, let it out on a shaky sigh, then dropped his hands and stretched his arms along the back of the bench once more. The sun had disappeared below the horizon now, the sky shifting from twilight to night. He tried to tell himself it wasn't some kind of hokey sign or omen, thinking of his sister just as the light disappeared from the sky and day turned to night. Or light to dark. Or something equally depressing and dismal and completely unlike him.

He had enough fucking darkness in his life right now, he didn't need to go adding more to it by turning everything into an artsy metaphor.

And fuck. He didn't need to be thinking of words

like *artsy* and *metaphor* either, especially not together. That was something Smurfette—Melanie!—would do. And he didn't want to go thinking about her, either.

What the fuck had happened to him? How the hell had his life gone to complete shit so quickly? He'd been coasting along, doing fine. Work, friends, the occasional no-strings-attached dates. He'd been happy. Or at least content.

He frowned then shifted on the hard bench, another breeze brushing across the skin of his bare arms.

Bullshit. Who did he think he was kidding? All he'd been doing was coasting and that was it. Content? Not really. He'd been miserable, especially the last six months. The only time he'd felt the stress and tension and worry leave him had been when he'd been with Smurfette.

Melanie.

Dammit, why couldn't he think of her as Melanie?

Because she was Smurfette. She'd always be Smurfette.

Not that it mattered because he doubted he'd be seeing her anytime soon, unless they happened to pass each other in the hall. Or unless she locked herself out of her apartment again and needed help getting back in.

Yeah, right. Somehow he doubted she'd ask him for help, not after what he'd done last week. Not after the way he'd used her then ran away.

What did it say about him that his little sister ended up having more courage than he did? After everything that happened, everything she had done, Lindsay ended up being the stronger one. What a fucked up commentary on his life.

"You staying out here all night?"

Dale turned his head to the side, not surprised to see Adam walking toward him. He sighed and slid over, making room for him to sit. "Let me guess. You drew the short straw?"

"No." Adam glanced over and grinned. "I'm the only one who hasn't given you the third degree yet."

"Because you haven't been here."

Adam shrugged then looked away. His gaze focused on the deepening night stretching out before them. A few minutes went by, filled with a comfortable silence broken only by the occasional chatter coming from the radio. Knock-on-wood, still nothing for them.

"So. You want to talk about it?"

"Not particularly, no."

"Yeah, didn't think so." Adam stretched his own legs out, his posture nearly a mirror image of Dale's. Except for the phone. Adam's phone was permanently attached to his hand, even right now. Dale glanced at it as the screen came to life with a ghostly glow, almost laughed when Adam's attention moved to the phone. He read whatever message had popped up, frowned, then started typing, his thumb moving at a rapid-fire pace across the screen.

"You know, it wouldn't kill you to put the phone down every once in a while."

"Hm?" Adam looked up from the screen, his face comically blank, as if he hadn't heard Dale. His face cleared and he grinned before shoving the phone into his pocket. "I was trying to set up a date."

"By text message? Really?"

"Someone I met online."

Dale rolled his eyes but didn't say anything. How

could he, when his own love-life was nonexistent now? Maybe he should look into that online thing. It couldn't hurt, right?

"So how's that work?"

"What?"

"The online thing. Is there somewhere you go or something?"

"Uh, yeah. Or something." Adam shifted, looking away. Dale got the impression he was suddenly uncomfortable, maybe even embarrassed. Why the hell would he be? Wasn't online dating the big thing now? He thought about pushing him, asking him why his face was turning red, then let it go.

"So how would I get started? If I wanted to do the online dating thing?"

"You?" Adam turned back, frowning. "I thought you had something going with your neighbor. What's her name? Melanie?"

"Yeah. No. I pretty much screwed that one up."

"That sucks. She was pretty nice."

Leave it to Adam to pare everything down to the bare basics. *Pretty nice*. No, Smurfette was more than *pretty nice*. But he couldn't tell Adam that, because then he'd ask for details and want to know what happened.

"You may as well go back inside. Just tell everyone I'll be fine. Just a few more days, and I'll be my old self again."

"Um, yeah. I'm thinking that's what everyone's afraid of."

"What the hell is that supposed to mean?"

"Nothing. I mean, you've just been—I don't know. Miserable or something. Even before all the shit with your sister."

Dale clenched his jaw and glared at Adam. The

look went unnoticed. "I'll be fine."

"Fine. But Mikey said she's coming out next so if you'd rather talk to her..." Adam shrugged and let his voice trail off, the threat loud and clear.

Damn his meddling, well-meaning, pain-in-the-ass coworkers. Why couldn't they be like normal coworkers, who didn't really care about each other? The kind who might go out for a drink or two on Fridays, complain about their boss, then head their separate ways.

Because they were family, that was why. And as much of a pain-in-the-ass they were being now, he wouldn't change a thing. That didn't mean he couldn't wish they'd just leave him the hell alone. At least for a little while longer.

"You're not doing a very good job of getting answers, Adam."

Dale looked over his shoulder, not surprised to see Mikey walking toward them. And she wasn't alone—Jay was right behind her. Of course he was. Those two were worse than twins.

"Don't blame me. He's more interested in learning about online dating than anything else."

"I hope to hell you're not giving him tips, considering the sites you hit are for hook-ups and not dating." Jay lowered himself to the sidewalk, stretching his legs out and leaning back on his elbows. Dale looked over, noticed how Adam seemed to be suddenly preoccupied with an invisible piece of dirt or something on his pants. If there had been enough light, Dale was fairly certain he'd see a blush staining the other man's cheeks.

Hook-up sites. He should have been surprised but he wasn't. Didn't they always say it was the quiet ones you needed to watch out for?

Mikey sat down between Adam and him, nudging them both so they'd move over. She reached over and grabbed Adam's phone, ignoring his weak protest as she tucked it under her leg. "I take it things aren't working out between you and your neighbor?"

Dale shrugged, not bothering to look at her. "Nothing there to work out."

"Hm." There was too much left unsaid with that little noise. Disbelief, curiosity. And the promise of more questions. "If you say so. We can talk about that later. Now what's going on with your sister? It's time to fess up."

"No, it's not."

"Yeah it is." Jay pinned him with a steady look, his gray eyes completely focused on Dale. "We left you alone our last night in, since her court date was just that morning. And we didn't say anything either day works, either, even though you had four days to stew."

"So now it's time to fess up." Mikey nudged him one more time, her elbow sharp against his ribs. "So what happened?"

Should he put them off some more? The idea held a temptation that was almost irresistible. But would it work? He looked at the three of them, saw expressions ranging from curiosity to concern. And support. No matter what, they were there to support him. Whether that meant giving him advice or just merely listening to him, giving him the chance to vent or talk or yell and scream, it didn't matter.

Dale leaned back against the bench and took a deep breath, let it out in a long sigh. "She didn't take the deal. And she, uh, changed her plea. To guilty."

"What?"

"No fucking way."

"Why'd she do that?" The last question came from Mikey. He turned to the side, his gaze meeting hers for a long second, then he looked away.

"I'm not sure." He paused, swallowed, looked down at the ground. "The judge gave her three years."

Silence greeted him, letting him know they were just as surprised as he was.

"Wait a minute. The deal would have been for a year, right?" Adam twisted to the side so he could look at all of them. "So why would the judge give her three years instead if she pled guilty? Wouldn't he have known about the deal?"

"I'm not sure. I know her lawyer is looking into it, seeing if they can get the sentenced reduced. Or whatever."

Jay sat up and hooked his arms around his legs. "I don't get it. Why would she change her plea instead of taking the deal? Did she think she'd get less time or something if she did that?"

"I don't know. I don't think so. And I think—" Dale paused, wondering if he should tell them what else had happened. How he had gone in to talk to her. How she had apologized. And what she had turned around to say before they led her away.

No, not that last part. That wasn't something he wanted to share, not even with these guys, no matter how close they were. It was too personal, too private. But he could share everything else with them, so he did.

Mikey leaned forward, frowning for a long minute where nobody said anything. Then she blew out a deep breath and sat back, watching him. "Do you think it was real? Her apology and all, I mean. Do you think she meant it?"

Dale hesitated before answering, not upset by the question. Why would he be, when that was how Lindsay had usually operated? Always sorry—until the next time. Always quick with an apology—as long as it got her what she wanted. They'd all been surprised that morning. Suspicious. Not quite ready to believe.

Dale closed his eyes, remembering the look on his sister's face. Remorse, honest and genuine. Nothing like her previous acts, where she did little more than pretend. "I think she meant it this time. No, I know she meant it."

Would she still mean it next month? Next year? Only time would be able to answer that but something told him she would.

"Maybe that means she's finally growing up. Taking responsibility." Mikey's voice was soft, thoughtful. Jay was more blunt. He snorted, shaking his head.

"Hell of a way to do it, if you ask me."

"No shit."

The four of them became quiet, the silence companionable. Demanding nothing, expecting nothing. Dale felt himself relax, for the first time in over a week. Maybe even longer.

Pete's voice came over the intercom, telling Jay he had a call on the station phone. He pushed to his feet and brushed off his backside, grumbling as he walked back into the station.

Dale heard Mikey laugh and looked over at her. "What's that all about?"

"He's getting suckered into working exchange time for one of the guys at Station One. Chippy."

"Oh shit. Why the hell would he do that? He

knows better. Chippy never pays back."

"Because he wants to take Angie down to Key West and the only week she can get off any time soon is when we're working. The calendar's already full so…" She shrugged, her voice drifting off.

"What people won't do for love."

"And speaking of love—"

"No. Nope, I'm out of here." Adam stood, holding his hand out. "Give me my phone back so I can go disappear before you even start that conversation."

"Wimp." Mikey laughed but tossed him the phone. He caught it, almost fumbled it, saved it at the last minute before it hit the concrete.

"Yup."

Dale tried to stand, figuring he could make his own escape by following Adam. Mikey was too fast for him and grabbed his arm, pulling him back. She kept her hand on his shoulder, preventing another escape attempt.

"So what's going on with you and your Smurfette?"

"Her name is Melanie. And nothing."

Mikey sat back, her brows raised in surprise. Yeah, maybe he'd been a little short, his voice a little too harsh. He hadn't meant to be, but maybe she'd take the hint and leave it alone.

"I thought you guys were…you know."

"What? Sleeping together?"

"Among other things, yeah."

"Well we're not. Not anymore." And fuck, why did he have to add that last part? It wasn't Mikey's business. It wasn't anyone's business.

And maybe he was more upset about it then he

realized.

Dale ran a hand through his hair and sighed, an apology hovering on his lips. He never got it out because Mikey kept talking, obviously not worried about an apology.

"So what happened?"

Dale hesitated, wondering if he could just blow her off. One glance at the determined expression on her face told him no. And she wasn't just determined—she was genuinely concerned. But why? It wasn't like she'd ever been curious about his love life before. Unless...

He leaned back, frowning. "Have you been talking to Lauren?"

A small smile teased the corners of her mouth and she shrugged. "Maybe. She's worried about you. Said you wouldn't tell her what was going on."

"Because there's nothing to tell. I thought we hit it off but I guess not."

"So what happened?"

"Christ. Are you always so fucking annoying?"

She laughed again, not fazed by his language or his question. "How long have you known me?"

Dale grumbled, her answer clear. He'd known her for quite a few years. Long enough to answer his own question. He watched her for a few more seconds then looked away, shaking his head.

"I'm not sure what happened. She just started acting like she wasn't interested." Right after her parents had come by that one day. He frowned again, thinking. Remembering back to the morning before Lindsay's court appearance, when she'd come out of her apartment to talk to him. To kiss him.

She'd completely surprised him, enough that he

didn't know what to say or how to act. He'd been too preoccupied with everything going on with Lindsay, too bewildered by how Melanie had acted when her parents had been there.

And then he'd been too wrapped up in his own feelings about his sister—confusion, guilt, sorrow, loss. Yeah, so wrapped up he'd ended up going next door and using Smurfette to forget, to lose himself.

Yeah, he'd definitely done that alright. He was such an ass.

He needed to talk to her. At least long enough to apologize. Maybe she'd listen to him, or maybe she'd slam the door in his face. But he had to at least try.

He looked over at Mikey again, noticed the way she was watching him. Almost like she knew, like she could see every single thought he was having.

"I need to talk to her."

She raised her brows. "Talking is always a good thing."

"Yeah, it is." He gave her a quick side-arm hug then stood. "Thanks."

"Uh, yeah. No problem. Glad I could help." Was it his imagination, or did she actually looked confused? He couldn't tell, was getting ready to ask her when the alarm went off. They both froze, heads cocked to the side, listening to the dispatcher strike out a box. A second later, everyone erupted into action, running for the engine, everything else forgotten.

Chapter Twenty-Two

"You really are conflicted, aren't you sweetheart?"

Melanie paused, the brush held in mid-air, and glanced at her mother. She was standing at her side, her head tilted, studying the painting with an odd expression in her eyes. Melanie sighed and put the brush down.

"It's awful."

"No, sweetheart, it isn't. A different style, yes. But not awful." She stepped back and titled her head to the other side, a few strands of her wavy hair falling against her cheek. She brushed them away with an impatient flick of her hand then smiled. "I understand why Anna wants to include additional paintings in the auctions. These are very powerful. You've captured something very…primal. Primitive."

Melanie pursed her lips and squinted, tilting her head back and forth. She stepped back and did the same thing again then let out another sigh, long and loud and full of frustration.

"You mean basic." She grabbed a rag to wipe her

hands, only partially aware that she was only succeeding in getting more paint all over herself. "Uninspired."

"Hardly. Your work has always invoked thoughts and emotions but this—" Her mom pointed at the canvas resting on the easel, then swept her hand to the side and pointed at the other two propped against the wall. "These are utterly breathtaking. The colors, the strokes, the technique. They're absolutely inspiring."

"Hm." Melanie spun away, tossing the rag onto the work table. She didn't want to look at the paintings any longer, couldn't stand to see them one more minute. Breathtaking? Inspired? No. They were more like angry splotches of emotion thrown onto a canvas, the strokes confusing and haphazard and making no sense at all.

What was the other word her mom had used? Conflicted. Yes, that word was more fitting. Everything was conflicted. Her thoughts, her feelings. Her painting. Conflicted was a perfect way to describe…everything.

All because of her neighbor. Her infuriating, hard-headed, stubborn, confusing, ingratiating neighbor.

Her soft-hearted, big-hearted, well-meaning, thoughtful, thoughtless, confusing neighbor. She didn't understand him. She didn't *want* to understand him.

And sweets, she was such a liar! Maybe she would never be able to understand him—he was man, after all—but she wanted to try. She wanted to hold him and comfort him and hit him upside the head with one of her equally-confusing paintings. How could one man create such a varying range of conflicting thoughts and emotions inside her? It didn't make sense. Nothing about him or the way he made her feel made sense.

"So how is Dale?"

Melanie jerked in surprise, her mother's question catching her off-guard. It shouldn't have, though. Her mother had always had an uncanny ability to read her thoughts and emotions, to know exactly what was going on inside Melanie. Mother's intuition or something more? She didn't know, had long-since given up trying to understand it.

"I don't know." The words were sharp, concise. She stepped around her mother and moved toward the kitchen, ignoring the knowing smile on her face. Ignoring her wouldn't work, though. Melanie knew that, knew her mother too well.

Just like her mother knew her too well.

She reached for the kettle and added water to it, then placed it on the stove to heat. Would her mother take the hint? No, she wouldn't. Melanie didn't expect her to, so she wasn't surprised when she followed her into the kitchen and pulled two teacups from the cabinet.

"And why is that, sweetheart?"

"Why is what?"

Her mom scooped some loose tea leaves into a tea ball then looked over at her, amusement and knowledge shining in her blue eyes. "I know you can sometimes be easily distracted, Melanie, but I also know when you're trying to avoid a subject. Now tell me, what's happened with you and Dale? He's such a nice man."

"Mom, how can you even say that? You only met him for a few hours."

"Because I can." She stepped forward and placed her slender hands on Melanie's shoulders, guiding her to the table. "Now sit. I'll finish making the tea, and you can tell me all about it."

Melanie propped her elbows on the table and rested her chin in her cupped hands. "I don't want to." Sweets, could she be any more pathetic? She sounded like a petulant, whiny child. Her mother laughed, the sound tinkling like fine crystal.

Melanie looked down, her gaze tracing the whimsical splashes of color that decorated the tablecloth. Bright pastels in gently swirling designs. Serene, soothing.

And boring. Oh so boring.

Is that what was wrong with her now? She used to love bright pastels, often used them in her paintings. But not recently, not since meeting Dale. Now her colors were bolder, more vibrant, daring and even edgy.

She had thought the change was because of him. Well, not *him* exactly. More like the frustration and confusion he caused her. But maybe it was something more than that. Maybe it was because she had been bored and never even knew it until she met him. Maybe she had been craving adventure and earth-shattering experiences all along and didn't realize it until she met him.

And maybe she was just being a teensy bit melodramatic—something else she had never really been until she met him. Well, mostly.

Her mother placed a steaming cup of tea in front of her then took the seat across from her, gently blowing on her own tea before taking a delicate sip. Melanie watched her, wishing she could be more like her mother. Confident, self-assured, comfortable with who she was.

She sighed then reached for her cup, taking a sip

without really tasting it.

"I remember when I first met your father—"

Melanie stifled a groan, causing her mother to smile. That didn't stop her from the telling the story Melanie had heard so many other times before.

"I was so frazzled, studying for finals, worried about my next showing, worried about my trip to Europe. I wasn't paying attention to anything else, my mind everywhere except on where I was walking—"

"And you ran into Dad, almost knocked him over and fell madly in love right then and there." Melanie finished the story for her, then looked up in surprise when her mother laughed.

"Well, not exactly, no."

"But I thought that's what happened!"

Her mother shrugged, a teasing smile on her face. "I may have left out a few details before, sweetheart. But your father enjoys thinking I fell madly in love at first sight."

"You didn't?"

"Of course I did. I just didn't realize it at first."

Melanie sat back in her chair, the cup of tea forgotten in the confusion that ran through her. "I don't understand."

"Your father was so…different. And oh so confusing. Stubborn and funny and strong-willed and sweet. I didn't understand how he could have so many opposing personality traits."

"Sounds like someone else I know," Melanie mumbled. She caught her mother's knowing smile and quickly looked away.

"I was so conflicted and torn and completely beside myself, not knowing if I wanted to hit him or hug him. Laugh or cry or tear my hair out in frustration."

"You never told me this! I thought you met him, fell madly in love, and married two months later!"

"We did, sweetheart."

"But—everything you just said…that doesn't sound like love at first sight."

"Of course it does, sweetheart. And you know what?" She leaned forward and placed a hand over Melanie's arm, giving it a gentle squeeze. "Your father still makes me feel that way. And I'm certain if you asked him, he'd say the exact same thing. Love can be stable and calming and steady. But it should also be exciting and surprising and keep you always guessing and never be boring. And if you can find someone like that, someone who inspires and delights and doesn't let you settle, you should hold onto him."

"Mom, I don't love Dale. That's just…that's…I don't. I just don't. That's insane."

Her mom smiled again, a small knowing smile that brightened her eyes. "Is it, sweetheart?"

Melanie looked away, trying to ignore the way her heart pounded in her chest, the way her palms grew a little damp. "Yes. It is."

"Hm." Her mother took another sip of tea then placed her cup in the saucer, the sound of clinking china somehow ominous. Final. She pushed back from her chair and grabbed Melanie's arm, urging her to her feet.

"Mom—"

"Hush." Her mother kept her hand on Melanie's arm and led her back to the living room, over to the completed paintings propped against the wall. "Look at them, Melanie. Really look. What do you see?"

Melanie sighed, knowing her mother wouldn't

release her until she looked. So she squinted her eyes and tilted her head and stared at the two canvases. "I see a mess."

Her mother sighed, a tinge of impatience in the sound. "Look again, Melanie. Really look and see what everyone else sees."

Melanie closed her eyes and took a deep breath, then opened them and stared back at the canvases.

Bold strokes of scarlet and smoky tangerine and bright violet. Vivid streaks of azure and emerald and pineapple. Stronger swirls of clashing color and chaos at the bottom, coming together in a gentle compatibility at the top. Soothing. Hopeful. Reassuring.

She blinked then shook her head, disbelief filling her. No, she must be seeing things. Imagining things. Her mother had put the idea in her head, that was the only reason she could see something so different now.

But now that she could see it, she wondered. Were the paintings real? Was she only just now seeing what she had really felt when she painted them? How could she have been so foolishly blind and not noticed it before?

She stepped away and shook her head, then brushed a curl away from her face with an angry swipe of her hand. Something like desperation and sadness filled her. "But it doesn't matter."

"Why doesn't it matter, sweetheart?"

"Because he doesn't even like me!"

That made her mother pause. She turned to face Melanie and gently folded her arms in front of her. "And why do you think that?"

"Because—" Melanie stopped and cleared her throat. "I don't know why. I must have done something because he practically ran away when he was here the last time and I haven't seen him since."

"When was this, sweetheart?"

"Over a week ago. The day after…" Her voice trailed off and her brows snapped together. The day after he had the thing with his sister. She still didn't know what had happened, but she knew he had been upset. So terribly upset that she could feel his pain even through the walls separating their apartments. Dark, violent, consuming. And for a little while, while they had been together, his pain had eased. Disappeared.

And then something had happened, something that filled him with horror and disbelief and regret. And he'd left, practically running from her apartment.

But what had happened? She didn't know but it must have been something she did. What else could it have been?

She looked over, saw the concern and curiosity mingled in her mother's eyes. "The day after something happened with his sister. He was upset and we…talked…and then he left and I haven't seen him since."

Her mother smiled and Melanie looked away, wondering if she knew what *talked* really meant. Of course she did. Her mother knew everything.

"And when you *talked*, did he seem better?"

Melanie looked away, her face heating under her mother's knowing look. "I think so, yes."

"Then maybe you should speak to him. You won't know what's wrong unless you ask."

"But what if it turns out he really doesn't like me? Or if he thinks *talking* was a mistake?"

"Melanie, I'm almost positive that won't be the case. But you won't know until you ask, now will you?"

"But…I don't know if I can do that."

"Sweetheart, you can do whatever you want, if it's something you really want. Now, enough brooding. Let's get these paintings into the car so we can get them to the gallery." Her mother stepped away, leaving Melanie standing there with her mouth partially opened. How could she just change the subject like that? Not change it—drop it. Just stop talking and walk away! Didn't she know Melanie needed to talk? That she needed her mother's advice and help and support and…and…oh, sweets. Her mother had already given her the advice. Now it was up to Melanie to decide what to do.

She didn't know what she wanted to do. Well, she did. Maybe. No, she did. She just didn't know how to do it.

"Sweetheart, enough thinking. Help me with these."

Melanie stomped her foot in frustration, a silent scream burning in the back of her throat. She swallowed it then reached for the painting her mother was holding out to her. Her mom opened the door and Melanie moved through it, walking sideways so the frame wouldn't hit the doorway. She adjusted the painting, holding it up in front of her to kick the hem of her skirt out of the way. There, that was better. Now she wouldn't trip and fall down the stairs.

Although maybe she should just fall down. Maybe she'd hit her head and develop amnesia and forget all about Dale. As long as she didn't break her arm or hand, that would suit her just fine.

"Easy there, Smurf—Melanie. You don't want to take a header down the stairs."

The sound of her name, spoken in *his* voice, made

her stop, one foot already in mid-air, searching for the first step. Melanie swallowed her gasp of surprise, nearly choking on it as her hands tightened around the edges of the frame.

Dale was right in front of her. She could actually feel him. All she had to do was lower the painting and she'd be looking at him. Would his deep brown eyes be amused? Shadowed? Carefully hooded or abysmally blank? Would dark stubble cover his chiseled jaw or would he be freshly shaved? It was early afternoon and he wasn't working today. At least, she didn't think he was. So yes, his jaw would probably be covered in a little of the masculine scruff that she found so appealing.

All she had to do was lower the painting. Just a few inches, that was all.

Her fingers gripped the edges of the frame, the canvas and wood biting into her flesh. Something sharp pinched the tip of her finger. One of the heavy staples she used, no doubt. A sudden image of Sleeping Beauty came to mind, succumbing to a silly prick of her finger from a silly spinning wheel, only to be saved by her Prince Charming.

Hysterical laughter bubbled in her chest and she choked, her breath catching in her lungs before rushing out in a sharp wheeze. She coughed, cleared her throat. Coughed again.

"Are you okay back there? You sound—"

"Fine. I'm fine." The words were rushed, too high-pitched and hurried. Melanie grimaced, suddenly thankful that she couldn't see him. That he couldn't see her. Surely her face had turned an embarrassing shade of ghastly tomato red.

"Sweetheart, do you have your keys? I don't want

to—oh. Dale. What a surprise. So nice to see you again."

Melanie glanced over her shoulder. Her mother was standing just outside her apartment, the other painting held carefully in one hand. She certainly didn't look surprised. In fact, she looked suspiciously cheerful. Had her mother somehow known Dale was coming in? No, she couldn't have. Could she?

"Mrs. Reeves."

"Please, call me Michelle. Could you do me a favor? Carry this out to Melanie's car while I grab her purse and keys."

Melanie's eyes widened and she shook her head, mouthing *No!* Her mother merely looked at her and smiled—then promptly ignored her. Sweets! What did she think she was doing? Her own mother!

She heard Dale move away from her, felt cool air brush over her as the heat of his nearness faded. A bare arm came into view, followed the short sleeve of a dark red t-shirt stretched over a muscled bicep and shoulder. Melanie almost squeaked and turned away before she could see his face, before he could see her.

She managed to hurry down the stairs without tripping or falling then pushed through the front door. The sun shone brightly overhead, so bright she squinted. The air was pleasantly warm, free of the humidity that would settle over them like wet wool in the coming months. Melanie paused to take a deep breath, enjoying the smells of early Spring, enjoying the sights of the spectacular colors swirling around her.

But only for a second. She didn't dare take longer than that, not when Dale was surely right behind her. She had to get to her car, open the back and get the painting inside. If she was lucky, she'd have that done quick enough so all she would have to do was stand aside while Dale put the other painting in the car.

Luck wasn't with her.

She was still struggling to get the painting into the backseat when Dale came up behind her. He was standing too close, the heat of his body, the warmth of all the colors that swirled around him too strong. Too near. Too powerful. Too *him*.

She finally got the painting inside then stepped back, her bottom bumping against his hip. Or maybe his thigh. She didn't know, didn't want to know.

"Sorry." She mumbled the apology and quickly moved out of his way, not daring to look at him. Was that a chuckle she heard? No, it couldn't be. Why would he be laughing? This wasn't funny. None of this was funny. And where was her mother? She should be here. As soon as she got there, they could get in the car and leave and she wouldn't have to stand here, pretending that Dale wasn't standing so close to her.

There she was, walking toward them, Melanie's purse and sandals held loosely in one hand and a bright smile on her face. Finally! Now they could leave...except why was she smiling like that?

"Sweetheart, something came up and I need to leave. I locked everything up for you so you wouldn't have to go back inside. I know you're in a hurry to get to the gallery."

What was her mother talking about? She wasn't in a hurry. It made no sense. But her mother was pushing the purse and sandals toward her, that wide smile still on her face. "But—"

"I know, but you don't need to worry." She leaned forward and pressed a quick kiss against Melanie's cheek then stepped back. "Dale has agreed to go to the gallery with you and help you unload. I'll talk to you later."

"But—" It was too late, her mother was already walking away, her steps much faster than her normal relaxed gait. Melanie stared after her, bewilderment and betrayal mixing inside her, leaving her stunned. Why? Why would her mother do that to her?

"Guess it's just us two, huh? I'm driving."

Melanie gasped as he grabbed the keys from her loose grip and climbed into the driver's seat of her little car. "But—"

"No buts. Climb on in, sweetheart. Your chariot awaits." He grinned, laughter shining in his eyes.

"But—" She never got a chance to finish because he winked then closed the door, shutting her off. Melanie pursed her lips then moved around to the passenger side, her steps slow, like she was in a daze.

How could her day have taken such a drastic turn like this? And what was she going to do about it?

What *could* she do about it?

Chapter Twenty-Three

Dale had thought that Mrs. Reeves' suggestion to drive Melanie to the gallery was a good one, one he'd gladly agreed to. Driving Melanie and helping her with the paintings should have given them plenty of chance to talk. It should have helped break the ice or bridge the gap or help fix whatever the hell had happened between them.

It didn't.

She barely spoke to him during the entire drive downtown, except to give him directions. And those were given at the last minute, which ended up with him doing some creative driving in the city traffic. There were a few times Dale wondered if she even knew where they were going. She'd look out the window and glance around, a frown on her face, like she wasn't quite sure where they were. And her hands kept twisting in the fabric of her skirt until the hem pulled up past her calves and she had a large wad of material bunched in her fists.

Every single time he tried talking to her, she either

ignored him, shook her head, or answered with a single-syllable reply.

How had she been the last week?

That one was ignored.

Are these the only paintings she'd have on display or for sale or whatever they were for?

She tossed him a dirty look at that one and shook her head.

Was she excited about the sale or auction or whatever tomorrow night?

Sure.

Then, after one last-minute instruction to make a turn had him cutting across two lanes of traffic on President Street, he'd made the mistake of asking if she knew where they were going.

She'd glared at him, her eyes narrowed and her lips pursed and something that felt like cold anger rolled off her. It would have been almost amusing, the fact that he could actually *feel* her anger, except for the fact that she was really angry. Angrier than what made sense.

She hadn't said a single word since then, wouldn't even look at him. She'd just point, left or right or straight ahead, until he finally pulled the car into a parking spot on lower Broadway in Fells Point. He cut the engine and got out of the car, looking at the storefronts lining the street. Most of the buildings were old rowhomes dating back to the 1800's, now converted into businesses or bars, some with apartments on the top floors. One building stood out from the others, its brick painted white with wrought iron handiwork framing the door and windows. A small sign hung above the door, neat and unobtrusive: Gallery 1900.

It didn't look like much but what did he know?

He moved to open the back door but Melanie beat him to it, already struggling to pull the paintings out from the passenger side of the car. He muttered under his breath, loud enough for her to give him a dirty look. She hesitated, which gave him time to lean in from his side and grab the first oversized canvas. He glanced down at it, frowning, wondering what it was even supposed to be. But he was smart enough not to say anything, especially considering the look she was giving him.

She fisted her hands and placed them on her hips, watching him with narrowed eyes. "I don't need your help."

The color of her eyes had gone from a deep ocean blue to that stormy gray again. He'd noticed it before, how the color changed whenever she was angry or frustrated. He kind of liked the way he knew that about her. It was like he knew something secret and private about her. Which was ridiculous, because anyone who was observant enough to know what color her eyes were would be able to see the difference. That didn't stop him from grinning, which only made her eyes darken even more.

"Too bad, because I'm helping." He pulled the first painting out the rest of the way and propped it against the car then reached for the second. Melanie came around to his side and grabbed the first one, mumbling something under her breath. He didn't catch the words, but he definitely caught the frustration in her tone.

Which only managed to turn his grin into a full smile.

He followed her across the old cobblestone street

to the gallery. There was one marble step in front of the door but she didn't bother using it. Instead, she turned to her side, the painting still held in front of her, and used her elbow to push the buzzer placed beside the door. Dale held his breath, ready to drop the painting and catch her if she lost her balance. She righted herself at the last minute and stood with her back to him, her hair blowing around her shoulders in the breeze coming off the water.

He squinted and looked closer, smiling again. "You have paint in your hair."

Her back stiffened but she didn't turn around, didn't even bother acknowledging him. He chuckled and stepped a little closer, leaning down until his mouth was close to her ear. "It's blue, like a cute little Smurf."

She made a low sound in her throat, a high-pitched cross between a groan and a growl, then stomped her foot and turned to face him. "Why do you always do that?"

Dale straightened, raising his brows and grinning. Finally, a reaction! "Do what?"

"That...that...whatever you're doing. Standing too close. Teasing me. It's annoying and I can't think straight when you do it."

He leaned closer, his voice low as held her gaze with his own. "Because I like you."

Her eyes widened and her cheeks turned a cute shade of pink. She opened her mouth but never got a chance to say anything because the door to the gallery opened. Dale stepped back, his eyes immediately going to the woman standing in front of them.

At first glance, she appeared to be in her late forties. Tall, thin, brown hair styled in a fashionable bob. She was simply dressed in a black skirt that hugged her lean body and a billowy blouse that accented her build. Heels that looked dangerously high to walk in completed the ensemble. There was something about her, sleek and professional. Almost regal. Like the gallery was her domain, ruled only by her.

Her eyes raked over him with a feminine appreciation that actually made him take a step back. A bright smile lit her face as she looked away, her gaze now focused on Melanie.

"Melanie, dear. I was beginning to worry you weren't going to show up. Come in, then, let's look." She stepped back to let them in, already studying the painting Melanie held in front of her. "Wonderful. Absolutely stunning. And this one?"

Dale looked over and noticed that she was watching him. No, not him. Her eyes were lowered, trying to see the paining he was carrying. He turned it around, watched as her eyes widened in appreciation when she studied the canvas.

"Melanie, dear, you continuously surprise me. The emotion, the vibrancy, the life. Wonderful, absolutely wonderful."

Dale looked down at the painting, frowning. He had no idea what the hell he was looking at except for a bunch of bright splotches that looked like running streaks of paint. But whatever it was, it was obviously good, if the way the woman was carrying on meant anything.

She closed the door behind them then walked toward the back, her heels clicking against the heavy planks of the wood floor. Melanie looked back at him, frowning, then followed the woman.

Dale hesitated, glancing around. The downstairs had been converted to one large room stretching to the very back of the building. Three walls boasted the original brick, carefully cleaned and restored. Artwork decorated the walls, displayed in clusters with lights accenting each piece. There was a break in the displays near the back of the room, separated by two comfortable seating arrangements. Beyond the seating arrangements was one more display, a pair of paintings fastened to the wall, the lights brighter, drawing his attention. An empty easel sat between the two paintings.

Even from where he was standing, Dale could tell they were Melanie's. He wasn't sure how he knew. There was just something about them. About the color, the strokes, the design. Something.

And then he realized that both women were standing at the back of the room, watching him. Waiting. He hurried across the room, not really paying any attention to them. His eyes were focused on one of the paintings, the larger one hanging to the left. There was just something about it...

Something tugged on the canvas in his hands and he stepped back, startled. Then he realized the woman was trying to take the painting from him, a small smile on her face. She noticed the direction of his gaze and looked behind her, the smile growing wider.

"It's very compelling, isn't it?"

"Hm? Oh. Uh, yeah." Dale shoved his hands into the front pockets of his shorts, somehow embarrassed that he had been caught staring.

"We're calling it *Elemental*. Fitting, don't you think?"

"Sure. I guess." Dale frowned and looked back at

the painting, studying it. Bold strokes of vibrant reds and oranges filled the canvas, broken by slashes of sulfur yellow and smoky black, each color fighting for dominance. Dark and light, negative energy fighting with positive. Chaos, confusion, desperation. How could something that was essentially nothing more than paint smeared across a canvas fill him with those emotions?

He cleared his throat and pulled his gaze away from the painting. "It looks more like someone who's been caught in a raging inferno and doesn't know how to escape."

Silence greeted his observation and both women turned to look at him. Melanie tilted her head to the side, a mixture of surprise and horror and even dismay on her face. In fact, she looked like a young child who had just had her favorite toy taken away. Or a teen who just had the deepest secrets hidden in her diary read out loud to the class.

But the other woman smiled, her eyes alight with satisfaction. She studied Dale for an uncomfortable minute then turned to Melanie. "Dear, who is your friend? You never introduced us."

"Oh. Um…" Melanie cleared her throat and looked away, a blush staining her cheeks. "This is Dale. He's my neighbor."

"I see. Your *neighbor*. Hm." The woman smiled again, something new shining in her eyes, something that made Dale even more uncomfortable. The woman extended her hand, taking his in a surprisingly strong handshake. "A pleasure to meet you, Dale. My name is Anna James."

She dropped his hand then turned back to the painting Dale had been studying. Her head tilted from side to side before she turned back once more, smiling at Melanie. "Dear, what would you think about changing the name?"

"Changing it?"

"Yes. We'll call it *Into The Flames* instead. Much more fitting, I think. Don't you?"

Melanie shifted, her hands again fisting in the material of her skirt. She looked at the painting for a long time before her gaze darted to Dale. Why did she look so awkward, so uncomfortable and even frightened? Maybe it was just his imagination because she looked away, a small smile on her face. A forced smile.

"That...that would be okay. I guess. You know I always have such a hard time coming up with names."

"Then it's decided. And how appropriate, that we get its name from the man who inspired it, don't you think?"

Dale blinked, his mind frozen for one scary minute. Inspired? Inspired what? She must mean the name. She couldn't be talking about the painting. Could she? No, impossible.

He looked over at Melanie, saw the fiery heat of a blush stain her face. She wasn't looking at him. She wasn't even looking at Anna. Her gaze was focused on the floor, her hands clasped together in a white-knuckled grip. He wanted her to look at him, wanted to see her eyes, to see what thoughts and feelings would be reflected in their deep blue depths. But she wouldn't look at him, no matter how long he stared at her, silently willing her.

"Will you be joining us tomorrow night. Dale?"

He tore his gaze away from Melanie, the question catching him by surprise. But he never got a chance to answer because Melanie spoke up, her voice too loud and a little shaky.

"No. No, he won't be coming. He's, uh, he's busy. And we need to leave now." She turned so fast that the hem of her skirt flared around her legs. The soles of her sandals smacked against the plank floor as she hurried toward the door, not bothering to wait for him.

Dale said a quick goodbye to Anna, surprised at her laughter. He didn't question it, just hurried after Melanie, wondering why she was suddenly in such a hurry.

To escape him, no doubt. To escape the questions she surely knew he had.

She was already standing by the car, her arms crossed in front of her, a long sweep of hair falling across her cheeks, hiding her face. Her body language was clear, screaming embarrassment and a desire to hide. He hesitated, something softening inside him as he watched her. There was something vulnerable about her, something that made him want to reach out and fold her in his arms and protect her.

To never let her go.

The realization slammed into him, freezing the air in his lungs and causing his heart to pound heavy in his chest. Fuck. When had it happened? When had it changed? He didn't just like her, didn't just want to spend time with her.

No. Impossible. He was simply imagining things. Yes, he enjoyed their time together. Yes, he wanted to spend more time with her, get to know her. She was different and funny and kept him on his toes. She saw things differently, made him see things differently. That didn't mean that he—

No. No way in hell.

Yeah, sure it didn't.

He took a deep breath, surprised by how fresh and clean the air seemed to be. By how clear the sky was, how vibrant and fresh the smells were. Yeah, he really was in trouble if he thought Fells Point smelled clean and fresh.

He took another deep breath then crossed the street, not stopping until he was close enough to her that he could feel the heat radiating from her body. He sighed and leaned against the car, his thigh brushing against hers. She didn't move away. That could be a good sign. It would be even better if she'd actually look over at him.

He thrust his hands into his pockets, his fingers closing over the keys to her car and jingling them. The noise was muted, almost swallowed by the sounds surrounding them.

The rumble of tires against the cobblestone as cars drove by. The call of seagulls swooping down over the water. The low moan of a tug nearby.

The steady thud of his heart. Melanie's harsh breathing. He took a deep breath and let it out slowly.

"So. Inspired, huh?" Probably the wrong to say because she stiffened and took a small step away from him. He sighed and jingled the keys some more. "I don't think I've ever inspired anyone before. I'm not sure if that's a good thing."

Silence.

"Would it help if I told you I liked the painting?"

She finally looked up at him. Pink still stained her cheeks but the color was fading. Was it his imagination, or did the barest smile tease the corners of her lips? Maybe, maybe not. But there was no doubting the amused disbelief that flashed in her eyes.

"You didn't even know what you were looking at."

He smiled then looked away. "Well, I could lie and say I did, but then you'd probably ask me to explain so I won't. That doesn't mean I can't like it."

This time she did smile. Just a small one, there and gone too quickly. He shifted, edging a little closer until their legs were touching again. She didn't step away, which he took as a good sign.

"Art has never been my thing but I think you already know that. But that doesn't mean I can't like something. And I did. I do. Like it, I mean. It's—" His voice trailed off and he looked away, frowning as his mind searched for the right words. "It reminds me of chaos and confusion and not knowing which way is up. Like…like when you're lost but it's okay because you know you're going to find your way out. And maybe it's not the way you thought you'd find, but it's a better way. And yeah, okay, that probably sounds stupid but—"

Dale didn't get a chance to finish because she was suddenly pressed against him, her mouth on his in a sweet gentle kiss. He hesitated for a split second then wrapped his arms around her, pulling her closer as he deepened the kiss, his tongue plunging into her mouth. Tasting, savoring.

Then she pulled away, leaving him breathless and confused and wanting—needing—more. She wrapped her arms around his neck and smiled, a bright beautiful smile that sent heat rushing through him.

Not heat of passion, heat of need. No, this was something more. Calming, reassuring, *right*. The heat of acceptance, of belonging, of finally learning where he wanted to go only to realize he'd already been there all along.

"You understand it!"

He blinked, his mind trying to focus on her words, trying to understand them. "I do?"

"Yes! That's it exactly."

The painting. She was talking about the painting. Not what she made him feel, not the amazing and monumental epiphany he'd just experienced. The painting.

He swallowed back his disappointment and forced a smile. "Well, I'm glad I understand."

"You do. Everything. The chaos, the confusion, the feeling lost. That's how you made me feel when I first met you. Not just how I felt, but how I saw you. Like you were lost in the chaos and confusion, too."

Dale frowned and leaned back, not sure if he liked the sound of that, even if it might have been true. "I had a lot of things on my mind."

"I know. But they're over now, aren't they? The worry and guilt you were carrying."

He froze. How did she know? How had she seen? He nodded, slowly.

"I knew they were. That night you came over. They were there at first, but then they were gone." Her smile faded and she dropped her arms, stepping away from him. "But then you left."

Fuck. Guilt swept over him, pushing away everything else he'd just been feeling. He reached for her, ran one hand down her arm until her their fingers entwined. He squeezed them then let go, dropping his hand to his side.

"I—" He paused, cleared his throat. "I need to apologize for that."

"For leaving?"

"Not just for leaving. For..." Fuck. The words

were sticking in his throat, full of regret over what he'd done, how he'd used her that night. "I shouldn't have...I wasn't thinking. I was just trying to..."

He couldn't say it. Couldn't get the words out. Hell, he couldn't even apologize the right way! He cleared his throat, determined to at least say he was sorry, but he didn't get the chance because Melanie grabbed his hands, squeezing them.

"You were upset and needed to find a way to heal."

"I used you."

"No. You turned to me. There's a difference. But I still don't understand why you left the way you did."

"Melanie—"

"Sweets!" She squeezed his hands again, hard, and stomped her foot. "Stop calling me that!"

"What? Your name?"

"Yes! I don't like it. It sounds weird coming from you."

"But I thought you hated when I called you *Smurfette*."

"No." She shook her head, her mouth pressed in a firm line. "I did at first because I thought you were teasing me but then I didn't. And I already told you that. So stop."

Dale watched her for a long minute, not sure if she was serious, if he should believe her. But she looked serious, with her brows lowered over eyes and her lips pursed in impatience. No, not impatience. A pout. She was actually pouting!

He chuckled, the sound deep and somehow freeing. She narrowed her eyes and tried to step away but he was faster. He caught her around the waist and pulled her close, the curves of her body pressed against him. Just where she belonged.

Then he dipped his head and claimed her mouth in a long deep kiss. It was too soon to tell her how he felt, but maybe he could show her. And maybe, just maybe, she'd be able to see how much she had helped him ban the darkness that had threatened to consume him.

And maybe, if he was very lucky, she'd eventually feel the same way.

Chapter Twenty-Four

No matter how many deep breaths she took, the knots in her stomach only grew worse. Big tight balls of nerves, sitting low in her belly, rough and hard and heavy. She curled her fingers against her palm, the edges of her short nails biting into her skin.

She didn't want to be here. She so didn't want to be here. Why did she have to be here? The people were buying her paintings, not her. It shouldn't matter if she was here or not.

She looked across the room, doing her best to ignore the mingling crowd as she searched for the door. Would anyone stop her if she suddenly took off? Maybe, if she just walked slowly, stopping occasionally to smile and nod, she could make her way to the door and just walk out. Surely nobody would notice her. And if they did, surely they'd think she was just stepping outside for a breath of fresh evening air. After all, it was a little crowded in here, the air a bit too warm and tight. Surely she wasn't the only one who thought that.

So she could just walk out. Get in her car and drive home and knock on Dale's door. He'd pull her into his arms and kiss her. Long deep kisses that made her forget her name, made her forget everything except how his body felt against hers. How he smelled and tasted. The way his eyes darkened, the gold flecks dancing in their depths when they filled with passion. The small moans he made when he grabbed her, held her, made love to her. The look in his eyes, the depth of emotion and feeling he tried to hide.

She almost smiled. He didn't say the words yesterday—or last night or this morning or this afternoon—but he didn't need to. She could see it, in the lazy swirl of colors that came to life around him when they were together. The darkness was gone. Well, mostly gone. She still saw a little of it, a faint whispery gray, when he finally told her about his sister and what she had done. But it didn't hover around him, didn't cling to him with the constant threat of smothering him. The darkness had been replaced by lighter colors. Still reds and oranges, but brighter. Calmer.

Melanie ducked her head and smiled. Calm? No, she didn't think that word would ever apply to Dale. And she was happy about that. She didn't want calm. She wanted wild and ferocious and dangerous and adventurous, everything that Dale was, everything that he offered.

Her fingers twitched, curling around an imaginary paint brush, the colors appearing on her mind's palette. She already knew how she'd paint it, how she would capture it and put it on canvas.

She sighed and uncurled her hand, pressing it against her stomach. Not yet. She couldn't do any of that yet.

Not until this agonizing night was over.

Her gaze flicked across the room once more, landing on the door. Maybe nobody would notice, maybe she really could just leave—

"Sweetheart, you will not make a run for the door so please stop thinking about it." Her mother came up beside her and placed a hand on her shoulder. Comforting? Or holding her in place, just in case? Why did her mother have to know her so well?

"I wasn't."

Her father came around her other side, his chuckle deep and affectionate. He pressed a kiss against the top of her head. "Don't deny it. We know you too well."

"It's just…it's so crowded. And what if nobody bids? What if everyone laughs and nobody likes them?"

"Don't be silly. Sweetheart, look around. All of these people are here specifically because of you. Because they want a chance to own something you created. Something you breathed life into."

Instead of reassuring her, her mother's words only succeeded in making her more nervous. Why, oh why, had she agreed to let Anna set up the auction? It had sounded so exciting at first, a validation of her work. But now she wasn't sure. She didn't need the validation. Her work sold, well enough that she was able to do what she loved the most and make a living at it.

She should have never agreed to it.

Her father placed an arm around her and pulled her in for a quick hug. "It'll be fine, sweetheart. You're worrying for nothing. Just like your mother does before one of her shows."

Melanie looked over at her mom, at the way she stood so poised and calm, so serene. Except for the way she was looking at her father, some secret silent communication passing between them. "You get nervous, Mom? Why?"

"Ignore your father, sweetheart. He's exaggerating. As usual."

Her dad laughed, which only earned him another look from her mother, this one sparkling with amusement. She stopped one of the passing waiters and took two glasses from the tray, passing one to Melanie. "Have a few sips, dear. It will help calm your nerves and stop you from eyeing the door."

Melanie didn't want the champagne, even though she knew it was a more expensive brand, reserved for the clientele that attended the auctions. Just one more reminder that she didn't quite belong here tonight.

Her mom took a small sip, watching her over the rim of the glass. "Where's Dale? I thought he'd be here."

"Oh. Um, no." Melanie looked away, her eyes darting to the door once more.

"Didn't you work things out yesterday?"

"We did. Yes." Yesterday, last night, this morning. "But, um, I asked him not to come."

"What? Why would you do that?" The surprise in her father's voice matched the surprise on her mother's face. Melanie wasn't sure how to answer. How could she, when she didn't understand it herself? She wanted him to be here, wished she had never asked him not to join her. But she had been afraid, worried the event would be a disaster. And she didn't want him here to be a witness to it if that happened.

Now she wished he was standing right beside her, his strong arm around her shoulders, supporting her. Standing by her. Sharing his strength with her.

She truly was an idiot. Maybe there was still time.

Maybe she could call him and ask. She glanced around, wondering what time it was, ready to sneak away to make a phone call. But then Anna appeared beside her, a bright smile on her face and excitement in her eyes.

"It's almost time, dear. It's going to be a huge success. I just know it."

"Anna, I don't think—"

"Nonsense. People are already talking, the anticipation growing. Now finish up and join me up front so we can get everyone's attention." Anna smiled once more then glided through the crowd, toward the back wall where Melanie's paintings were displayed.

Her hand tightened around the stem of the glass as she fought the urge to finish the champagne in one long swallow. No, that wouldn't do. So she took one last small sip and passed the glass to her father, then gave them both what she hoped was a smile before turning away.

The sooner they started, the sooner the nightmare would be over with.

If only she hadn't told Dale to stay home.

Chapter Twenty-Five

"Are you sure this is a good idea?"

Dale didn't bother to look at Lauren as they pushed through the door. He paused, frowning as his eyes skimmed the crowded room. "Of course. Why wouldn't it be?"

"Maybe because she asked you not to come."

"Only because she was nervous. I think she's afraid the auction will be a bust."

"Uh, you wouldn't know it by looking at this crowd. Wow. Holy crap." Lauren pushed closer, caught between him and Kenny as someone jostled them from behind. Kenny grunted and placed his hand in the middle of Lauren's back as he moved behind her, protecting her. Dale would have smiled his approval if he wasn't so busy looking for Smurfette. She was probably near the back wall. Of course that's where she would be. That's where her paintings were. At least, where they were yesterday.

Lauren was right, though. The gallery was crowded. More crowded than he had expected. Not that he'd ever been to an art auction before. Hell, before yesterday, he'd never really been to a private gallery before. He didn't know what to expect, but this crowd hadn't been it.

There had to be more than seventy people mingling around them, making the large room feel oddly small. Hell, it was crowded enough that it probably exceeded what the maximum occupancy allowed. Well, maybe not. They weren't exactly crammed in elbow-to-elbow. There was still room to move, room to breathe. Mostly.

"Kenny, you're taller than me. Do you see her?"

"Taller? Yeah, by what, an inch?" Kenny rolled his eyes then raised up on his toes, looking around. "She's over by the back wall talking to another lady."

"Does it look like they started yet?"

"Do you see anyone bidding?"

"Kenny, stop." Lauren laughed and placed a hand on Kenny's arm. "Can't you see he's nervous? Look at him. He's worried because he just realized he's in love."

"Yes, I know." Kenny leaned over to kiss Lauren, the kiss a little too long, a little too deep. Dale stepped closer and cleared his throat, half-tempted to pull Kenny away from his sister. But Kenny stopped on his own, his eyes dancing with laughter when he looked at Dale. "I'm just getting him back for what he did all those months ago."

Lauren laughed then looked away when Dale scowled. So maybe he had been wrong to tell Kenny how his sister felt about him. He couldn't do anything about it now. Besides, if he hadn't told Kenny that Lauren loved him, the two of them would probably still be dancing around each other, neither one of them taking the first step to let the other know how they felt.

That didn't mean he appreciated being teased about what he was going through now, though.

He moved deeper into the room, angling across and toward the front so he could see better. Yes, there she was, standing to the side, talking to Anna. And her parents were there as well. Good, she had moral support with her. She still looked nervous, her face a little too pale in the overhead lighting. Her hands twisted in front of her the way they always did when she was worried or upset about something.

"Why'd you stop? Aren't you going up there?"

"No, not yet."

Lauren gaped at him, surprise and impatience flaring in her eyes. "Why not? I thought you wanted to get here early enough to surprise her. You know, to support her?"

"No. I mean yes. I know. But not yet."

"Dale, how are you going to show her support if she doesn't even know you're here?"

"I'm going to show my support by buying that painting right there." He pointed to the one on the far left. What were they calling it now? *Into The Flames*. He didn't care what they called it. He inspired it, and now he was going to buy it.

"You're going to bid on a painting?" Lauren looked at him as if he had just lost his mind. He nodded, then reached for a glass from the passing waiter's tray.

"Yes. What's wrong with that?"

"Nothing. I just never figured you'd actually buy real art, that's all."

"It's Smurfette's. Why wouldn't I?"

"Um, Dale. Have you ever been to one of these things before?"

He looked over at Kenny and shook his head. "No, why?"

"Ever been to a gallery like this before? No, don't look at me like that, I'm not insulting you. I'm just wondering how much you think art work like this goes for." Kenny looked around the room, nodding at the different pieces on display around them. "Some of the prices are pretty steep."

That made him hesitate. Steep? How steep? No, Kenny must be exaggerating. Or his definition of *steep* was a bit different. He was a cautious spender, saving and investing, never buying anything he didn't really need, never spending more than he had to. Lauren said it was because he still couldn't believe the Banners were keeping him, that he wasn't going to have to play in the minor leagues anymore.

Dale just liked to tease him and call him cheap.

"Doesn't matter. I inspired Smurfette to paint it, so I'm buying it. That's all there is to it." Dale took a long swallow of the champagne and looked around again. Everyone seemed to be shifting toward the back wall. Sure enough, Anna had stepped closer to the crowd, a bright smile on her face as she started speaking. Her voice was clear, projecting over the entire room, commanding everyone's attention.

"Ladies and gentlemen, thank you so much for coming tonight. I know many of you have been waiting for this opportunity for a long time. Well, your wait is over." There was a slight spattering of applause, a few chuckles. Anna turned to the side, her arm outstretched, motioning for Smurfette to come forward.

Dale's heart thudded, with excitement, with some of the same nervousness Smurfette obviously felt. She smiled, her lips trembling just the slightest bit as her gaze swept across the crowd. Dale ducked his head and stepped behind the gentleman in front of him. He didn't want her to see him, not just yet. He didn't want to spoil the surprise.

"I've had the tremendous honor of showcasing Melanie's work for the last few years. The honor of watching her work take on a life of its own. And like many of you, I knew it was only a matter of time before her wonderful renditions became more than collector items we treasured so dearly. So much more."

Dale shifted, the first wave of discomfort washing over him as he looked around. Many in the crowd were smiling and nodding, as if they knew exactly what Anna was talking about. As if they, too, had been waiting for…whatever was about to happen.

Lauren eased closer, her voice a low whisper. "Are you sure you want to do this?"

"Yes, I'm sure. Now be quiet."

"Ladies and gentlemen, you've all had a chance to view the two selections for this evening. Now it is time to start the bidding. We'll begin with *Into The Flames*."

Dale glanced at Lauren and Kenny, a grin on his face as Anna described the painting. Smurfette was going to be so surprised when he bought it. He drank the last of the champagne then passed the empty glass to Lauren. He wanted both hands free, he needed to concentrate. He didn't want to get distracted and let someone outbid him by mistake.

"Dale, I don't think—"

He shook his head, trying not to let Lauren distract him. What had Anna said? He missed it. Probably just something else about the painting, that was all. It didn't matter because she had paused, coming closer to the crowd, her smile all business now.

"Who will start the bidding—"

Dale grinned and stepped forward, ready to raise his hand. Smurfette would be so surprised.

"—at eight?"

"Eight."

"Eight five."

"Nine."

"Nine five."

"Ten!"

Dale stood frozen as people around him called out bids. What the hell? It was like a frenzy, people shouting, the number getting higher and higher. He still hadn't had a chance to raise his hand, numbers ringing in his ear. Fifteen. It was up to fifteen now. Fifteen hundred dollars? He looked around and started to raise his hand, but Kenny and Lauren were suddenly beside him, holding his arms down.

"Dale, don't."

"It's thousands, not hundreds." Lauren hissed the words in his ear but it took him a second to understand.

Not hundred. Thousands.

As in dollars.

Someone else called out, their bid immediately topped by someone else. Nineteen. Twenty.

Holy shit. Twenty thousand dollars.

He felt weak, like his knees were going to collapse. The number kept climbing, a little slower now but still climbing.

Twenty-five thousand dollars.

Holy fucking shit.

He tried to straighten, struggled to focus his eyes and search out Smurfette. There she was, next to Anna, her eyes wide and her mouth slightly parted. Her expression was pure bewilderment, shocked and pleased and slightly anxious at the same time.

He must have been staring too hard, or maybe the crowd shifted and she just happened to be looking in the right direction at the right time. It didn't matter because their gazes suddenly locked. He tried to smile, tried to move, but he couldn't. He was held in place by the look in her eyes, soft and wide and bright. And by the bright smile that grew wider with each second as she watched him.

Applause broke out around them, mingled with a few good-natured groans as the bidding came to an end. Dale didn't hear the final number, was almost afraid to know. An older gentleman with thinning sandy blonde hair, dressed in a suit that didn't quite fit, stepped out of the crowd to join Anna and Smurfette as someone else took the painting from the wall.

Disappointment pulsed through him. His painting, gone.

No, not his. And the painting didn't matter. What mattered was Melanie. Smurfette. No painting could compare to her. Now he just needed to tell her that.

He pushed his way through the crowd, not caring that he left Lauren and Kenny behind, not caring that maybe he was just a little too forceful as he moved forward.

And then he was there, standing in front of her, the words a mangled mess in his mouth. She looked up at him, that soft smile on her face, happiness and joy dancing in her eyes.

Tell her. Just tell her. Three words, that was all he had to say.

He reached for her hand, stepped a little closer

when someone jostled him. Took a deep breath and looked into her eyes, felt himself drowning in the ocean blue of her expectant gaze.

Just tell her!

He opened his mouth but then it was too late, she was being pulled away, back toward the crowd as Anna announced the bidding for the second painting would be starting soon.

No. Not yet. Didn't they know he had something to say? He stepped forward but felt something close around his arm, pull him back. Dale almost yanked his arm away, ready to swing out in frustration—until he saw Melanie's father standing next to him, an understanding grin on his face.

"Sometimes, son, it pays to be a little quicker."

Chapter Twenty-Six

Melanie's face was numb from smiling. Even her mind was numb, not quite able to grasp how well her paintings had done. Anna had tried telling her. So did her mother. But she didn't believe it, wouldn't let herself believe it.

The night had proved them both correct but she was still having trouble believing it. She'd wake up in the morning and this would all be a dream. A glorious, wonderful, spectacularly perfect dream.

Well, not quite perfect.

She thanked Mr. Leiken again for buying her painting and shook his hand for what seemed like the hundredth time. He truly was a nice man, even if his breath did smell like onions left in the sun too long. Who was she to judge, after he'd spent all that money?

And finally he was gone, as well as all the other patrons. Everyone except Anna, her parents—

And Dale.

She took a deep breath, her first real breath of the entire crazy wonderful night, then turned to face him.

He was sitting in one of the small cozy chairs of the small seating area to her left, saying something to his sister and her boyfriend. He looked over at her and smiled, drawing her own wide smile in return.

He had shown up. He had really shown up! She still couldn't believe it.

Her smile grew wider as she walked over to him, as he reached out for her hand. Instead of just giving it a reassuring squeeze and letting go, like she had expected, he tugged and pulled her onto his lap. She stiffened in surprise then relaxed against him. His arms came around her waist, holding her close, the broad expanse of his chest warm and solid against her.

Kenny and Lauren congratulated her on the show, said something else that she didn't pay attention to, that she barely heard. How could she, when all her attention was on Dale? On the gentle look in those deep warm eyes? On the way the gold flecks danced in their depths? On the warm tenderness of his mouth as he nuzzled her ear?

He chuckled, the sound deep and rich, resonating throughout her limp body, warming her with a tiny thrill. He pressed another kiss just below her ear, his voice soft when he spoke.

"They said goodnight."

"Hm? Oh. Goodnight."

"They're gone now."

She opened her eyes and looked around, then turned back to see Dale smiling. He kissed her again, a quick one at the corner of her mouth, then leaned back.

"You're famous."

"Who, me? No I'm not."

"I think you are."

A blush heated her cheeks and she almost looked

away, wanted to look away, but his eyes held her in place. Captivating, mesmerizing. Full of her deepest dreams and wishes. Or was she only imagining that?

"Thank you for coming. It meant a lot."

"I wanted to be here."

"Why? Especially after I asked you not to?"

"Because I did. I wanted to surprise you."

"You did. Thank you." She leaned forward and gave him a quick kiss. Too quick, too fast. He pulled back, a frown on his face, shadows filling his eyes for a brief second in time.

"Not as much as I wanted to."

"Wanted to what?"

"Surprise you."

Melanie tilted her head, studying him. Why did he look disappointed? "I don't understand."

He pursed his lips and for a second, she didn't think he'd explain. Then he blew out a quick breath and shrugged, not quite meeting her eyes. "I was going to bid on the one painting."

"You were? Which one?"

"The, uh, the first one."

Warmth spread throughout her, tingling low in her belly and shooting out to her limbs. "Dale! That's so sweet!"

"Yeah, not really. I didn't even manage to get one bid in. Like I said, you're famous."

He was disappointed! He was trying not to show it, but she knew anyway. She could see it floating around him like some misty cloak, could feel it in the way his fingers touched her arm, just a little too stiff. She smiled and leaned forward, capturing his mouth with hers, kissing him. Sweet, warm. She pulled away, her heart racing, and smiled again.

"Thank you. That means so much." She rested her head against his shoulder and sighed, her body relaxing, molding to his. Almost like they were one. "But I don't understand. Why did you want it?"

He shrugged, the soft material of his dress shirt sliding under her cheek. "I don't know. Uh, sentimental, I guess."

"Sentimental?"

"Yeah. Because, you know, uh—" He cleared his throat and lowered his voice. "You, uh, said I inspired it. That's all. Stupid, huh?"

She raised her head and gave him her most ferocious scowl—which wasn't very ferocious at all if the grin on his face meant anything. "It most certainly is not stupid. How can you even say such a thing?"

His grin widened. "Sorry."

She hopped off his lap and grabbed his hand, pulling him from the chair. He tugged back, not quite following her as easily as she thought he would. She placed her free hand on her hip and frowned. "I want to show you something."

"Yeah?"

"Yes." She tugged again and this time he followed her, his hand wrapped around hers. She led him to the far wall then released his hand and pointed. Leaning against the wall was a third painting, tucked back in the corner where nobody could see it. That didn't mean people didn't. Some had. And some had even offered to buy it, promising sums of money that left her blinking in astonishment. But it wasn't for sale.

At least, not unless the perfect buyer came along with the right price.

"What's that?"

"It's a painting, silly. Anna wanted to include this

one in the auction tonight as well but I wouldn't let her. I pulled it at the last minute." She hadn't understood why at first, only knew, for some reason, that it wasn't meant to be sold. Intuition? Instinct? Or something even stronger?

She picked the painting up and held it out for Dale. "What do you see?"

His eyes locked with hers for several heartbeats, the curiosity and unasked questions clear in his gaze. The muscles in his strong throat worked as he swallowed. She felt his mood shift to something more serious as he dropped his gaze to the painting and looked.

Really looked.

Melanie held her breath, wondering what he would see in the smooth strokes and fluid lines. In the rough textures that faded to perfection. In the slashes of rusts and gingers and lapis and corals that should have clashed but somehow came together in a symphony of emotional depth.

"I see—" Dale cleared his throat, his eyes darting to hers for a brief second before focusing on the painting once more. "I see frenzy. Uncertainty. Excitement and fear. Hope and resolution."

"Anything else?" Her voice was barely a whisper but he still heard her. Did he see it? Could he tell? She didn't know, couldn't be sure.

He stepped closer, his eyes searching hers. "I think so, yes."

Sweets! How could she be certain he saw it? What should she say? She didn't know, was so awful at this kind of thing. New and exciting and frightful and energizing all at the same time. She chewed on her lower lip, thinking, wondering, arguing with herself.

Then she blew out a quick breath, the sound soft and sharp. But she didn't look at him. She couldn't.

"You inspired this one, too."

"Yeah?"

She looked up, surprised to see him standing so close. His gaze locked on hers, holding it, refusing to let her look away. "Y-yes. And...and it's for sale. For, uh, for the right price."

No! No, those were the wrong words. They sounded...well, too wrong. Like she was selling something different. Sweets, why was this so hard? "I mean—"

"What price?"

Her hands tightened around the edges of the canvas, the wooden frame cutting into her palms. "I...I could only sell it to someone who sees everything in it."

"You said I inspired it. What about you?"

"I don't understand."

"Did a part of you inspire this one as well? Is there a part of you in here?"

"There's always a part of me in every painting I do."

"That's not what I'm asking, Smurfette." His voice was low, a little rough and uncertain. No, she knew what he was asking, knew it so clearly. And she could see the need for the answer in his eyes, overwhelming, leaving her breathless as he watched. Waited.

She nodded, her mouth too dry. She ran her tongue along her lips and tried to clear her throat, nodding again. "Y-yes. Yes, there's a part of me in this one. A very large part."

He nodded and stepped back, his eyes lowering to the canvas one more time. Then he closed the distance between them, each movement lightning fast and certain as he eased the painting from her hands. She had no idea what he was going to do with it, didn't care. Not when he was looking at her like that, his gaze direct and intense. And hot, so very hot.

"Love. I see love."

His hands cupped her cheeks and tilted her head back as his mouth closed over hers. Warm, hot, giving and taking. Seeking reassurance even as it gave the same. She sighed, losing herself in his touch, in his kiss.

No, not losing. Finding. Finding herself

Dale pulled away then reached down for her hand, dragging it up and resting it on his chest. Over his heart. The steady *thump thump* beat against the palm of her hand, its rhythm echoing her own racing pulse. His gaze captured hers, holding it with a gentle ferocity and determination.

"I love you, Smurfette. It might be too soon and it might not make any sense but it's right. I'm as sure of that as I am of my need to breathe. And I need you even more than I need breath."

Melanie gasped, her eyes filling with tears at the soft words. At the emotion, thick and heavy, that laced each one. Colors swirled around them, glittery and pearlescent, red and orange and pink and blue, broken with the flare of diamonds and the gentle fire of opals. She leaned up on her toes and brushed her mouth against his.

"I love you, Dale. All of you. Light and dark, your flame and fire and vibrancy. I love you."

He grinned, a heart-stopping grin that filled her with warmth and need. Then he pulled her more tightly against him, his mouth on hers. Breathing life into her. And hope. And love.

On the other side of the room, standing far enough away so as not to intrude, Michelle Reeves smiled up at her husband then placed her own hand over his heart. "Oh Michael, how beautiful. I think he may be almost as wonderfully romantic as you."

Michael Reeves pressed a kiss against his wife's forehead and pulled her close. "It takes a special woman to teach a man how to love, dear. And Melanie is, after all, her mother's daughter."

Epilogue

Dale pushed through the door, the cool air of the apartment washing over him as the smell of oil paint and turpentine wrapped around him. He took a deep breath then smiled when he realized what he was doing. If anyone had told him eight months ago that he'd come to enjoy those smells, he would have laughed in denial. Just like he would have laughed if anyone had told him he'd come to enjoy his Smurfette's taste in music. Not that he would ever admit that to her. He'd never live it down.

He walked across the living room, pausing as he approached the cloth-covered easel. Temptation grabbed him, its grip tight, and he stepped closer, his hand reaching for the end of the cloth. He wasn't sure why Smurfette suddenly wanted to hide her work from him, not letting him see it until she was finished. Not from embarrassment, he knew that much. But he wasn't sure if he really believed her when she said she wanted him to be surprised by each one. It had become a game of sorts. She'd unveil the completed painting then stand back, her hands twisted in her long skirt and her lower lip pulled between her teeth as she waited, watching as he studied each painting.

Waited as he told her what he saw. A huge smile would spread across her face whenever he was right. Then she'd run across the room and throw herself in his arms and they'd make love.

Dale didn't know if he was actually right all the time, or if she was just appeasing him. And he didn't care.

But he still wanted to peek. One tiny look. She'd never know.

His fingers caught the edge of the sheet, closing over them. One tiny peek—

"Don't even think about it!" Smurfette's voice called from the bedroom. Dale jumped back, dropping the sheet. How had she'd known?

The music stopped and he waited, expecting her to come out of the room. A minute went by but there was still no sign of her so he headed down the hallway, his fingers undoing the buttons of his uniform shirt as he went. He heard a small thud, followed by an odd swishing sound. Dale paused, his head cocked to the side.

"What are you doing back there?"

"Um, nothing."

It didn't sound like nothing. He frowned, listening again. Was that a splash? It almost sounded like one. Maybe she was taking a bath. Images of Smurfette stretched out in the tub played through his mind. Her sleek body would be covered in translucent bubbles, her fiery hair damp with steam, her eyes burning with desire as she waited for him. His fingers fumbled with the buttons, suddenly in a hurry to undo them as he moved closer to their room.

"Lauren called. We're meeting her and Kenny for lunch before we go see Lindsay."

Dale stumbled to a halt, remembering what day it was. Once a month they would meet for lunch then visit Lindsay. The visits had been awkward at first, full of discomfort and distrust as they tried to get to know their sister again. It hadn't been easy, and there were still times when the visits were hard, too full of emotion and bitterness that had developed over the years.

But Lindsay was trying. Really trying. And going to counseling as well. She had changed. They had all changed, the darkness slowly easing, replaced with something lighter, reassuring.

It would take time, they all knew that. But as long as they kept working at it, as long as they didn't give up…

No, he wasn't going to give up. Smurfette wouldn't let him.

He glanced at his watch. Not quite eight thirty yet, plenty of time. They'd had a quiet night at work so he was wide awake, no need for a nap.

Unless he happened to take a quick doze after making love to Smurfette. He grinned and continued down the hallway. There it was, that splashing sound again. And no, it wasn't coming from the bathroom.

"What are you doing back there?"

"Um, nothing. I mean, just playing with some new paint I got."

"New paint? Why are you playing with it in the bedroom—" Dale stumbled to a halt, nearly tripping as he entered the room. His eyes widened as he looked around, taking in the sheets of plastic that covered the bed and floor. Smurfette stood in front of him, her hair a wild mass of fiery curls, her eyes sparkling with laughter and a wide playful smile on her face.

Paint dripped from her gloriously nude body, pooling in a bright blue puddle at her feet.

"It's body paint." She glanced down at herself then looked up at him, her lower lip pulled between her teeth. "Do you like it?"

He watched as a drop of paint rolled across the swell of one full breast to her nipple. It clung to the hard peak, tantalizing, mesmerizing, until finally dropping to the plastic beneath her feet with a small wet plop. He swallowed and dragged his gaze up her body, taking in each delicious inch of her bared curves. He swallowed again, his mind completely blank as the blood moved from his head in an urgent race to reach his cock.

"Do you like it?"

Somewhere in the back of his mind, he realized she had already asked him that. Realized that she was shifting, moving her arms as if to cover herself. He hurried forward, grabbing her hands to stop her.

"I love it."

She smiled again, wide and beautiful, the sight filling him with peace. "You always call me Smurfette. I thought maybe I could really be one for just a little bit."

Dale laughed then pulled her to him, his mouth crashing against hers. Her hands were fast and efficient, shedding his clothes, smearing his own body with the paint. Cold at first, then growing hotter as they moved together, the plastic smooth and slick beneath their wet bodies.

Later, as they lay in a tangled heap on the plastic,

Smurfette raised up on one elbow and smiled down at him. He reached up and tucked the damp hair behind her ear, smiling at the paint smeared over her face.

"You know, some artists actually use this technique to paint."

Dale dropped his hand and frowned. "Uh, what technique?"

She stretched her arm out, indicating their paint-smeared bodies. "This. They strip down and cover themselves in paint, then use their bodies to decorate the canvas."

"Seriously?" No, she was messing with him. She had to be. But one look at her eyes let him know she was being serious. "No. Don't get any ideas."

"But we could do it together. Just think how much fun it would be. And how many colors we could create, how unique it would be. It would open a whole new world of possibilities. Take my art in a whole new direction."

Dale laughed, the sound more like a choke, then reached for her. She gasped, her hands clinging to his slick shoulders as he rolled, tucking her beneath him.

"We can try it. Once. Together. But it'll be just for us. Deal?"

"Deal." Smurfette smiled, her breath escaping in a short gasp as he plunged into her a second time.

As they lost themselves in each other, creating their own masterpiece together.

*****

ABOUT THE AUTHOR

Lisa B. Kamps is the author of the best-selling series *The Baltimore Banners*, featuring "hard-hitting, heart-melting hockey players" (USA Today), on and off the ice. Her newest series, *Firehouse Fourteen*, features hot and heroic firefighters who put more than their lives on the line.

In a previous life, she worked as a firefighter with the Baltimore County Fire Department, then did a very brief (and not very successful) stint at bartending in east Baltimore, and finally served as the Director of Retail Operations for a busy Civil War non-profit.

Lisa currently lives in Maryland with her husband and two sons (who are mostly sorta-kinda out of the house), one very spoiled Border Collie, two cats with major attitude, several head of cattle, and entirely too many chickens to count. When she's not busy writing or chasing animals, she's cheering loudly for her favorite hockey team, the Washington Capitals--or going through withdrawal and waiting for October to roll back around!

Interested in reaching out to Lisa? She'd love to hear from you, and there are several ways to contact her:

Website: www.LisaBKamps.com
Newsletter: www.lisabkamps.com/signup/
Email: LisaBKamps@gmail.com
Facebook Author Page:
www.facebook.com/authorLisaBKamps
Kamps Korner Facebook Group:
www.facebook.com/groups/1160217000707067/
Twitter: twitter.com/LBKamps

Goodreads: www.goodreads.com/LBKamps
Amazon Author Page:
www.amazon.com/author/lisabkamps
Instagram: www.instagram.com/lbkamps/
BookBub: www.bookbub.com/authors/lisa-b-kamps

DANGEROUS PASSION

Shelby Martin's life is as dry, dull and dusty as the artifacts with which she works, but all that changes when she accepts a dare by her friends: pick up a sexy stranger for one unforgettable night of uncharacteristic passion.

Josh Nichols is a no-nonsense vice cop used to the seedier side of Baltimore. When he's picked up in a bar by Shelby, he realizes the move is out of character for her—and is immediately surprised at the instant chemistry between them. He doesn't count on her disappearing after one hot night—before he gets her full name or even a phone number.

Neither of them had expected to see the other again—or to have their worlds turned upside down when they're thrown together as a result of a crime at Shelby's museum. Can two people from completely different worlds look beyond suspicion and build a relationship from one night of unprecedented passion? Or will those differences pull them apart...especially when there's someone else who wants nothing more than to see Shelby fail?

Turn the page for an exciting sneak peek at DANGEROUS PASSION...

Shelby looked over at Chrissy and winced at the gleam in her friend's eyes. Coupled with the several shots Chrissy had already slammed back, the look could only mean trouble. Trouble for *Shelby*. Amanda's low groan confirmed her instinct.

But trouble or not, Chrissy's words stirred something to life in Shelby, a flicker of want, a spark of yearning. She didn't *want* to be so consumed by her work that she let everything else—let life—pass her by. But she didn't know to fix that, didn't know how to claw her way out of the dusty, boring existence that had become her life.

Pretending to be someone she wasn't...yes, the temptation was as appealing as a ripe strawberry dipped in dark chocolate.

"Maybe. I mean, it's tempting but...I couldn't do it."

"What?" Amanda's surprised shock was drowned out by Chrissy's sudden excitement as she leaned forward and grabbed Shelby's wrist again.

"Yes you could. Just pretend the last few years never happened. You can do it, I know you can."

Shelby laughed, and even she could tell it sounded forced. She took another sip of the wine then sat back, eyeing Chrissy and ignoring Amanda's muttered warnings. "Okay, I'll try. So what do you want me to do? Match you shot for shot? Go get crazy on the dance floor? Pretend the two of us are a couple so you can get the guys to hit on you?" Shelby was pretty sure she could do any of those things—all she had to do was pretend the last few years had never happened, pretend that she hadn't really changed. The three of them used to do crazy things like that all the time together. It wouldn't be too difficult. At least, she didn't think it would.

But Chrissy was shaking her head with enough energy that strands of her platinum hair flew around her face. She impatiently brushed them away and grabbed Shelby's hand again. "No. You need to do something you've never done before. You need to pick out a guy and go have wild sex with him. *Tonight*."

"What? No. That's crazy."

"That's what you get for encouraging her."

"Amanda, stop. This is exactly what Shelby needs. And yes, Shel, it's crazy. That's the whole point. Look around. There's tons of gorgeous guys here. Just pick one and go. See what happens."

Shelby glanced around the crowded room. Yes, there were tons of guys here tonight. But not a single one stood out. Not a single one remotely struck her with the urge to walk over and strike up a conversation, let alone have a one-night stand with him.

A one-night stand. Oh dear Lord, what was she even thinking? She must really be losing her mind if she was sitting here even thinking about contemplating Chrissy's crazy words. She shook her head and turned back to face her friend.

"I'm sorry Chrissy, but that's not going to happen. I can't. I'm not like you, I can't just go up to some stranger and—"

"Oh my God. Him. You have got to go talk to him."

"Who?" Shelby glanced around, trying to see who had caused the look of feral hunger in Chrissy's eyes. Amanda drew her breath in with a sharp hiss, which made Shelby turn in her seat and look behind her.

And she realized why her two friends were suddenly on high alert. Her own pulse kicked up several notches and she swore her face was heating as well.

The newcomer had just walked through the door, and his presence was already drawing appreciative glances from the female occupants of the room. At first glance, Shelby thought he was tall and broad, but she blinked and realized that had been an illusion. Yes, he was a bit bigger than average, but not like she had first thought. No, it was his presence that made him seem larger than life.

And presence the man possessed. Just over six-feet tall, with broad shoulders, narrow waist, trim hips, and muscular legs. All packed into black leather and faded denim that hugged him in just the right spots. Shelby wanted to run her hands over the denim, to see if the material was as soft as it looked. To feel if his thighs were as hard as they looked.

She blinked again and let her eyes wander back up, pausing for a long second at waist-level before raking higher, appreciating the snug fit of the black polo shirt stretched tight across his chest. She would have loved to see his arms, to see if his biceps were as toned and muscular as she thought they must be, but they were encased in black leather, hidden by the motorcycle jacket he wore.

And Shelby realized that must be why he stood out in the crowd. It wasn't just his presence, an aura of power and authority and strength surrounding him, it was his clothes as well. He was the only one wearing jeans and motorcycle leather in a singles crowd of young professionals outdoing one another in a hapless effort to impress everyone else.

This man looked like he didn't care if he impressed anyone, as if he didn't care if he fit in or not.

Shelby's eyes drifted higher, finally resting on his face, and her pulse quickened even more. The slightest hint of beard shadowed his strong, square jaw; his dark hair was swept back off his face and curled just above the collar of the leather jacket. Coupled with his high cheekbones, he had a classic, rugged face that advertised adventure and screamed danger all at once. But his eyes...from where she sat, they looked dark in color. And intense. He shifted slightly, coming further into the club and surveying everything around him in one long sweep of the room.

Including her.

Shelby's heart paused as their gazes met in the briefest touch. Heat instantly filled her. Heat...and awareness. She swallowed and shifted in her seat, turning away from the searing touch of that all-too-brief look.

"Wow." Amanda turned around and fanned herself, a small grin on her face.

"Oh, yes." Chrissy's murmur was sly, determined. Her eyes remained glued to the newcomer long enough that Shelby had time to finish her wine in several long gulps. Chrissy finally pulled her gaze away and fixed Shelby with a long look. "If you don't talk to him, *I* will. And if I have my way, we won't be talking for long."

Shelby stared at her friend, at her thick blonde hair and toned, voluptuous build, at the confidence that she wore like a cape, and opened her mouth to wish her luck.

And just as quickly, she snapped her mouth closed.

Chrissy, who never hesitated at taking chances.

Chrissy, who saw what she wanted and went after it.

Chrissy, who always had fun.

And Shelby suddenly wished *she* was the one who wasn't afraid to take chances and always have fun.

Chrissy gave her a pointed look, then held her hand up between them, raising her index finger.

One...

Was Shelby willing to take a chance?

Two...

Was Shelby willing to go after something she wanted and have fun?

Three...

Chrissy lowered her hand and shifted, ready to stand up. And Shelby knew if she did, that would be it. Her chance would be over. Chrissy would walk over to Mr. Tall, Dark, and Dangerous then walk out the door with him moments later.

Shelby slid out of the chair and stood so fast that she had to grab the back of it to keep it steady. Amanda turned and looked up at her, her brows furrowed in a funny combination of concern and surprise.

"Shelby! What are you doing? Are you insane?"

Insane. Yes, quite possibly. But Chrissy's earlier words came back to her. She *was* just skirting the edges of life. Tonight, she wanted to live.

But she had no idea what to do. Her grip tightened on the seat back and she looked quickly at Chrissy, silently asking for advice.

"Just go over and offer to buy him a drink. Flirt a little. See what kind of vibe you get from him."

"Chrissy, don't tell her that! He could be dangerous. He *looks* dangerous!"

"So she can trust her instincts. It's just a drink, for crying out loud. She doesn't *have* to leave with him." She turned back to face Shelby, raising her glass in a mock toast. "Just talk to him, see what happens. Follow your gut and do what feels right."

Do what feels right. Shelby nodded. She could do that. She glanced down at the empty wine glass and suddenly wished it was full. But then she realized she could order another one.

At the bar.

When she offered to buy the stranger a drink.

Shelby nodded and straightened, then took a deep breath and turned away from her friends.

To walk head-first into an exciting new chance. Into unknown passion.

*****

Amber "AJ" Johnson is a freelance writer who has her heart set on becoming a full-time sports reporter at her paper. She has one chance to prove herself: capture an interview with the very private goalie of Baltimore's hockey team, Alec Kolchak. But he's the one man who tries her patience, even as he brings to life a quiet passion she doesn't want to admit exists.

Alec has no desire to be interviewed--he never has, never will. But he finds himself a reluctant admirer of AJ's determination to get what she wants...and he certainly never counted on his attraction to her. In a fit of frustration, he accepts AJ's bet: if she can score just one goal on him in a practice shoot-out, he would not only agree to the interview, he would let her have full access to him for a month, 24/7.

It was a bet neither one of them wanted to lose...and a bet neither one could afford to win. But when it came time to take the shot, could either one of them cross the line?

Forensics accountant Bobbi Reeves is pulled back into a world of shadows in order to go undercover as a personal assistant with the Baltimore Banners. Her assignment: get close to defenseman Nikolai Petrovich and uncover the reason he's being extorted. But she doesn't expect the irrational attraction she feels—or the difficulty in helping someone who doesn't want it.

Nikolai Petrovich, a veteran defenseman for the Banners, has no need for a personal assistant—especially not one hired by the team. During the last eight years, he has learned to live simply...and alone. Experience has taught him that letting people close puts them in danger. He doesn't want a personal assistant, and he certainly doesn't need anyone prying into his personal life. But that doesn't stop his physical reaction to the unusual woman assigned to him.

They are drawn together in spite of their differences, and discover a heated passion that neither expected. But when the game is over, will the secrets they keep pull them closer together...or tear them apart?

BLUE RIBBON SUMMER

THE BALTIMORE BANNERS (BOOK 5)

LISA B. KAMPS

Kayli Evans lives a simple life, handling the daily operations of her small family farm and acting as the primary care-taker for her fourteen-year-old niece. She knows the importance of enjoying each minute, of living life to its fullest. But she still has worries: about her older brother's safety in the military, about the rift between her two brothers, and about her niece's security and making ends meet. And now there's a new worry she doesn't want: Ian Donovan, her brother's friend.

Ian is a carefree hockey player for the Baltimore Banners who has relatively few worries—until he finds himself suddenly babysitting his seven-year-old nieces for an extended period of time. He has no idea what he's doing, and is thrust even further into the unknown when he's forced to participate in the twins' newest hobby. Meeting Kayli opens a different world for him, a simpler world where family, trust, and love are what matters most.

BODY CHECK

Baltimore Banners defenseman Randy Michaels has a reputation for hard-hitting, on and off the ice. But he's getting older, and his agent has warned that there are younger, less-expensive players who are eager to take his place on the team. Can his hare-brained idea of becoming a "respectable businessman" turn his reputation around, or has Randy's reputation really cost him the chance of having his contract renewed?

Alyssa Harris has one goal in mind: make the restaurant she's opened with her three friends a success. It's not going to be easy, not when the restaurant is a themed sports bar geared towards women. It's going to be even more difficult because their sole investor is Randy Michaels, her friend's drool-worthy brother who has his own ideas about what makes an interesting menu.

Will the mismatched pair be able to find a compromise as things heat up, both on and off the ice? Or will their differences result in a penalty that costs both of them the game?

Jean-Pierre "JP" Larocque is a speed demon for the Baltimore Banners. He lives for speed off the ice, too, playing fast and loose with cars and women. But is he really a player, or is his carefree exterior nothing more than a show, hiding a lonely man filled with regret as he struggles to forget the only woman who mattered?

Emily Poole thought she knew what she wanted in life, but everything changed five years ago. Now she exists day by day, helping care for her niece after her sister's bitter divorce. It may not be how she envisioned her life, but she's happy. Or so she thinks, until JP re-enters her life. Now she realizes there's a lot more she wants, including a second chance with JP.

Can these two lost souls finally find forgiveness and Break Away to the future? Or will the shared tragedy of their past tear them apart for good this time?

Valerie Michaels knows all about life, responsibility--and hockey. After all, her brother is a defenseman for the Baltimore Banners. The last thing she needs--or wants--is to get tangled up with one of her brother's teammates. She doesn't have time, not when running The Maypole is her top priority. Could that be the reason she's suddenly drawn to the troubled Justin Tome? Or is it because she senses something deeper inside him, something she thinks she can fix?

On the surface, Justin Tome has it all: a successful career with the Banners, money, fame. But he's been on a downward spiral the last few months. He's become more withdrawn, his game has gone downhill, and he's been partying too much. He thinks it's nothing more than what's expected of him, nothing more than once again failing to meet expectations and never quite measuring up. Then he starts dating Val and realizes that maybe he has more to offer than he thinks.

Or does he? Sometimes voices from the past, voices you've heard all your life, are too strong to overcome. And when the unexpected happens, Justin is certain he's looking at a permanent Delay of Game--unless one strong woman can make him see that life is all about the future, not the past.

Sometimes it takes a sinner...

Nicole Taylor has been fighting to get on the right side of the tracks all her life, but never as hard as the last two years. Finally free from an abusive relationship, her focus is on looking forward. Her first step in that direction? A quick get-away to immerse herself in her photography--and a steamy encounter with a gorgeous green-eyed stranger.

To love a saint...

As a forward for The Baltimore Banners, shooting fast and scoring often is just part of the game for Mathias "Mat" Herron. Off the ice is a different story and this off-season, he has a different goal in mind: do whatever it takes to rid himself of the asinine nickname he was recently given by some of his teammates. An encounter with a beautiful stranger helps him do just that.

And life to teach them both what's important...

When reality collides with fantasy, will passion be enough to see them through? Or will it take a shoot-out of another kind to show them what matters most?

Kenny Haskell's hard work and determination finally paid off last season when The Baltimore Banners called him up from the minors. That doesn't mean the quiet defenseman is willing to stop proving himself. Each day is a new fight, a new opportunity, to prove to his coaches, to his team—and to himself—that he belongs with the Banners. Kenny is convinced he'll be able to keep his head in the game with no problems—until he gets thrown out of a youth hockey game by one unforgiving ref who proves to be more of a distraction than he anticipates.

Lauren Gannon approaches life with a single successful mindset: take no prisoners, never give up, and always rely on yourself. At least, that's what she likes to think. The last year has been a little different. Being saddled with her younger sister who refuses to grow up and take responsibility for anything is turning Lauren's world into one crazy disaster after another. The last thing she needs to deal with is a professional hockey player who's too attractive for his own good—or for her sanity.

The one thing Lauren has learned in life is to never underestimate the unexpected, and falling for Kenny definitely fits into that category. Can they really be friends and lovers? Kenny does his best to prove they can. But when a sudden family obligation forces Lauren to choose between what she knows is right and what she thinks is expected, will she find herself skating on thin ice and risking the happiness she really wants?

Jake Evans has been in the Marine Corps for seventeen years, juggling his conflicting duties to country and his teenage daughter. But when he suffers a serious injury and is sent home, he knows he'll be forced to make decisions he doesn't want to. Battered in spirit and afraid of what the future may hold, he takes the long way by driving cross-country.

He never expected to meet Alyce Marshall, a free-spirited woman on a self-declared adventure: she's running away from home.

In spite of her outward free spirit, Alyce has problems of her own she must face, including the ever-present shadow of her father and his influence on her growing up. She senses similarities in Jake, and decides that it's up to her to teach the tough Marine that life isn't just about rules and regulations. What she doesn't plan on is falling in love with him...and being forced to share her secret.

Michaela Donaldson had her whole life planned out: college, music, and a happy-ever-after with her first true love. One reckless night changed all that, setting Michaela on a new path. Gone are her dreams of pursuing music in college, replaced by what she thinks is a more rewarding life. She's a firefighter now, getting down and dirty while doing her job. So what if she's a little rough around the edges, a little too careless, a little too detached? She's happy, living life on her own terms--until Nicky Lansing shows back up.

Nick Lansing was the stereotypical leather-clad bad boy, needing nothing but his fast car, his guitar, his never-ending partying, and his long-time girlfriend--until one bad decision changed the course of two lives forever. He's on the straight-and-narrow now, living life as a respected teacher and doing his best to be a positive role model. Yes, he still has his music. But gone are his days of partying. And gone is the one girl who always held his heart. Or is she?

One freak accident brings these two opposites back together. Is ten years long enough to heal the physical and emotional wounds from the past? Can they reconcile who they were with who they've become--or will it be a case of Once Burned is enough?

Angie Warren was voted the Most Likely to Succeed in school. She was also voted the Most Responsible. And responsible she is: she made it through college on a scholarship and she's even working her way through Vet School. She has an overprotective older brother she adores and a part-time job tending bar that adds some enjoyment to her life. In fact, that's the only pleasure she has. She's bored and in desperate need of a change. Too bad the one guy she has her sights set on is the one guy completely off-limits.

Jay Moore knows all about excitement and wouldn't live life any other way. From his job as a firefighter to his many brief relationships, his whole life is nothing but one thrilling experience after the other. Except when Angie Warren enters the picture. He's known her for years and there is no way he's going to agree to give her the excitement she's looking for. Even Jay knows where to draw the line—and dating his friend's baby sister definitely crosses all of them.

Too bad Angie has other plans. But will either one of them remember that when you're Playing With Fire, someone is bound to get burned?

Dave Warren knows all about protocol. As a firefighter/paramedic, he has to. What he doesn't know is when his life became nothing more than routine, following the rules day in and day out. Has it always been that way, or was it a gradual change? Or did it have anything to do with his time spent overseas as a medic with the Army Reserves? He's not sure, but it's something he's learned to accept and live with—until a series of messages upsets his routine. And until one spitfire Flight Medic enters his life.

Carolann "CC" Covey has no patience for protocols. Yes, they're a necessary evil, a part of her job, but they don't rule her life. She can't let them—she knows life is for the living, a lesson learned the hard way overseas. Which is why her attraction to the serious and staid Dave Warren makes no sense. Is it just a case of "opposites attract", or is it something more? Will CC be able to teach him that sometimes rules need to be broken?

And when something sinister appears from Dave's past to threaten everything he's come to love, will he learn that Breaking Protocol may be the only way to save what's really important?

INTO THE FLAMES

Dale Gannon has sworn off women. He's seen more than his share of crazy and not all of it has been during his job as a firefighter. His youngest sister, Lindsay, is currently in jail awaiting trial for the attempted poisoning of his other sister, Lauren. Guilt still eats at him, making him wonder if there was something he could have done to prevent Lindsay's fall. Could he have been more supportive? More encouraging? What if...no, he was done with what-ifs. Done with women. Done with people, period. What he needs is peace, quiet...and time to come to grips with everything that's happened in the last six months.

And then he meets the neighbor from hell: a sassy free-spirited woman who quickly turns his life upside down.

Melanie Reeves has always seen things differently, viewing life as an array of color. Bright and vibrant, dark and moody. She captures them, breathes them, gives life to them on canvas. But her obnoxious neighbor is a mystery, one she can't solve, one she can't even read clearly—and one she tries her best to ignore.

Until she discovers the deep guilt that plagues him—guilt he won't admit to or even acknowledge. Can she help him find his way to the surface before the darkness completely engulfs the inner vibrancy she senses in him? Or will he drag her with him into the flames, where they both run the risk of losing who they really are?

Shelby Martin's life is as dry, dull and dusty as the artifacts with which she works, but all that changes when she accepts a dare by her friends: pick up a sexy stranger for one unforgettable night of uncharacteristic passion.

Josh Nichols is a no-nonsense vice cop used to the seedier side of Baltimore. When he's picked up in a bar by Shelby, he realizes the move is out of character for her—and is immediately surprised at the instant chemistry between them. He doesn't count on her disappearing after one hot night—before he gets her full name or even a phone number.

Neither of them expected to see the other again—or to have their worlds turned upside down when they're thrown together as a result of a crime at Shelby's museum. Can two people from completely different worlds look beyond suspicion and build a relationship from one night of unprecedented passion? Or will those differences pull them apart...especially when there's someone else who wants nothing more than to see Shelby fail?